SANITARY CENTENNIAL
and Selected Short Stories

The Texas Pan American Series

FERNANDO SORRENTINO
SANITARY CENTENNIAL

*A*nd
Selected
Short
Stories

Translated by Thomas C. Meehan

UNIVERSITY OF TEXAS PRESS, AUSTIN

First Edition, 1988

Requests for permission to reproduce material from this work
should be sent to Permissions, University of Texas Press,
Box 7819, Austin, Texas 78713-7819.

*The Texas Pan American Series is published with the assistance
of a revolving publication fund established by the Pan
American Sulphur Company.*

LIBRARY OF CONGRESS CATALOGING-IN-PUBLICATION DATA

Sorrentino, Fernando.
    Sanitary centennial and selected short stories / by
Fernando Sorrentino; (translated by Thomas C.
Meehan). — 1st ed.
        p.   cm. — (The Texas Pan American series)
    Contents: Sanitary centennial — A lifestyle — In
self-defense — Piccirilli — The life of the party — The
fetid tale of Antulín — Ars poetica.
    ISBN 0-292-77608-X
    I. Title. II. Series.
    PQ7798.29.06A25 1988
    863 — dc19   88-4972 CIP

CONTENTS

INTRODUCTION
TO FERNANDO SORRENTINO
vii

TRANSLATOR'S NOTE
xxvii

ACKNOWLEDGMENTS
xxviii

SANITARY CENTENNIAL
1

Short Stories

A LIFESTYLE
95

IN SELF-DEFENSE
100

PICCIRILLI
106

THE LIFE OF THE PARTY
110

THE FETID TALE OF ANTULÍN
123

ARS POETICA
150

NOTES
177

*H*umor has tended to be a rare commodity in Spanish American fiction. Indeed, until fairly recent times, approximately the 1960s, an authentic tradition of humor has been conspicuously absent in the general literary output of our neighbors to the south. For genuine mirth to flourish in literature, it may be that nations and individual writers must acquire not only a relatively high level of cultural sophistication but also that quintessential capacity for detachment that enables artists to stand back and laugh at the absurdities of human existence as well as at themselves. Notwithstanding a number of significant but isolated exceptions over the centuries (Del Valle y Caviedes, Terralla y Landa, Ricardo Palma, Lizardi, Payró, the Chilean Genaro Prieto's newspaper articles, Felisberto Hernández, and a few others), such a development was slow in coming to Spanish America where writers have tended, in the main and for varying reasons, to take matters and themselves very seriously. Moreover, the tone in the complete works of these figures and others is not consistently or homogeneously funny; it would be difficult, if not impossible, to single out any Spanish American author and classify him or her solely as a humorist. However, the presence on the contemporary scene of an expanding group of impressive narrators (Arreola, García Márquez, Augusto Monterroso, Jorge Asís, Humberto Costantini, Mireya Robles, Luis Britto García, the late Julio Cortázar, Jorge Ibargüengoitia, and so on), whose writings often contain generous doses of comic wit, suggests that the foundations of a solid "house of humor" are now being laid. As a relatively new and invigorating trend in Spanish American prose fiction, the ring of laughter in the pages of these authors may well signal one of the latest and surest signs of the maturity of Latin American literature and culture.

Busy at work in the "construction crew" erecting that edifice of laughter is an Argentine author, Fernando Sorrentino, about whom one reader has remarked: "The point is that Fernando Sorrentino opens his windows to the world, looks out to contemplate men and things, and simply dies laughing." That Sorrentino has compiled an edition entitled *36 cuentos argentinos con humor siglo XX* [36 humorous Argentine short stories of the 20th century] is evidence of his attraction to the comic mode, and he reaffirms his commitment to merriment upon choosing as an epigraph for that anthology these revealing words from J. D. Salinger's *The Catcher in the Rye:* "What I like best is a book that's at least funny once in a while." I should like to introduce to the reader this talented and refreshing artistic personality whom I had the pleasure of getting to know during the summer of 1981 in Buenos Aires. I warmly recommend his creations, the few extant translated tales as well as the Spanish versions, some of the best of which I have rendered into English here.

Short story writer, novelist, teacher, editor, and literary critic, Fernando Sorrentino was born in Buenos Aires on November 8, 1942. He has one sister, Adela. In an autobiographical letter of April 1985 he writes that he is "the son of Argentine parents, the great-grandson of seven Argentine great-grandparents and one Italian great-grandparent, and the great-great-grandson of sixteen Italian great-great-grandparents," thus not only affirming his Italian ancestry, quite common in Argentina, but also emphasizing, perhaps even more, his pride in his Argentine heritage. The Sorrentino family belonged to the lower middle class, but, as the author observes, "everybody we knew belonged to that class then." In a manner reminiscent of Galdós' keen knowledge of Madrid, Sorrentino, even as a boy, was beginning to acquire the remarkable familiarity with his city, its topography, streets, parks, avenues, *barrios* (or quarters), and neighborhoods that crops up so frequently in his subsequent writings. Recollecting his childhood years, the author states: "I grew up in that subsection of the Palermo quarter they call 'Pacífico' because of its proximity to the tracks of the former Buenos Aires–Pacific Railroad." His family lived on Costa Rica Street, as he points out, "in the stretch that runs between the former Maldonado Creek (channeled, before I was born, into an underground storm drain running under Juan B. Justo Avenue) and the switching yard of the Mitre Railway." Like many little boys, Fernando played in the vacant fields and lots near his home in the burgeoning capital city. Magnified by memory, such areas he now nostalgically recalls as "immense tracts of empty terrain (that's how I seem to remember them today) covered by uneven ground, dips and plateaus; there were soccer fields, flooded areas, big wooden spools for wire abandoned by the telephone company, horses, sheep, and dogs. For us, that was an enchanted world, a world for games and adventures. Those of us who were kids then spent the greater part of our time outdoors."

Sorrentino's sharp intellect and superior intelligence were revealed during his earliest schooling when, as he states, he was the best student in his class throughout the seven years of primary school. "I don't say this," he writes, "with any special pride or shame. I'm simply pointing out a fact. I became aware then of something I've continued to observe until the present day: most people have difficulty in understanding even the simplest things." The last year of the boy's elementary education, 1955, also saw the revolutionary overthrow of Juan Domingo Perón, an event the author wryly recalls: "That's when we found out that yesterday's saints were today's devils, and vice versa; those dichotomies continued to divide Argentina down to the present time, perhaps with changes in the names of the contenders." Playing soccer or reading novels and short stories, the only two things Fernando liked at the time, filled his rather typical boyhood days; yet his lifelong love of literature was already in evidence and discriminating tastes were even then being formed. "My early readings of Salgari and Verne faded into the background when I read *David Copperfield*; I thought then that nothing superior to that novel by Dickens could be written. It was the first time I had found in one book a whole, extremely rich gamut of verisimilar details. Even today I can reread it with pleasure, disregarding, of course, its tear-jerker tendency and other hypocritical vices so dear to the English heart." Sorrentino's high school years remain somewhat blurred in retrospect but are similarly linked in his memory to soccer games and further readings in prose fiction; the latter, however, were now broadening out and becoming more sophisticated: "It was like a dream about which I remember nothing except an occasional face or some teacher's last name. I didn't make friends, either, except one who is still my friend today. I liked adventure novels in the Anglo-Saxon tradition: Stevenson, Rider Haggard (I think I read no less than six of his stories set in Africa), Conan Doyle, and one or two others. At the age of fourteen or fifteen, I read *Don Quixote* in the Biblioteca Mundial Sopena edition, that is to say, an edition without a single explanatory note; nevertheless (or perhaps for that reason), I was delighted by that book, although later I became aware that a large part of its textual meaning had escaped me." Sorrentino spent his first two years in the university studying law and simultaneously fulfilling his compulsory military service obligation. He refers to those two years as "wasted" time, for his life was now about to change direction.

In 1963, at the age of twenty-one, Sorrentino entered the Escuela de Profesores Mariano Acosta, the same normal school attended earlier by his compatriots and fellow authors Leopoldo Marechal and Julio Cortázar. Although he didn't know it at the time, Fernando was about to follow in their footsteps in more than one way. At Mariano Acosta he began the necessary course work in language and literature preparatory to a career in secondary teaching. While at this teacher-training institution, the future author became, as he tells us, "a completely different person, a person seriously interested in literature, in linguistics, in Latin, even in mere grammar." There was one instructor who had a profound effect on his intellectual life: "I had the good luck to have, as my professor of the Spanish language, Julio Balderrama, the *wisest, most intelligent* man I have known in my life—and I say that without exaggeration. If there's anyone in the world of the living whom I intellectually *adore*, it's Julio Balderrama."

In 1968, Sorrentino graduated from Mariano Acosta with a degree in the teaching of Spanish, Latin, and literature. That same year he won a grant from the Argentine National Foundation for the Arts, which enabled him to continue, while teaching, other literary activities he had now initiated, the writing of short stories. Unfortunately, the enthusiasm he felt for his language and literature studies while in college was never to be duplicated in the matter of his teaching, for he had already discovered that his true vocation lay not in the teaching of literature but in its creation. This explains the completely negative attitude toward his academic career, which Sorrentino expresses in these words: "I graduated in 1968 and began then that gray, monotonous life of the high schools, that teaching of things to people who aren't interested in learning them. At any rate, I can say (with shame?—absolutely not) that I never paid the slightest attention to teaching, except as an (inadequate) means of making a living. I feel a natural repugnance for 'schoolish' things, for pedagogy, and for books on methodology." Sorrentino views teaching only as a means to an end; it has allowed him (barely) sufficient time and money to support himself and his family while composing the fiction that brings him greater personal rewards, recognition, satisfaction, and self-fulfillment.

In the year following his graduation from Mariano Acosta, Sorrentino published his first book of short stories, titled *La regresión zoológica* [Zoological regression], a work he now practically disowns: "I had the misfortune of immediately finding someone who wanted to publish it; it didn't take me long to realize it was deplorable book, a book written out of inexperience, ignorance, vanity, and pedantry. It's an embarrassing book that I'll never republish. However, there is to be found in it the seed (but a flawed seed) of my subsequent literary output, for which I have no regrets." Despite the vehemence of this rejection, the author did see fit to bring out carefully revised versions of two of the fourteen stories of *La regresión zoológica* seven years later in another collection of tales. The same year that saw his debut as an author, 1969, Fernando was married. He still lives in Buenos Aires with his charming wife, Alicia, and their three children, a teenage boy, Juan Manuel ("Juanín"), and little twin girls bearing the almost regal names of María Angélica ("Geli") and María Victoria ("Vicky"). When I visited the ever hospitable Sorrentinos, they lived in an apartment they owned on Teniente Matienzo Street in the *barrio* Palermo, not too far from the Pacífico subsection of Palermo where the author grew up. They have since moved to a more spacious residence on Ceretti Street in Villa Urquiza, another quarter of the sprawling city. The family usually vacations each summer at the resort areas on the Atlantic coast. Over the years, in addition to teaching Spanish Peninsular literature and Spanish American literature in the capital city's secondary school system, Sorrentino has also worked in business offices as an advertising writer and as an editor for the Plus Ultra Publishing Company, which has published four of his books. At this writing, Sorrentino has almost completely given up teaching except for what he calls "a few symbolic classes" he still gives; he is proud and happy to be master of his time now and, as he says, "his own boss." At present, he is busily engaged in preparing a volume of his best short stories, some previously published in books, magazines, or newspapers and some as yet unpublished.

Sorrentino's second collection of short stories, *Imperios y servidumbres* [Empires and servitudes], came out in 1972. The newer volume, however, had the distinction of seeing the light under the imprint of the prestigious Spanish publishing house Seix Barral of

Barcelona in its well-known Nueva Narrativa Hispánica series. This was the same company that was responsible for the publication of many of the significant works of fiction appearing during the so-called Boom in Spanish American prose fiction, and hence *Imperios* enjoyed greater dissemination throughout the Spanish-speaking world. The publisher's eminence, however, also bespeaks the excellent quality of the thirteen tales included in the collection, for it contains some of the author's finest stories and represents one of his best efforts to date. Good was, indeed, born out of adversity and desperation this time, for the three years intervening since the appearance of *La regresión zoológica* had been a period of hardship for Fernando and Alicia as they struggled to make ends meet on the author's meager salary as a beginning schoolteacher, and they were faced also with the responsibility of their first child. Sorrentino speaks of that trying time and offers an explanation for the success of his latest book: "Between the age of 27 and 29, plagued by dire poverty, I wrote the short stories included in *Imperios y servidumbres*, to which I quickly succeeded in giving a form that I consider gratifying to the present day. I overcame the essential error that had presided over the writing of my first book; the latter had been written with me thinking about pleasing hypothetical readers; conversely, with *Imperios*, I thought only about pleasing myself. Since then, I have proceeded in this way; I write the stories I would like to read, without concerning myself with what some vague readers would like to read."

To date, Fernando Sorrentino has published eight books. In addition to the two previously mentioned collections of short stories, he has produced three more: *El mejor de los mundos posibles*, 1976 [The best of all possible worlds], *En defensa propia*, 1982 [In self-defense], and *El remedio para el rey ciego*, 1984 [The remedy for the blind king]. Among the contents of these volumes are many humorous tales that poke fun at various aspects of contemporary human existence. A sixth book, despite its title, *Cuentos del mentiroso*, 1978 [Stories of the liar], is more than merely another compilation of short stories; in reality, it is a lengthy (77 pages), connected narrative. Bipartite in structure, its contents are composed of a tongue-in-cheek, rollicking spoof of the clichés of American cowboy novels (and films) plus a humorous continuation of the fantastic oriental adventures of Aladdin from the *Thousand and One Nights*. As in the picaresque novel (with which *Cuentos del mentiroso* has certain features in common), the work's two large, symmetrical sections, each consisting of five chapters, are unified by the presence in both of the peripatetic narrator-protagonist. Named Lelio García, alias "the liar," he is an obvious alter ego of the author; even the humorous drawing of Lelio that decorates the front cover of the book bears a zany, almost uncanny resemblance to Fernando. Lelio García is depicted in the story, however, as a bothersome but loveable, prevaricating neighbor of Sorrentino who brazenly interrupts the author's creative writing sessions and obliges him to listen to his far-fetched, totally fabricated adventures. These consist of García's incredible travels through the nineteenth-century American Wild West and through China in the days of a supposedly legendary rule of Aladdin over that country. Needless to say, Lelio García, "the liar," casts himself in the role of the gallant, romantic hero of the dual tales he relates to the author. While this work purports to be for children, it is really, as the dedication states, not only "for all children" but also for those adults who still retain from their childhood that special "pleasure in the game, the joke, the gratuitous." Indeed, *Cuentos del mentiroso* sometimes contains humor marked by a subtlety beyond the usual comprehension of children. The extended treatment of the material and the unity of the two halves of this lengthier adventure tale suggest that the author was already moving toward the more protracted form of the novel. In light of this, it seems noteworthy that *Cuentos del mentiroso* appeared the year preceding the publication of Sorrentino's first and only novel to date. He is now, however, working on a second, which he hopes to bring out very soon. It is, according to the author, an adventure novel in the Fantastic vein, which is to be titled *La infantina Soledad* [The little Princess Soledad] and in which "the heroes, who are always presented to us by the centers of world power, will appear as I believe they [really] are: as sinister personages."

With the comically alliterative title, *Sanitarios centenarios* [Sanitary centennial], Sorrentino brought to fruition his first effort in the novelistic genre in 1979. (The reader of the present English edition of the novel should know that the Spanish word *sanitario* does mean "sanitary," but as an adjective; as a plural noun, it also means "bathroom fixtures." I have attempted, I hope not in vain, to retain the conciseness of the original title as well as some of its alliterative cleverness.) In this genuinely funny short novel, a corporation that manufactures bathroom fixtures uses a gigantically inflated centennial celebration of its founding as a pretext to increase sales of its bathtubs, toilets, washbowls, and bidets; the author uses his talent, imagination, and wit to create a hilarious satire of the corporate mentality as well as of the high-powered, often unscrupulous advertising techniques of the popular mass media. Even the narrator-protagonist's name, Hernando Genovese, broadly hints that there is no small part of Fernando Sorrentino himself in this character, who laments having to prostrate his artistic talent as a short story writer to the composing of commercial advertising copy in order to eke out a living. (One is immediately reminded of Sorrentino's attitude toward teaching and other work he has done.) Try as he may, the emotionally stirring or fantastic tales that Genovese sets out to write always seem to turn themselves perversely into stories that provoke laughter, in much the same way that many of Sorrentino's own fictions do. In this regard, it is worthwhile observing that Sorrentino does not consider himself primarily a humorist, despite the highly amusing quality of perhaps the majority of his stories to date, but rather simply a man who refuses to take life (or himself) too seriously. As he has stated with characteristic modesty in an interview: "No, I don't consider myself a humorist. I consider myself a narrator who has, *moreover*, a sense of humor and, hence, sufficient common sense not to assume he is a member of the illuminati, an envoy of the gods, or an everlastingly tragic figure." However, Sorrentino does recognize, albeit almost reluctantly, the comic element in his fiction: "As for the humor in my stories, I believe it's there, that's undeniable." Like Hernando Genovese, his fictitious counterpart in the novel, our author also finds it difficult to reconcile himself to the fact that he is, perhaps above all else, a superb humorist, and that his greatest and unique contribution to Latin American literature may well lie in that direction. Were Sorrentino to accept this supposition, he might justifiably find himself, at the end of his career, in the distinguished company of all the great literary humorists and satirists of past and present. But, like a siren song to the artist, there always beckons the allurement of so-called serious literature.

Some of the novel's thematic content had been partially foreshadowed in two of Sorrentino's funniest short stories, both included in the present volume: "La pestilente historia de Antulín" ["The Fetid Tale of Antulín"], with its scatological humor and its principal setting in the bathroom of a Buenos Aires *pensión*, or boardinghouse; and "Ars Poetica," another richly textured parody, a similarly farcical lampoon of a rich, business-minded father's all-out mass media campaign to make a best-selling author out of his son, a mediocre poet. Once again, art is viewed as being sacrificed on the altar of expediency, and the reader begins to understand such pained statements by Sorrentino as the following, again from his autobiographical letter: "Those who assume they know me think I'm extremely modest; in reality, I suffer from pride. I look with resignation upon this world of the 'business of literature,' in which there are people who take seriously the writings of, for example" (and he mentions three well-known contemporary Argentine authors whose books have become best sellers and whose writing he deplores).

As literary critic, Sorrentino has published *Siete conversaciones con Jorge Luis Borges* (1974), translated by Clark M. Zlotchew as *Seven Conversations with Jorge Luis Borges* (Troy, N.Y., 1982). This work is an informative, book-length series of interviews in which Fernando skillfully draws out the author of *El aleph* on a broad range of literary and intellectual subjects. In 1986, Sorrentino collaborated as co-editor with Juan José Delaney, another Argentine writer, in the founding of an excellent scholarly journal, *Lucanor*, which is dedicated to articles on and reviews of modern and contemporary Argentine narrative. Sorrentino is also the editor of nine compilations of short stories by other Argentine and Spanish American authors, the themes of which run the full gamut from tales of stark realism to those of fantasy, animals, the grotesque, the absurd, and the humorous; from lengthy narratives to the Argentine *microcuento* (the mini-or micro-story, usually one page in length). In addition, he has prepared annotated editions of such Spanish and Argentine classics as *El libro de buen amor* [The book of good love], *El conde Lucanor* [Count Lucanor], *La verdad sospechosa* [The suspicious truth], *Artículos de costumbres* [Local color sketches], and *Martín Fierro*, the celebrated Argentine gaucho poem. To all this scholarly work Sorrentino brings his lengthy teaching experience and his vast knowledge and love of Spanish classical literature as well as the literature of his native land. It is no wonder the reader constantly encounters, scattered throughout the author's narratives, quotations and paraphrases of verses, stanzas, phrases, and sentences taken from those literatures. As Fernando declares in his inimitably facetious yet simultaneously serious way: "I like Borges, I like Bioy Casares, I like Denevi. I like Cortázar's early books. I like humor, fantasy, irony, subtlety. I like Spanish poetry of the Golden Age. I could recite from memory almost the whole *Martín Fierro*, almost all of *La vida es sueño* [Life is a dream]. Without being Funes, I have a very good memory; I have considerable aptitude for learning and mental association. I'm incapable of understanding a book on physics, chemistry, or philosophy."

Besides the earlier recognition by the National Foundation for the Arts, Sorrentino's creative writings have been accorded additional honors. His third collection of stories, *El mejor de los mundos posibles*, was awarded the Second Municipal Prize in the Narrative for 1976. Alluding to the increasing attention he was beginning to attract from important literary critics in Argentina, Fernando informs us, with his characteristically self-effacing manner, that "around that time I became aware—without knowing how it came about—that there was a certain number of critics interested in what I was writing." Two years later, in 1978, *Cuentos del mentiroso* won the Faja de Honor de S.A.D.E. (Sash of Honor of the Argentine Society of Authors). In June of that same year, the author took first prize in the short story category of a literary contest sponsored by the Troquel Publishing Company for his strange tale entitled "El nuevo juez" [The new judge], one of almost five hundred entries.

Sorrentino's eighth book, *El remedio para el rey ciego* (1984), is another collection of short stories, but, like *Cuentos del mentiroso*, this work too is unique. In *El remedio*, the author experiments with a kind of *refundición* (adaptation), or what he calls a *reelaboración*, of traditional medieval and renaissance exempla and of other ancient, brief narrative forms drawn from various cultures. The reader will usually find, either within the individual texts of the eight tales or at their end, an occasional nodding acknowledgment of a literary source— *The Thousand and One Nights*, Juan Manuel's *El conde Lucanor*, *Don Quixote*, Juan de Timoneda, and so on—but the stories all bear the unmistakable stamp of Sorrentino's original voice and personal vision. The artist adds, subtracts, and changes names, circumstances, and details of the venerable old tales with complete freedom and with what he calls "the parodic spirit with which I came into this world." Dedicated to the author's three children, most of the fablelike narratives of *El remedio para el rey ciego* are, indeed, intended primarily for children, and in this, too, they somewhat resemble *Cuentos del mentiroso;* however, Sorrentino believes that adults can also read them "without feeling guilty of childishness." It is quite apparent that the author views this book as a digression from his usual creative trajectory, a pleasant parenthesis in his literary career, or what he has, during an interview, more metaphorically termed "a landing on the stairway": "This little book is, let us say, a landing on the stairway; I simply wanted to write those slightly ingenuous tales characterized by rigorous conventions and a traditional, peremptory form. Naturally, I don't disavow them; I love them very much. But I would like the reader to see them for what they are: merely an exception."

Sorrentino's writings to date are characterized by certain formal and thematic constants: allegorical animal stories (several of which deal with birds, sheep, mice, and insects, especially spiders and scorpions); stories about laws, bureaucracies, life in offices, and professional white-collar workers; realistic stories; fantastic stories; tales of the absurd with *situaciones límites* (on-the-brink situations); an assemblage of very funny stories; and another corpus of strange, Kafkaesque narratives that reveal a darker side of the author's vision. Sorrentino's predominant voice, however, resonates with his sparkling, multifaceted sense of humor, which manifests itself in exaggerated, ludicrous situations, ridiculous characters, witty dialogue, satire, word play, and parodies of linguistic forms and pop culture. Reading Sorrentino's fiction, one may be reminded, almost simultaneously, of Rabelais, Quevedo, and, above all, yet strangely enough, Kafka: the first, for his hyperbolic, exuberant, sometimes even coarse humor and parody; the second, for his mordant satire; and the last, for his nightmarish ambiences and absurd predicaments, which communicate a somber, ironical statement on the alienating, dehumanizing machinery of our complex, often impersonal world.

Sorrentino profoundly and openly esteems Kafka. One of his strange yet humorous stories, found in *El mejor de los mundos posibles* and titled "Nuevas leyes inmobiliarias" [New real estate laws], is unmistakably dedicated "a la memoria de mi idolatrado K." [to the memory of my idolized K.]. And when queried in an interview, the author responded: "Yes, I am an ardent admirer of Kafka. When I read and reread him, I never fail to be fascinated by his stylistic precision, by the richness of his plots. I admire precision exceedingly, and, conversely, I don't like ambiguity at all. In my stories, despite the strangeness of many situations, I try to make the images very concrete, very precise." Sorrentino shares other experiences with the German-speaking, Czechoslovakian author of *The Metamorphosis*.

While the inspiration for some of Kafka's literary works came from his bureaucratic position in the workmen's compensation division of the Austrian government, the Argentine writer tells of somewhat similar work involvements. In the same interview, Fernando refers to literary approaches and procedures utilized by Kafka that shape his own stories as well: "As my point of departure, I work with common situations and well-known circumstances. I was an office worker for several years and at present I am a literature teacher. My human experience is, then, of a common, ordinary kind. But, as a storyteller, I am convinced that any environment, no matter how simple and conventional it may seem, represents a world susceptible to various interpretations, and it is the task of the writer to suggest them. It's all in knowing how to scratch the surface of reality to see what lies beneath." There is, however, a very significant difference between Kafka and the Argentine author. As one commentator notes, Kafka makes of the absurd a vehicle for expressing the pity he feels for his wretched characters, who are ground up and devoured by powerful, inscrutable forces in a tenebrous, unequal struggle, the outcome of which seems inevitable. By contrast, in Sorrentino's fictional world, from his realistic, almost trivial initial situations, the author slips, at times imperceptibly, into an absurdity freighted with satire, irony, parody, caricature, and sly, good-natured winks of complicity at the knowing reader. The Argentine writer's humor functions in part, therefore, to attenuate his potentially Kafkaesque situations and atmospheres, the essential ingredients of which usually tended to be, as one observer noted, "a nightmarish sense of having lost one's identity . . . and of a bewildered helplessness" in the face of overwhelming odds in a dark game whose rules the character never seems to know or understand. In Kafka, the protagonist confronts a "vast, sinister, impersonal bureaucracy, which is intuitively felt to be evil yet which appears to have a crazy kind of transcendent logic on its side." On the other hand, in Sorrentino's more luminous world, the potent adversary in the struggle (his stories are often about competitions and rivalries) is more tangible, familiar, and humanized, because he or she is frequently a relative, friend, neighbor, colleague, or co-worker. Familiarity, as the saying goes, breeds contempt, and through this familiarity such personages are quickly unmasked for the reader, compelled to reveal their foibles, silly aberrations, and vulnerabilities, thus laying themselves open to ridicule, satire, and laughter. In Kafka, the main player in the game, the protagonist, is always a defeated man; in Sorrentino, the contest's central participant, almost always a first-person narrator, may be a winner or a loser. In a word, it's the difference between the tragic Weltanschauung projected by Kafka and the comic vision emanating from Sorrentino's creations. Sorrentino's skilled humor, then, while deftly avoiding Rabelais' vulgarity, Quevedo's bitter, caustic wit, and Kafka's stern despair, steers a middle course and seems to draw eclectically and mysteriously on all three. The end product, novel and unique, reveals an artist with a distinctly original, highly personal voice and vision.

A genuine literary humorist plays a dual role; he is, paradoxically, an amused yet serious spectator of life as well as an artist. As dispassionate but critical onlooker, he observes mankind's foolish foibles and the disparities and absurdities of social existence and endeavor. As artist, he interprets and shapes. He enjoys a special, detached outlook on life as well as the genius to mold that aloof yet tickled vision into expressive, appealing forms. The targets of Sorrentino's humorous satire, like his themes and forms, have remained constant: hypocrisy, stupidity, mediocrity, ignorance, and foolishness in any shape or manifestation; excessive materialism and infatuation with power, titles, possessions, prestige, and status symbols; groundless attitudes of superiority; the senseless, bureaucratic complexity of large business corporations and other hierarchical institutions; phony public relations and advertising; the mindless insipidness of many types of popular entertainment—television, radio, certain films, and popular magazines, such as *People, Reader's Digest*, and the like; and, furthermore, the exploitation of all this mass media for exclusively commercial ends. A special mark for Sorrentino's satirical barbs is any form of pretentious, inflated, or just incorrect language, including snobbish speech, clichés, *frases hechas* (fixed or set expressions), the ostentatious abuse of professional jargon, and certain types of unintelligible literary language and criticism. He takes great glee in poking fun, for example, at such practically untranslatable Spanish critical jargon as *praxis, problemática, fáctico*, and the overused and/or mistaken usage of such phrases as *pienso de que* (literally, "I think [*of*] that," the preposition "de" being superfluous in Spanish), and *a nivel*, a much misused Spanish phrase somewhat akin to our American English abuse of the suffix "-wise," as in terms like "weatherwise."

The satirical humorist's detached aloofness may be adroitly used to conceal his scorn and derision for things that are objectionable to him. This procedure may be seen at work when one contrasts such vehement personal assertions by the author as the following with their counterparts in his fiction: "I became familiar with the literary milieu; I attended an occasional meeting of writers: as good a way as any of wasting time. I loathe writers' statements about literature, debates, roundtable discussions, polemics. The soccer player is valued for his playing; the writer for his writing. Statements add merit neither to the one nor to the other. I usually avoid people I dislike, even though I might garner some advantage from being around them. And the fact of the matter is that I dislike the majority of people. I detest stress, greed, vanity, and stupidity." When such attitudes and feelings, which may seem to take on the tones of what is only an apparent antisocial bitterness, are collated with the merry mirth clothing them in Sorrentino's stories, one appreciates the distance separating real sentiments and their cleverly disguised expression in artistic form. When he or she turns, then, to the translated narratives included herein, the reader will soon discover (and will do well to remember) that thoughtful human concerns and other serious feelings, enumerated above as targets of Sorrentino's barbs, lie embedded, for example, in the gleeful satire of the corporate and commercial world seen in *Sanitary Centennial*; in the good-natured ridicule of certain social conventions, attitudes, and human types in "The Life of the Party" and "In Self-Defense"; or in the uproarious parodic mockery made of the debasement of art in "Ars Poetica." Even lurking behind the apparently insignificant, absolutely silly circumstances depicted in "A Lifestyle," barely hidden beneath its absurd surface, is one of those sober, typically Kafkaesque situations in which an innocent individual falls victim to the nameless, faceless, and omnipotent forces with which he is powerless to cope. This brief tale is a superb example of the creative sorcery with which a master of wit can transform an essentially serious set of circumstances fraught with grim potential into a ludicrous farce. Kafka's influence is in evidence, but the story is stamped with Sorrentino's original irony and wit. Only after reading through to the end, for example, will the reader fully appreciate the subtle humor of the narrative's opening sentence.

Although unique among the stories in this anthology, "Piccirilli," like the other stories, is also representative of another sizable sector of Sorrentino's writings, and it belongs to a genre with a long and illustrious tradition in Argentina—the Fantastic. Not only has Sorrentino edited an anthology titled *17 cuentos fantásticos argentinos siglo XX* [17 Argentine fantastic stories of the 20th century], including narratives by as many authors, he has also written a goodly number of first-rate fantastic tales. Indeed, even his more realistic stories occasionally incorporate wild, fantastic elements; the denouement of "In Self-Defense" is a case in point. Within the canon of fantastic themes, that of the homunculus, or diminutive man, is somewhat unique, although it too has enjoyed a long, illustrious tradition in myth, legend, and literature (Swift, Goethe, Carroll, Maugham, Tolkien, Mann, Darío, Mujica Láinez, Bioy Casares). "Piccirilli" marks Sorrentino's second treatment of the homunculus theme; the first was a story titled "Cosas de vieja" [Ramblings of an old woman] appearing in *Imperios y servidumbres*. "Piccirilli" is a charming little tale that achieves perfection as a fantastic story (according to Todorov) insofar as it offers absolutely no explanation for the apparently supernatural appearance of a tiny man five centimeters in height; the reader is left in suspense, hesitating and wondering to the end about the possibility of such an event. Moreover, Piccirilli's unintelligible language only adds to the mysterious enigma, for he, himself, can tell us nothing.

"The Fetid Tale of Antulín" is sheer fun. The narrator, one of Sorrentino's refined, sensitive, but pathetic "losers" in life, finds himself pitted against a seemingly invincible antagonist, the boorish, eternally unwashed, but ever triumphant Antulín. The reader should not miss the supremely ironic little detail, tucked unobtrusively into the scene in the second café (Chapter 6), of the supposedly dumb Antulín's swift working out of the most difficult parts of the sad narrator's crossword puzzle. The arena for their unequal combat is the bathroom of one of those traditional old *criollo* boardinghouses of Buenos Aires with a central open-air patio. The story appeared in *Imperios y servidumbres*, and in a kind of epilogue to the collection, titled "Four Paragraphs," Fernando waggishly (and again self-effacingly) recounts the origin in reality of the famous "Antulín" and at the same time discloses one of his preferred narrative techniques, that of hyperbole, or exaggeration: "The tortures to which he was submitted by the maneuverings of Antulín were described some three years ago [ca. 1969] by Juan Angel Scarsi—Uruguayan, bohemian, vocational actor, and, above all, boardinghouse lodger—to my friend Juan Manuel González Servat. The latter—an unbeatable teller (and twister) of crazy stories—related them to me, suitably exaggerated, and I, in turn, set them down in written form, with my own appropriate exaggeration. It should, then, be made quiet clear that Antulín's circumstances belong more to Scarsi than to González, and more to González than to me." The humor of the term "Antulín's circumstances" will become abundantly apparent to the reader in the first paragraph of Chapter 15 of this wildly entertaining tale.

Accentuated in Sorrentino's statement quoted just above is the double dose of exaggeration that went into the crafting of "The Fetid Tale of Antulín." Hyperbole has traditionally been one of the main tools of the humorist, the satirist, the parodist, and the caricaturist. I mentioned earlier the author's reference to "the parodic spirit" with which he came into *this* world and which now infuses large cross sections of his *fictional* world. During one of my conversations with Fernando in Buenos Aires, while we worked together on the translation of *Sanitarios centenarios,* he told me that two of his favorite techniques or approaches to storytelling are parody and what he calls "crescendo." Both entail exaggeration of one kind or another. Crescendo is a type of gradation; it is akin to a stylistic figure of speech called "climax," consisting of a series of related words, phrases, or thoughts so arranged that each surpasses the preceding in force or intensity. It may follow an ascending or descending progression. One recalls, for example, Sor Juana Inés de la Cruz's well-known sonnet, "Este que ves, engaño colorido . . ." [This colored deception that you see . . .], which ends in the descending climax, "es cadáver, es polvo, es sombra, es nada" [is a corpse, is dust, is a shadow, is nothing]. As a device of narrative discourse, crescendo creates anticipation, tension, and suspense, contributes to rhythm and pacing, and may even determine structure and organization.

Crescendo, for Sorrentino, denotes a steady increase and/or intensification of usually (but not always) zany elements, leading to a climax of high jinks and boisterous merriment. Any reader of the author's substantial repertoire of comical stories (as well as his novel) will observe how these narratives often rise and culminate in "crescendos" of fun-filled humor of the rollicking, farcical type. It is a pattern discernible in many of the artist's tales, but, of those assembled here, "In Self-Defense" perhaps offers the best illustration of its mechanisms. As in a game of one-upmanship or a war of nerves, Mr. Wilhelm Hoffer and the narrator gradually, even literally, "escalate" the value and magnitude of the gifts they bestow upon one another to extremes of the absurd, the impossible, and, finally, the unreal. But most of the other narratives, too, display an analogous design in one way or another. For example, the entire plot trajectory of *Sanitary Centennial* builds to a giddy climax, a crescendo of frenzied revelry. In retrospect, it all seems to have pointed "upward," toward the gargantuan centennial festivities of Spettanza Bathroom Fixtures, which were promised at the end of the first chapter ("With the works!"), culminate the action in the last chapter, and there give the novel its title. Similarly, each successive attempt of the narrator to "execute" Antulín in "The Fetid Tale" contributes to a rising action and intensifies the reader's anticipation while, at the same time, providing structure and pacing for the narrative. Each successive nasty trick played by Arthur and Graciela on the Vitavers in "The Life of the Party" seems to the reader the height of grossness and audacity—until they unveil their next prank, that is. In an ascending climax of fun-filled but sharply pointed tomfoolery in "Ars Poetica," the author ludicrously satirizes each and every one of the complex parts of the vast public relations machine that literally creates celebrities. One after another, all the agencies and entities involved in the commercialization of art (the "business of literature," to use the author's term) come in for a lambasting: well-heeled, overly ambitious, unscrupulous fathers; vapid television roundtable discussions; mercenary literary critics and historians; author and book debuts; the "intellectual" community; superficial newspaper book reviews and literary criticism; popular magazine interviews (and interviewers); the readers (purchasers) of such magazines; corrupt literary contests and judges; ghost writers; and, finally, to cap it all and bring it full circle, a second, infinitely more raucous TV talk show.

Parody, the author's other favorite technique, is usually defined as a written composition that burlesques or imitates another, usually serious literary work. More specifically, parody is the imitative use of the words, style, attitude, tone, and ideas of an author or a work in such a way as to make them ridiculous. As with crescendo (or climax), this goal likewise is accomplished by exaggeration, since the writer exaggerates and disfigures certain features of the author's style or the work imitated in the manner of a caricaturist. Indeed, parody is to literature what caricature and the cartoon are to art, for the original model is deformed and made funny or grotesque. In short, parody is a satirical verbal (linguistic) mimicry, and, as a branch of satire, it usually seeks to deride and/or to correct. Parody is difficult to bring off successfully, since it demands a very delicate balance between a close resemblance to the model combined with a deliberate distortion of the original's main characteristics. It is best accomplished by authors who are imaginative and creative themselves; indeed, the best parodists have been gifted writers (Cervantes, Fielding, Beerbohm).

It has been pointed out by Margaret A. Rose that there are two main theories regarding the nature of the parodist's attitude toward his or her imitated text: the first holds that, motivated by contempt for that text, he or she writes to mock it; the second maintains that, feeling sympathy with the targeted work, the author imitates it out of admiration for the style of that text. As the reader may already have guessed, Sorrentino's attitude belongs to the first category, for he obviously disdains his targets and writes to ridicule and belittle them humorously, to call attention to their vacuity and stupidity in hopes of annihilating them, literally "to laugh them away." Although Rose maintains that the requisite comic effect in parody is achieved both through the mere simulation of other styles and through the incongruous juxtaposition of the parodying text with the imitated work, the latter is probably more vital. The essence of parodic humor lies largely, then, in raising the reader's expectations to receive one thing, by means of evoking the text alluded to, and then serving up something else. As in jokes and much other humor, this mechanism involves our anticipations and their deception through an unexpected surprise. Although not absolutely necessary, the reader's recognition of the "signals of parody," that is, the mismatched discrepancies between the parodist's model (the object of the attack) and the ridiculing imitation of it, will greatly enhance the reader's appreciation of the parodist's art of distortion and its subtleties.

Most theories of traditional parody tend to limit the original model copied and/or mocked to an individual work of "serious literature" or to a specific "literary" author's peculiar stylistic idiosyncrasies. Although Sorrentino occasionally engages in this kind of conventional parody as well, he generally circumvents the limitations implicit in such considerations because his choice of targeted texts also happen to be some of his "pet peeves," and as such they guarantee almost instant reader recognition. (The parodies of the "literary world" in "Ars Poetica" might be an exception.) It is apparent, then, that when referring to his "spirit of parody" and to the corpus of his works, Sorrentino greatly extends the term "parody" far beyond formal literature to include bantering mimicry of almost any mode of discourse, but especially those represented in most forms of "pop culture," the popular entertainment fields, the mass media, sports, advertising, and numerous other types of speech. We can easily picture the necessary incongruent juxtapositions between his parodying stories and the originals he is imitating precisely because we are all (most of us anyway) so familiar with his models, which constitute such a large part of our contemporary mass culture. We quickly pick up the signals of his parody and laugh with him at the objectives of his satire. Suffice to state for the record that the following are a few of the devices at the service of parody within the author's stylistic repertoire: hyperbole, incongruity, distortion, irony, repetition, contrast, neologisms, caricature, reductio ad absurdum, deliberate abuse of synonyms and nonexisting words, use of *porteño lunfardo* (Buenos Aires underworld words and other slang expressions), jargon, plays on words, intentionally wrong use of Spanish words as well as of Latin and other foreign languages, and funny proper names.

At present, Fernando Sorrentino is considered one of the brightest new talents in the contemporary Argentine narrative. While he is without question an outstanding humorist, his writings also embrace, as we have seen, serious, universal thematic considerations and significance. His admirable, carefully crafted tales of the Fantastic qualify him, moreover, as a worthy successor to the well-known writers of fantastic fiction, usually referred to as the "Grupo de Sur" (because of their affiliation with *Sur*, the well-known Argentine journal founded by Victoria Ocampo): Borges, Bioy Casares, Silvina Ocampo, Enrique Anderson Imbert, and so on. In an interview published in the Buenos Aires daily *La Prensa*, as early as 1978, the eminent Argentine critic Juan Carlos Ghiano had already singled out Sorrentino and included him among the few writers who managed to escape what Ghiano perceived as a "general state of exhaustion" beginning to afflict contemporary Spanish American writing. These exceptional authors are able, according to the critic, to admire a Borges or a Cortázar "without fanaticism," that is, without slavishly imitating these two internationally prestigious artists and others. Ghiano goes on to say that Sorrentino, Héctor Lastra, and Jorge Asís represent a select group of narrators in Argentina, then aged 25 to 35, who "define themselves through the cautiousness with which they seek to be original," who are intensely aware of the fact that they must seek their uniqueness "along other paths." Writing two years later in *El Día* of Montevideo, Jorge Oscar Pickenhayn, another distinguished arbiter of Argentine literature, concurs with Ghiano's favorable assessment of the quality and singularity of Sorrentino's creativeness. Pickenhayn numbers Sorrentino among other important writers of prose fiction (Borges, Sábato, Denevi, Bioy Casares, etc.) who are, the critic declares, "capable of representing the [Argentine] narrative of our century."

This talented artist, Fernando Sorrentino, continues to construct his highly entertaining, imaginary *world of fiction* and to publish its components in respected magazines and newspapers of the Spanish-speaking world, such as *Papeles de Son Armadans, Revista Nacional de Cultura, La Nación, La Prensa.* When he has accumulated a sufficient number of stories to make up a collection, he assembles them in volumes like those referred to here. With remarks that ring strikingly similar to the narrator-protagonist's concluding words in "A Lifestyle," Fernando closes his autobiographical letter with these cheery, optimistic thoughts, which accurately characterize him as a good and genuine human being and situate him comfortably in his *world of reality:* "I like good food, I like idleness and leisure, I enjoy a good time. I like the virtues and the defects of the Latins. I love my country deeply. In a word, let's say that I'm relatively happy."

Thomas C. Meehan

TRANSLATOR'S NOTE

$\mathcal{F}$ernando Sorrentino's style is generally quite clear and unambiguous. From that point of view, translating his stories has been a labor of love. His works, however, can present a translator or reader with problems of other kinds. In the Introduction, the reader will have become aware of the author's academic training and teaching, his broad reading, his prodigious memory, and his love of native city and country. In his writings, Sorrentino draws very freely upon these personal experiences, characteristics, and qualities, as well as upon his considerable general knowledge and culture. All of this material frequently crops up, identified or unidentified, in textual quotations, references, and allusions, which may be literary, linguistic, historic, or geographic in form or simply of a general sociocultural nature. Such references are never pedantic, nor are they used merely for adornment; rather, they are always skillfully integrated into the characterization of a personage or the plot development of a given story. I have used in-text explanations and paraphrasing wherever possible to clarify the author's allusions. However, without some type of help, the English-speaking reader with no knowledge of Spanish or experience with general Hispanic (and, more specifically, Argentine) culture, could find difficult, even meaningless, passages containing such referential contexts. I have, therefore, appended some notes, which will, it is hoped, be of assistance to such readers. Other readers may safely pass over the notes. Unless otherwise indicated, all streets and *barrios* mentioned in the stories are to be found in Buenos Aires.

It is my hope that the reader will find these English renditions of Fernando Sorrentino's tales as enjoyable and entertaining as I found the Spanish versions. I also hope that this collection will draw the attention of the North American reading public and the Latin American scholarly community of the United States to the art of this unique literary figure. The realization of these hopes would be due to the Argentine author's excellence and talent as a writer; any failure would be attributable solely to the undersigned's shortcomings as a translator.

ACKNOWLEDGMENTS

I wish to express my appreciation to a number of individuals who have been very generous with their time and most helpful to me in resolving certain translation problems as well as those related to references and allusions of different types appearing in Fernando Sorrentino's fictions. I am deeply indebted to my good *porteño* friend and faculty colleague Horacio Porta for identifying and clarifying many references to people, places, and things in and near Buenos Aires. In this same regard, Marianela Chaumeil, an Argentine graduate student in my department, was also particularly helpful. To Santiago García-Castañón, a graduate student from Spain, I am very grateful for his invaluable aid in tracing and identifying several of Sorrentino's quotations from and allusions to Spanish Golden Age literature. Sincerest thanks also to my research assistant, Olga Uribe, for her helpful suggestions on "Ars Poetica" and on the translation of Sorrentino's autobiographical letter, several passages of which appear in my Introduction. Special gratitude is due also to another translator of Sorrentino, Clark Zlotchew, for his encouragement and for his assistance with a particularly "thorny" passage in "Ars Poetica," his imaginative rendering of which has been incorporated practically verbatim. I am very grateful to Pamela A. Patton for her generous help in the preparation of the final manuscript of the volume. Thanks go to Editorial Plus Ultra, Editorial de Belgrano, and Editorial Seix Barral for their cooperation in granting permission for these translations. Finally, but above all, I wish to convey my deepest gratitude to Fernando Sorrentino for his gracious permission to translate his stories, for all the hours of invaluable help he gave me while I was working on both *Sanitarios centenarios* and "La pestilente historia de Antulín," and for the infinite patience he has shown while waiting to see this project brought to fruition. To both Fernando and Alicia Sorrentino I send my sincerest thanks for the kindness, hospitality, and generosity they extended to me during my stay in Buenos Aires.

T.C.M.

SANITARY CENTENNIAL

Furthermore, I don't remember
all those stupid symbols;
they were all in the same style,
to the point that I finally
felt ashamed.
                        —DOSTOYEVSKY
                The Possessed, III, II

Prologue

*I*t must have been about twenty years ago. Yet I, a person who tends to forget more important things, retain that memory clearly in my mind, as if it happened to me just yesterday. Or, even better than if it belonged to yesterday, I safeguard the essential part of it, keeping it free from the accumulation of any superfluous details.

It was on Costa Rica Street, it was siesta time, and it was autumn; a nice, warm, but indecisive sun was keeping me cozy. I was squatting on the edge of the curb, stirring the sewer water in the gutter with a little stick. A zoological mystery had aroused my curiosity: some tiny white worms were wriggling around in the blackness of that slime in the spaces between the paving stones. They looked like vermicelli or like slender strands of thread. What were those little worms? How could I catch them? They would appear and then hide, appear and hide. They seemed to form part of that shiny, black muck; but, no, they weren't part of it because, when I picked up a bit of it and smoothed it out with my little stick, I found to my surprise that the little worms were no longer there. Was it possible that I couldn't gain possession of those little worms?

A sudden chill nipped my ears. Something had come between me and the sun. I looked up. A big, wide, square truck had just parked. I read the emphatic yellow letters against a green background: *Spettanza Bathroom Fixtures*. And, below, in somewhat smaller characters: *Reliable Products*.

There appeared four men enveloped in blue overalls. They opened the rear doors of the truck and folded out a wooden ladder worn down by countless feet. One of the workers said to me: "Hey kid, move away a little bit, we have to unload."

And unload they did. I stood up and, leaning against the rough bark of a tree, I watched a long, snow-white procession of washbowls, bathtubs, toilets, and bidets as they emerged, ghostlike, from that inexhaustible truck and disappeared, on the shoulders of the workmen, into the depths of the tall building under construction, in front of which I, perched on the curb, had been stirring the sewer water with a little stick in an attempt to capture the uncapturable, little white worms.

I. The Coming of the Spettanza Brothers

*I*t hasn't been twenty years since the culmination of the story that is now beginning. I should like to assign to these events the rarefied apocryphal time of fiction; hence, no one is unaware of the fact that around that imaginary date the Spettanza Bathroom Fixtures Company attained the age of one hundred years. Twelve or fifteen months in advance, its owners prepared to celebrate that occasion befittingly. They concluded, therefore, that the most appropriate thing to do was to wend their way to Carlos Pellegrini Street, pass through a certain door, travel by elevator to the third floor, and there have recourse to the already quite renowned services of the Persuasive Conviction Advertising Agency, where at the time I—in one of my many incarnations—was carrying out the functions of a copywriter.

My office door opened and a secretary named Irene came in and said to me: "Hernando, McCormick wants to know if you can come to his office."

"Listen, Irene, will you marry me?"

"Don't you ever weary of uttering the same drivel all the time?"

Having learned from experience, I took a sheet of paper and a pencil and went into McCormick's office. He was standing behind his huge desk, dominating with his imposing stature a group of three gray backs crowned by three partially gray heads.

"New clients," I thought with annoyance, "and, consequently, new work."

I put on that languid, blank face that precedes introductions.

"Hernando Genovese," McCormick proclaimed emphatically, as if he were announcing "His Majesty, King George V."

McCormick is a quick-witted individual, and he is also a great actor, skilled in the art of impressing the cleverest person with words or posturing; at his pronouncement, the three men, with an ostentatious and disorderly scraping and pushing back of chairs, stood up with the same resolute swiftness that would have corresponded to the actual entrance of King George and his entourage of nobility.

But McCormick wouldn't even dream of limiting himself to the enunciation of my name; he needed to issue a value judgment. "Hernando," he added, "is one of our three creative geniuses."

I smiled indulgently, as if saying in effect that McCormick was 100 percent right, but that my modesty might have preferred my status as a genius to remain a secret nevertheless.

The visitors examined me attentively, trying to discover outward signs of my genius. Then McCormick dealt them another blow: "Thanks to the creative brilliance of Hernando's writings, our clients are sick of counting their money."

I saw amazement on the faces of the three men. What magical writings mine must be!

But McCormick, implacable, was already moving on: "Mr. Peter Spettanza."

I smiled, shook his hand, and declared that I was very pleased to meet Mr. Peter Spettanza.

"Mr. John Spettanza."

I smiled, shook his hand, and declared that I was very pleased to meet Mr. John Spettanza.

"And Mr. Luke Spettanza."

I smiled, shook his hand, and declared that I was very pleased to meet Mr. Luke Spettanza.

"Three of the six proprietors," McCormick summed up, "of Spettanza Bathroom Fixtures."

"Reliable Products," I emphasized.

This phrase produced a foreseeable beatific effect on the three Spettanzas. McCormick's face lit up with joy.

"Ah, I see you're already acquainted with our firm," John Spettanza said complacently.

"Gentlemen, please be seated," said McCormick, as though fearful the promising beginning might fizzle.

He passed around cigarettes with the intention of creating an adequate prologue of silence for his next words: "Not to boast about the functioning of our agency . . ."

His voice had taken on that slight edge of a friendly threat. The three Spettanzas hastened to protest: "No, no, of course not."

"Not to boast about the functioning of our agency," McCormick repeated energetically, thus invalidating the Spettanzas' words, "but I can assure you that here at Persuasive Conviction, everyone, absolutely everyone . . ."

The Spettanzas looked tense, ashamed.

". . . absolutely everyone, from Arrambide and Violini, my partners (presently on a business trip in Europe), and from me right on down to the lowest office boy, everyone, absolutely every single one of us, is deeply involved in the matter."

He emphasized the enigmatic word *matter* with a rap of his knuckles on the glass top of his desk. Peter Spettanza blinked slightly, and I sensed that he was on the verge of asking what, exactly, was the *matter*. So as not to let him talk, I said: "And not only that. The fact is that I, too, have Spettanza bathroom fixtures installed in my home."

"You're not the only one," replied Peter Spettanza, forgetting his original intention. "Just imagine, practically 80 percent of all the bathroom fixtures installed in this country bear the Spettanza trademark."

"Then with good reason they're called 'Reliable Products,'" I concluded, smiling.

How pleased the Spettanzas were! How artfully McCormick and I pretended to share their delight! All you could see were smiles from ear to ear.

"The fact is, there are reasons, a surplus of reasons," added Luke Spettanza, fatuously straightening his tie, "for Spettanza Bathroom Fixtures to be the *assoluta* leading firm in our area."

"The best advertising agency for the best firm," McCormick declared sententiously.

The ice was broken. Indeed, more than broken, it had been turned into tiny bits of crushed ice. Due to this gushing enthusiasm, there now ensued a slightly chaotic scene. No one waited any longer with respectful courtesy his turn to talk, and simultaneous crisscross conversations took place among the five speakers. Through some mishap, each found himself talking to his least near neighbor. Carried away by the give-and-take of his conversation with John Spettanza and McCormick, Luke Spettanza would regularly interject his profile between Peter Spettanza and me. Every so often Peter would emerge from behind his brother's nose and show me now his left eye and half of his mouth, now both eyes and his whole mouth. I should mention in passing that I didn't like the latter at all: it was a tiny, little mouth pleated like an accordion bellows, the folds of which were repeated in the almost vertical nostrils of his boxer's nose, a nose that turned upward and always seemed to be smelling some unbearable odor. When he smiled, the folds of his little mouth would spread open a bit, as if Peter Spettanza were ruefully musing: "Yes, it's true that I'm smelling a most unpleasant odor, but it can't be helped: it's part of my destiny and I'm now resigned to it." Just then, Peter Spettanza was going through one of those moments of serene resignation, because his little mouth was smiling as he stretched his neck out from behind Luke Spettanza and punctuated his words with a chubby index finger. He was uttering some stern, instructive phrases of which there reached me, confused in the general din, only fragmentary expressions like *faith in the future, we've never let down our guard* (I especially liked this one, because it matched his boxer's face), *vim and vigor, enterprising vision, oppressive tax burden, individual initiative.*

The arrival of a tray with five cups of coffee in Irene's hands called us all to order. For several seconds our voices were stilled by the distribution of cups and lumps of sugar. As we entered a brief interlude of spoon tinkling, I took advantage of the lull to ask Irene, in a very low voice, if she would marry me; and, immediately, before the conversation could again diversify into unforeseeable—and unprofitable—channels, McCormick said: "I'll fill you in on what it's all about, Hernando."

And he did so. I put on that concerned face which also showed intelligent discernment, a face that pleased McCormick no end whenever I adopted it in front of clients. He began to explain what the Spettanzas expected of our professional expertise. He was looking at me, but out of the corner of his right eye he attentively watched the Spettanzas' facial expressions, even the most imperceptible ones, and guided by these he amended here and there the sense of his phrasing, supplely adjusting it to their taste and liking and saying precisely the words they expected to hear.

I, in turn, wasn't idle. What a wonderful hypocrite I am when I'm in a good mood! Every so often I would interrupt McCormick with some shrewd but phony question, the answer to which both he and I knew beforehand; the purpose of such a question was to convince the

Spettanzas that I really was deeply concerned with understanding, even in their finest details, the desires and aspirations of the aforesaid Spettanzas.

"You gentlemen will let me know if I've interpreted you correctly or not," McCormick summed up, casting a humble learner's glance from one Spettanza to another.

"Yes, of course, we think that, uh . . ."

In a word, McCormick had interpreted them to perfection, but the Spettanzas were jumping out of their skins to talk, and we had to let them blow off steam; this circumstance too had been foreseen. So they repeated McCormick's presentation, but with more words and less precision. What emerged clearly was that the Spettanza Bathroom Fixtures Company was, as they say, rounding out one hundred years of *quiet, productive work* in the rather competitive field of sinks and bathtubs, of bidets, urinals, and toilets, and that it had thus established itself, in a highly commendable manner and thanks to a *clean, outstanding business record*, always *with their head held high*, as the *leading firm in the above-mentioned field*. The Spettanzas *were of the opinion that* such an event should be celebrated in a resounding, perhaps even glorious way, by *pulling out all the stops and painting the town red*, without regard for the *economic factor nor for a few pesos more or less, since it isn't every day you turn a hundred years old, but rather you only turn a hundred years old after a hundred years have passed, if you'll allow us the joke*. Despite its heavy nostalgic charge, capable of stirring the heart of more than one expert in bathroom fixtures, the program of festivities should, nevertheless, attend simultaneously (and perhaps even *in a predominant yet sensitive way*) to another very important aspect—*the promotional, business factor* . . .

"After all, we do make a living from it," noted Luke Spettanza.

. . . so that a *marked increase* in the demand for those reliable products was expected as a *logical consequence* of the centennial celebration. In short, what did Spettanza Bathroom Fixtures expect from the Persuasive Conviction Advertising Agency? They were eagerly seeking a broad publicity campaign, to be carried out in all the communications media: newspapers, magazines, radio, television.

"What about motion pictures?"

Yes, of course, it could be done in the film industry, too. The essential thing was that—before, during, and after the centennial festivities—the Argentine people should feel moved to renovate every bathroom in the country: from La Quiaca in the far north to the Antarctic in the south, and from the Atlantic Ocean to the Andes Mountains, there shouldn't survive a single one of the old, outmoded, inauspicious, and despicable bathroom fixtures that constituted a shameful and tragic remnant of a happily bygone era. Hence, some months before the great centennial festivities, Spettanza Bathroom Fixtures *would launch onto the market* some very modern sanitary *appliances*, whose exclusive blueprint was the work of the combined talents of three world-renowned designers.

"Why don't you explain to Hernando that business about the four lines?"

"O.K.," said Peter Spettanza. "The fixtures are divided into four lines. Even this isn't anything new, but we kinda thought it'd be nice to identify each line with a slogan, which more or less follows a tradition deeply rooted in the company."

"The lines," Luke Spettanza clarified, "are *Northampton, for the Exquisite; Royal, for the Exclusive; Majestic, for the Exacting; and Buckingham, for the Connoisseur.*"

At this point I thought it worthwhile to make a suggestion. Would it not *impact* more to replace the slogan *for the Connoisseur* with another that, like its three companion mottoes, also began with *ex?* That way we would succeed in giving the four lines a *more solid image of uniformity and coherence.*

"Do you think so?"

"Undoubtedly. Just now I'm reminded of the well-publicized campaign we put on for Hercules Trusses. Do you gentlemen recall it? No? That's a pity, because . . ."

And right then and there I launched into an erudite synopsis that traced the struggle waged between hernias and trusses from the Middle Ages to the Atomic Era. I even explored its antecedents in prehistoric times and made a brief digression into the use of multiple colors in the painting of trusses on the walls of the Caves of Altamira, a subject to which Doctor Ludwig Boitus, professor emeritus of the University of Göttingen, had dedicated more than one detailed monograph. I then went on to an in-depth analysis of the Hercules truss and aptly and opportunely related its name to several aspects of Greco-Roman mythology. I had already begun to recite in Latin some hexameters by Virgil when McCormick, who up to that point had listened attentively while inwardly bursting with laughter, became alarmed: "Experience, our experience, demonstrates," he stated eruditely, making a slight sign for me to shut up, "that Hernando is completely right. Because, in effect, numerous studies on market motivation tend to establish in a trustworthy way . . ."

"Trustworthy?" asked John Spettanza, just to say something.

"Absolutely trustworthy," McCormick retorted severely, and he fell silent, as if offended.

The three Spettanzas looked at each other, dismayed. Luke salvaged the situation: "You were saying, sir, that studies on market motivation . . ."

"Yes," McCormick continued peevishly, thus showing that he had lost all interest in the subject. "I was saying that market motivation studies have established in an absolutely trustworthy way," he glared at John Spettanza, "that the public, the consumer public, tends to identify the products of a single line by the elements common to all of them, so that . . ."

"Ah, fine," interrupted John, now anxious to redeem himself, "in that case, not another word. What slogan would the gentleman suggest?"

The "gentleman" turned out to be me. I innocently proposed *Buckingham, for the Excremental.* Distressed, the Spettanza brothers adduced, in annoyance and opposition, that such a slogan could lend itself to fanciful and even counterproductive interpretations. We then discussed for quite a while (I was now amused by McCormick's restrained impatience as he cast sidelong looks at the clock) what would be *le mot juste*, and, after weighing the relative beauty of the words *expensive, extemporaneous, exceptional, exclusivist, excessive,* and *excommunicated*, we decided on the euphonic slogan, *Buckingham, for the Expert.*

"Is that better than *for the Connoisseur?*" (This guy, John Spettanza, was turning out to be a rebel without a cause; we had to teach him a lesson.)

"Oh, much better," I replied. "Notice that, when you say *for the Expert*, you are connotating, at the level of subconscious semeiology" (the things I'm capable of at times!), "that Buckingham toilets agree to receive into their bosom only the waste of a certain class of individuals: the expert."

John Spettanza was impressed. I felt like adding something more, but McCormick gave me an imperceptible wink, which a layman would take as a nervous tic; it was best not to waste any more time on the Spettanzas since, from all the evidence, they now formed part of the growing number of admirers of the Persuasive Conviction Advertising Agency.

"Mr. Luke Spettanza, who is the poet of bathroom fixtures . . .," said McCormick.

So as not to explode in an uproarious outburst of laughter, I feigned a violent coughing fit. McCormick's face was stony, but he was laughing inwardly.

". . . has prepared a written report," he handed me some typewritten pages, "so you can read it and start immersing yourself in the history of Spettanza Bathroom Fixtures."

"Mmm-hmm"—I put on a serious expression.

"I've recorded there a short history," Luke explained proudly, but also timidly, "of the life of Spettanza Bathroom Fixtures. What we'd be most interested in stressing is how our products are inextricably linked to world history."

"Mmm-hmm," I repeated, frowning even more and riveting my gaze on the paper; I had just discovered that Luke had an ugly ruptured blood vessel in his left eye, and I wanted to avoid that gory sight.

"Just think, since eighteen seventy something to the present, our firm has established an outstanding record of constant excelling, ever onward and upward, without letting down our guard, in continuous expansion of personal property and real estate."

"At first," recalled Peter Spettanza, "the going was really rough. Who would have dared to struggle in the market against a Pescadas, against a Flussometer, would you mind telling me? They were the best toilets of their time. Noble toilets they were!"

"Even today," Luke added impartially, "I see a Pescadas and I doff my hat."

"In those days," sighed John Spettanza, "state agencies would accept no toilet from you that wasn't a Pescadas."

"But the city government," clarified Peter, "preferred the Flussometer, who knows why."

"They probably bribed the mayor," I suggested.

"No, sir!" retorted Luke almost indignantly. "The manufacturers of bathroom fixtures don't bribe anybody; making bathroom fixtures is an apostolate, a high priesthood. What happened was that there was bad blood between the mayor and the commissioner of public works. I remember that, once, the mayor's office paid to publish a full-page personal statement in *La Prensa* and *La Nación*, the two major newspapers, defending to the four winds Flussometer's victory in a public bidding that had taken place. The mayor really gave the commissioner a piece of his mind. It was tremendous, unnerving. Who knows what went on behind the scenes, in high circles. The thing is that a week later the mayor had to resign and escape by night to Montevideo in a rowboat. Then, with a clear field, the commissioner of public works really went all out. Two weeks later there wasn't a city hospital or garbage dump without its elegant Pescadas toilet. The saddest part was that groups of roughnecks paid by the commissioner stormed city hall and smashed all the Flussometers to pieces with sledge hammers. It was really an awful massacre."

"But were you on Flussometer's side, then?" I asked.

"No, no," he replied, holding his hands up, "not at all. I wasn't partial to either Pescadas or Flussometer. I was just an observer of that struggle between two colossal giants."

"And the mayor?" I thought to inquire.

"He committed suicide in a hotel in Montevideo. Asphyxiation by immersion. He just couldn't get over the defeat and stuck his head in a Flussometer. There was a man true to his convictions to the end. There aren't any men like him left anymore."

All of us were moved and observed a moment of silence.

"The first bid we won," said John Spettanza, in search of less gloomy subjects, "was a contract with the Argentine Central Railroad."

"Just five little old urinals." Peter Spettanza's mood was nostalgic, tearful.

"And not all along the whole line either; just in the station at Acassuso," concluded John.

"I was just a lad then," Luke recalled. "And if I tell you something, you're all gonna laugh. Well, it's just that I was so proud of that first public triumph of our firm that at least once a week I used to get the train at Belgrano and ride as far as Acassuso just to pee in a Spettanza urinal."

Luke had said we were going to laugh, so I etched a little smile on my lips, but McCormick, who hates to do things halfway, let out such a cordial guffaw that it even seemed spontaneous. However, it so happened that the Spettanzas weren't in the mood for laughter. They had suddenly turned melancholy, and McCormick's outburst was abruptly truncated, left floating in the air like a gross, irreverent statement.

"Those were the good old days," sighed Peter Spettanza.

"We were younger then," John added.

"With many years still ahead of us," concluded Luke.

Resentful now over that change of mood, McCormick had run out of patience, and he had no intention of listening to this sad reminiscing. He furtively pressed a button three times, and Irene came in immediately. "Mr. McCormick," she said, "excuse me for bothering you, but . . ."

"Yes, what's wrong?"

"Wrong? Nothing's wrong, really. But Mr. Mandelbaum, the engineer, is waiting to see you."

McCormick looked at me as if asking, "What the hell can that guy possibly want? Is he going to prevent me from enjoying the delightful company of these charming fellows?"

"Does he have an appointment?" he added, peeved.

"At five," Irene pointed out. "And it's already five-thirty."

I had seen this farce about the engineer named Mandelbaum enacted so many times that it now bored me. So I quickly wrote on a slip of paper, *Irene, won't you please marry me?* and handed it to her.

"Since Mr. Mandelbaum is here," I said, "would you please give him this message for me?"

"Good heavens!" McCormick looked at his watch, fumbled with some papers, and pretended to be annoyed. "Irene, please ask him if he'll be so kind as to excuse me for just one more minute. I'll finish up with these gentlemen and see him immediately."

The Spettanzas, now contrite, stood up instantly. There were additional but now quick handshakes, renewed smiles, reiterated scraping of chairs, and, finally, they left hastily and happily.

"Irene," McCormick ordered, "could you please show these gentlemen to the elevator and tell Mr. Mandelbaum to come in?"

"And will you also ask him if there's a positive response to my message?"

Irene threw me a disapproving little smile and I thought to myself, "What a doll!" McCormick already had a brush out of a desk drawer and was energetically buffing his shoes. "I have to get out of here right now," he said, putting on his jacket. "These guys are prepared to spend in a big way. You start reading that little history and try to put together for them a celebration *with the works*."

He picked up his briefcase, put some papers in it, and headed for the door.

I asked him: "With an elaborate party, with dancing, a banquet, the selection of a queen and princesses of this or that? Do we have it at the Bow-Wow Club?"

And from the door, he reaffirmed: "*With the works.*"

II. The History of Spettanza Bathroom Fixtures

*L*uke Spettanza had written his history on sheets of very high grade paper, that kind of pure white, heavy, crisp bond paper that usually awakens in me an irrepressible desire to write something—to copy a line of poetry, a sentence, or a word. Not type it, but write it slowly with a fountain pen full of fragrant, dark black ink.

Centered at the top, a kind of aristocratic letterhead literally screamed out for attention. It was a coat of arms elegantly stamped in full color, with gold edging, and engraved in high relief. I examined it carefully. First of all, it was made up of a large oval divided into heraldic quarters. In the first of them, in the upper-left-hand corner, against a bloody field of gules, there figured a snow-white Spettanza washbowl crowned with noble chrome faucets. In its counterpart to the right, a limpid Spettanza bathtub cavorted rampant on an ocher field of sable. Below, and to the left, the vairs, with their jaunty little bells of argent and azure, jubilantly framed the curvilinear Spettanza bidet. Finally, in the lower-right foreground, the severe, pragmatic forms of the dignified Spettanza toilet were set off against a subdued, republican green.

The heraldic oval was enhanced by Hellenic garlands of interwoven branches of bucolic laurel and the Arcadian olive tree, which appeared among the harmonious folds of six flags—three on each side—six very strange banners which I could attribute to no country on our planet; their colors seemed to recall those of certain soccer team jerseys. To round out my amazement, an animal, this one real, that one imaginary, stood watch on each flag: a rampant lion; a menacing eagle; a spirited hippogryph; a striped tiger; a fiery dragon; and a jumping frog. Another disconcerting detail: the forehead of each animal bore the stigma of a letter, in this order: L, M, M, J, P, P. I thought of Roman numerals and translated: 50, 1,000, 1,000 . . . I stopped; there were no Roman numerals J and P. Moreover, I was thoroughly confused by that unfathomable series of two Ms and two Ps. Dazzled, I postponed the deciphering of this enigma and went on observing.

Above the coat of arms gleamed a multipointed golden crown— very similar to that of the king of clubs; and, on this crown, a green baroque monogram proclaimed its truth: S. B. F. "Spettanza Bathroom Fixtures," I said to myself, pleased with my perspicacity. Beneath the coat of arms, an austere red, white, and green bunting ("for the flag of Italy," I discerned, feeling more and more vain) enveloped in its maternal folds the six flagpoles and the laurel and olive stems, thus joining them all into one fraternal whole. As a finishing touch, on the bunting was written *Spettanza Bathroom Fixtures*, and on its ribbons, *Reliable Products*.

In its totality, the heraldic device seemed unclassifiable to me. No matter how hard I thought, it was impossible for me to link it to any civilization, any region, or any era. In its own way, it was nonspatial; it was, also in its own way, timeless and, hence, eternal.

I sat there for a while, perplexed, without the strength to begin reading the history. In an effort to raise my spirits, I had some coffee and drank a glass of water; then I lit a cigarette and made up my mind. The title read:

Ref: (SPETTANZA BATHROOM FIXTURES) CENTENNIAL

Another pause was now required to unravel the meaning of those parentheses; in the light of my reading of the text, however, I concluded that they were to be interpreted as quotation marks. Now calm in this regard, I got up my courage, plunged ahead, and read it straight through to the end.

What follows is a true copy of Luke Spettanza's history:

The (Spettanza Bathroom Fixtures) Corporation that was fownded, by Don Massimo Spettanza my actual graygranfather who arrived in Argentina from Italy; around 1860 on the frayter (Princess Appiciafuoca) and who fownded it in 1,873 establishing hisself at whats actually Cochabamba Street in the 300 block a place actually demolished by the pick and shovel of progress and in its place is a cabaret that plays tangos, almost at the coarner of Defensa Street this firm dedicating itself in its early years to the importing of (Pescadas) and (Flusometer) bathroom fixtures and other presteedjus brands being imported from England and France.

Upon ocuring the demise by death of my actual graygranfather in a traffic axident hit by a buckboard with horses from the open-air market held in (Dorrego) Square; the firm of (Spettanza Bathroom Fixtures) passes into the hands of my actual granfather Italian like his father but a naturlised Argentine citisen called Pietro trancelating his name to Peter on his identity papers, this new owner afecting important improovments due to change of owner like, for ezample the new line of iron water tanks for toilets pull-chaines being added to them whitch in that epoc were a genuwine advanse in the feeld of toilet tanks, all so imported from England.

My actual father who didnt dye and is now 103 vigrus years young having reetired from the bisness two years back for reesons of helth: that is roomatism and lumbaygo. Having given to (Spettanza Bathroom Fixtures) a great push foreword mooving in 1,935 to Maure Street "in that tipicle Buenos Aires naiberhood of Chacarita" aqiring a big yard and a shoroom for (Spettanza Bathroom Fixtures); where the actual shoroom of (Spettanza Bathroom Fixtures) actually is on Maure Street.

My actual father what was the one that gave the bisnes the actual push foreword because he had great faithe in the fyutur of the countrie, he being Argentine and not a (Dago) as he used to afexionatly call his actual father Don Pietro. With enreprizing vision he incorperates in 1,936 the manufactchering of the first washtub for washing cloths bilt totaly by Argentine Industry the latter turning out much cheeper than the ones imported from Europe: that is England, the traidmark of that tub being (Royal) so that peeple can see its a English product maintaning the name or registred traidmark in one of the actual lines of bath fixtures for the bathroom.

As a funny acnedote those (Royal) tubs were made of cemetary marbel that the marbelworker nextdoor who bilt toombs for the dead use to sell us at cost and they dont make such fine tubs now cause they make em out of cement or concreat and not out of cemetary marbel.

During the epoc of the 2nd World Comflagration of Europe the importation of (Pescadas) and (Flusomeetors) is no longer propheta-

ble so that my father called (Don Carmelo) and well known in the
feeld of Bathroom fixtures being elected for three consecyative terms
hornerary Pressedent of the Manufactcherers of Bathroom Fixtures
and Reelayted Products Club, being recieved in private audiense by
the Minester of Public Helth but I cant think of his name rite now,
by the Pressedent of the Argentine Republic of that epoc General
Agustin Pejusto.[1] By reason of the importation of (Pescadas) and
(Flusometeors) not being prophetable my father who lawnches hisself
with optamism and faithe in the fyutur of the countrie lawnches hisself into bilding bathroom fixtures for the bath room and he bilds em
so exelent wining a exhabition held in Bolivia "la Paz" of bathroom
fixtures, having compeeted in it even American firms from the Usa
and German companys and all so from that little sister countrie Nic-
araqua (Spettanza Bathroom Fixtures) tryumphing by the unanamous
vote of the Jewry.

My father (Don Carmelo) as we afexionatly call him in the (Spettanza Bathroom Fixtures) company who gave to this blessed Argentine soil 6 mail sons, not having 7 for fear it will turn out a warewolf
on him and be tranceformed into a wolf on nights of the full moon;
all of them with good helth and with faithe in the fyutur of the countrie and being actually at the head of the firm who: are I whose the
oldest, Matthew the second Mark the 3rd, 4th John, 5th Peter and
6th Paul the youngest of the 6 whose only 35 years old and pozesses
great entreprizing vision and faithe in the fyutur, having these names
cause my deceesed mother who allready dyed was a very cathlic
woman from the South of Italy and she gave us names from the
(Bible), but discusing this with my father (Don Carmelo) who had
advansed ideas being a anarkist and a socialest, none of we 6 not
having actually any political Cathlic nor union activety, being men
of bisnes entreprize at the servise of the greatness of this blessed
Argentine soil and membres of the Lions Club of Chacarita and
Mark all so of the Rotary Club.

The last few years which were years of unseasing expancion and
were carachterized by the aqisition of a modren (IBM) brand com-
puter the perssonnel calling it with that hyuman warmth that pre-
vales at (Spettanza Bathroom Fixtures) they call it kidingly by the
name of (Looloo) the actual blue coller perssonnel being arrownd
600 workers contrary to the adminstrative perssonnel that amownts
to the nice round figyure of 87 perssons among the veryous Departments 36 being women of the oposite sex, thus giving to woman the

place she desserves to fullfill herself on the working plain of our
actual soceyety.

When my father reetires from the (Spettanza Bathroom Fixtures)
corporation it was in 1971 and he hisself created the logo-tipe base-
ing hisself on the Knites of the Cathlic Crusaids in desserving hommige to the memry of my deceesed mother who was very Cathlic and
had given us those names of Cathlic Saints and (Don Carmelo) called
them the Knites giving them the Italian name (Bersaglieri) whitch is
how its said in the Italian Langwidge, putting as a hommige to my
deceesed mother (Dona Concetta) the inishals of our 6 names of the
sons on the animals on the flags of the logo-tipe, whitch when a
sicolygist freind Doctor Maurice Felber saw them he gave it the
folowing cycleanalitical intrepatation, saying that the lion sim-
bolyzed comercial dygnity whitch comes to be me because of the
great expeeriance I have in bisnes, the tiger being John whitch simbolyzes the agresive spirit in marketing. The eegle coresponding to
Matthews' lawfty flites of immagenation in comercial planing completely the opossite of the griffin whitch means (fawcet) in latin and
simblyzes the reealistic spirit of Mark, the griffin simbolyzing the
fawcets that are on our fixtures.[2] The Dragon: It simbolyzes Peter
who has in his spirit the sacred fire of bisnes inishative just as the
dragon has a lit fire in the inteerior of its mouthe. The green Frog: It
simbolyzes the youngest "The Baby of the Famly" whitch is Paul and
this young man having a dyenamic and playfull spirit like the frogs
that leep in the mud to eat insecs and its an animal thats usefull to
man just as Paul is all so usefull to his fallow men being a membre
of sevral school-ayd Co-ops of that tipicle Buenos Aires naiberhood
of (Chacarita).

In conclusion Gentelmen of that esteamed Advurtyzing Agensy,
what we 6 want to have done is the dezire that their be held a great
celabration and a good publisety campain of advurtyzing to push the
new lines (Royal) (Buckingham) (Majestic) and (Northampton) in all
the bath rooms of the homes of this blessed Argentine soil, remayning
at the servise of your esteamed Agensee ready to amplefy verbly
these facts and data and greeting your Agensea most atentivly, I am
your faythfull servent.

Luke Spettanza
Senior Parcner

Overwhelmed, I slowly spread open my fingers in a tragic theatrical gesture, and the pages of the senior partner's history took flight with the aid of the breeze from the fan. For a few moments they fluttered among the typewriters, desks, and filing cabinets and finally landed with a slight swishing sound.

I pondered them for a few seconds, scattered here and there. Then I picked them up, punched two little holes in them with my paper punch, and inserted them in a brand new, clean, pink loose-leaf binder. In a very firm hand I wrote *Spettanza Bathroom Fixtures* on the cover, and placed the binder in my in-basket.

After reflecting briefly, however, I took the binder out, and in smaller letters I added: *Reliable Products*.

III. The Axiom of the Twelve Lines

A week later, the Persuasive Conviction Advertising Agency illustrators had finished the sketches destined for the graphic media and I had written the matching copy.

In accordance with the guiding principle that inspired the philosophy of Spettanza Bathroom Fixtures, there was enunciated the *Axiom of the Twelve Lines*, more popularly known as the *Parallel Postulate of Three Times Four*, the formula of which was as follows:

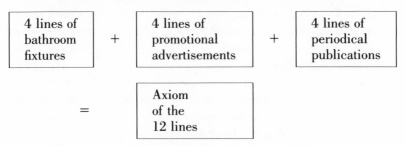

Let us now analyze how this theory was implemented in practice. First of all, we must remember that the four lines of bathroom fixtures were, in order of decreasing exaltedness:

1. NORTHAMPTON: *For the Exquisite*
2. ROYAL: *For the Exclusive*
3. MAJESTIC: *For the Exacting*
4. BUCKINGHAM: *For the Expert*

As can be seen, the British names of the lines of bathroom fixtures were lacking in any connotation whatsoever. In fact, the word Northampton, for example, expressed no more delicate notion than the word Buckingham; but neither did it express any less delicate notion. They expressed absolutely nothing.

Conversely, the gradation with regard to their possible recipients was indeed significant and accurate:

1. In the term *expert* there lurks the idea that an expert will be able to appreciate duly the quality of Buckingham fixtures. But nothing more; that virtue bestows upon him no prerogative. He must, therefore, limit himself to recognizing the values of Buckingham fixtures, but without even dreaming of selecting another line.

2. On the other hand, the *exacting* are simultaneously—by definition—experts, but they are also in a position—having once ascertained the undeniable quality of the Buckinghams—to demand even greater merits and, in the exercise of these powers, to opt for the Majestic line.

3. When he reads *exclusive*, the consumer justifiably appropriates unto himself the qualities of expert and exacting, but he adds to them still a third—that of his economic potential. The latter allows him to acquire the Royal line, which, just as its slogan indicates, is not for everyone.

4. Finally, we come to the *exquisite*. Without repudiating their attributes of expert, exacting, and exclusive, these privileged people achieve such a degree of eminent refinement that they couldn't—even in the most dire circumstances—appeal to the services of any fixture that wasn't a Northampton.

To sum up the idea in a more or less syllogistic way: every exquisite owner is exclusive, exacting, and expert, but no exclusive, exacting, or expert owner is exquisite; every exclusive owner is exacting and expert, but no exacting or expert owner is . . .

McCormick and I hammered all this into our heads so well that we were absolutely convinced that matters were, in fact, so. Then we sat down to think about how we would organize the four groups of publications in which the four lines of advertisements would be distributed. With pencil in hand, we elaborated a kind of table that systematized the presumed reading preferences of expert and exacting, of exclusive and exquisite. According to this document:

A. The *expert* would be recruited among the readers of comic books, romance magazines, certain sports magazines, magazines dwelling on murders and rapes of minors or adult women, and magazines about film, theatrical, radio, and television gossip.

B. On the other hand, we had to seek out the redoubt of the *exacting* among those who read women's magazines, certain other sports magazines, and magazines of general current events printed in multicolor.

C. The *exclusive* were "thinking people"—that's what McCormick called them. That is, they were the aware readers of political commentary magazines, those publications that generously entrust the most hidden secrets of national and international politics to office employees.

D. Finally, the *exquisite* were—who could doubt it?—members of a certain fauna, which are grouped generically under the name of "executives." These creatures quench their intellectual thirst in magazines dedicated to economic themes, full of charts and graphs.

The foregoing structure, in the form of an inverted pyramid, should be interpreted in the same manner as the previous one. The readers in group D also make incursions into groups C, B, and A, but those in groups C, B, and A don't enter into group D, etc., etc.

According to this plan, the campaign would be quite simple. Consequently, the advertisement sketches were four variations on the same theme. They represented, in a multicolored photograph, four bathrooms progressively less luxurious and imposing; the respective copy bore a close relationship to each bathroom.

To understand this clearly, notice the marked difference between:

Le Corbusier dreamt of it long ago.[3]
The bathroom should be a warm, inviting, artistic retreat
wherein each detail reflects the homeowner's personality
as one of the beautiful people.
Le Corbusier dreamt of it.
Spettanza Bathroom Fixtures made it reality.
NORTHAMPTON: *For the Exquisite*

and the following:

You are a clean person.
You know the pleasure of tepid water
caressing your body.
You can interpret better than anyone
the hygienic message of the washbowl.
You understand the level-headed honesty of a solid toilet.
You know, in your innermost being, the mischievous,
tickling sensation of the bidet's little spray.
Because you are an expert person.
BUCKINGHAM: *For the Expert*

"Do you think it'll go?" I asked McCormick.
"On a scale of 1 to 10, I'd give it a 10," he replied, very pleased with himself. "Now, put together four film scripts for the movies and T.V., but always keeping in mind the *Axiom of the Twelve Lines.*"
"Yeah, but that'll be *mutatis mutandis*, right?"
"Of course."
I thought for a little while, put a sheet of paper in the typewriter, thought for another little bit, and then wrote the four film scenarios. They really turned out beautifully. I shall again illustrate by using the two extreme ends of the scale. First, the script for the Northampton line; then that of the Buckingham line. Anyone with a minimum of imagination can figure out what the scenarios for the Royal and Majestic lines were like.

FILM SCRIPT FOR THE NORTHAMPTON LINE.
TITLE: "BEFORE THE PARTY"

Scene. The living room of a luxurious mansion, magnificently decorated, but with exquisite taste. At stage rear, large windows allow the view of a beautiful green, wooded estate. At stage right, a circumspect door leads to one of the residence's fourteen bathrooms.

Dramatis personae. JOHN DUBOIS. His wife, MARIE LOUISE. And an ENGLISH BUTLER.

VIDEO   *AUDIO*

JOHN—handsome, manly face; dressed in severe formal attire. He paces impatiently about the living room. He looks repeatedly at an XVIIIth-century pendulum clock with gold, pearl, and diamond relief. Finally, he gives three delicate little raps with his knuckles on the bathroom door.

LITTLE RAPS. Knock, knock, knock.

MARIE LOUISE (off-camera). Occupied, John.

JOHN (*in a pleasant voice, but with a slightly reproachful tone*). Will you be much longer, Marie Louise? Remember, the duke is waiting for us and it's getting late.

MARIE LOUISE (*obligingly*). I'll be right out. (*Immediate noise of the toilet being flushed, followed at once by a joyous torrent of water.*)

JOHN smiles understandingly. Out of the bathroom comes MARIE LOUISE. She'a a tall, svelte blonde, dazzling with jewels and beauty. She's wearing a white evening gown. She kisses JOHN.

JOHN (*discreetly eager*). Well?

MARIE LOUISE (*circumspectly satisfied*). Faaabulous.

JOHN (*off-camera; in a warm, loving voice*). Marie Louise, I could never have imagined that Northampton would make us late for the duke's reception.

Cut. Panoramic view of bathroom. Immediate foreground shot of toilet and a very tight close-up shot of commercial trademark.

MARIE LOUISE (*off camera; still warmer, in a trembling voice, now close to orgasm*). Northampton has that certain something that . . . that seduces one.

Rapid shot of the couple leaving the mansion, on their way to the

duke's party. An ENGLISH
BUTLER, characterized as an English butler, precedes the couple
and opens the door for them, with
a solemn bow. But then JOHN and
MARIE LOUISE look at each
other with a questioning glance.
They are joined in a deep communication that goes beyond words.
They understand each other. They
smile and go back to the
bathroom. They take one last, enraptured look at the toilet. They
kiss once more and finally leave,
followed by the ENGLISH
BUTLER's paternal look.
When the door closes, the scene   PLEASANT BARITONE VOICE
darkens to complete blackout. But   (*off camera*). Northampton: For
at once brilliant light on a very   the Exquisite. The meaning of
tight close-up of the sparkling   life.
toilet.

This was the film script for the Northampton line. For the Buckingham, I wrote the following:

FILM SCRIPT FOR THE BUCKINGHAM LINE.
TITLE: "BEFORE THE PICNIC"

Scene.   An interior covered flagstone patio with grape-
                         vine, flower pots, terra cotta statues of little
                         dwarfs, and canaries in cages. Three large
                         wicker chairs. Several doors—some covered
                         with rolled matted blinds—open on the patio.
                         One, with a painted window, is the bathroom
                         door.

Dramatis personae.   BUTCH. His wife, FANNY. And DOÑA
                         GERTRUDE, Fanny's mother and Butch's
                         mother-in-law.

          VIDEO   *AUDIO*
BUTCH paces impatiently about
the patio. He displays the strong

face of a butcher. He's wearing a sleeveless undershirt and, around his waist, a wide black belt; he has on socks and sandals and is sporting a pair of dark, leather wrist straps. He's chewing a toothpick and is busily concentrating on cleaning his fingernails with a jackknife. Prompted by his bad mood, every few moments he lets out a rhinoceroslike snort. Finally, sick of waiting, he lets fly three violent kicks at the bathroom door.

BUTCH. Har-umph! Har-umph!

KICKS. Whump! Whump! Whuuump!

FANNY (*off-camera*). Don't rush me, Butch, 'cuz ya just make me nervous and then it don't come out.

BUTCH (*urgent and encouraging*). C'mon, Fanny, try harder, push. Look, we're gonna be late and Jake's a'ready loaded the pickup truck for the picnic at Ezeiza woods, he's a'ready loaded up.

Having said this, BUTCH nervously pokes at an ear with the toothpick and lets out a hurricanelike snort.

BUTCH. Ooooooofffff!!!!!
(*Immediate noise of the toilet being flushed followed at once by a cheerful torrent of water.*)

With these favorable signs, BUTCH's sullen expression sweetens somewhat. At once, out of the bathroom comes FANNY: short, big breasted, wearing curlers, anklets, and slippers. She kisses BUTCH.

BUTCH (*touching* FANNY'S *lower abdomen playfully*). Everthin' come out a'right?

FANNY (*entranced, rolling her eyes*). Like a gem.

Cut. Panoramic view of bathroom. Immediate foreground shot of toilet and a very tight close-up shot of commercial trademark.

BUTCH (*off-camera; in a contemplative tone of voice*). If I'd a known you was gonna go nutty over the Buckin'am, I'd a kep' Jake waitin'. I'd a . . .

FANNY (*off-camera; in a shrill voice and, in her own way, also close to orgasm*). Well, it's jus' that the Buckin'am is so faaaberlous that a gal goes tuh the toilet even when she don't feel like it, even when she . . .

Rapid shot of the couple crossing the patio on their way to Jake's pickup truck. DOÑA GERTRUDE interrupts the making of a shawl she is knitting and accompanies the pair to the street door. But then BUTCH and FANNY look at each other with a questioning glance. They are joined in deep communication that goes beyond words. They understand each other. They smile and go back to the bathroom. They take one last, enraptured look at the toilet. They kiss once more and finally leave, followed by DOÑA GERTRUDE's maternal look.

When the door closes, the scene darkens to complete blackout. But at once brilliant light on a very tight close-up of the sparkling toilet.

PLEASANT BARITONE VOICE (*off-camera*). Buckingham: For the Expert. The toilet for happily married couples.

I should state—without vanity or modesty—that the Spettanza brothers were delighted with both the printed advertisements and my film scripts. Except that, in the text corresponding to the advertisement for the Northampton line, Luke insisted on adding the adverb *actually* in the second-to-the-last sentence. We did it to please him, and so it read as follows: *Spettanza Bathroom Fixtures actually made it reality.*

The scenarios were filmed very successfully, and they turned out to be really beautiful movies, faithful to the spirit and the letter that had inspired them—my spirit and letter. Executed in brilliant color in huge CinemaScope for gigantic screens, the films were strategically distributed to the various movie houses according to a rule that took into account two factors, which we had to coordinate with exquisite tact and devilish ability: a. the program; b. the location of the movie house.

In some cases, it was quite simple to make a decision. Without the slightest doubt, the film dedicated to the Buckingham line corresponded to grossly pornographic movies, coarse comical ones, and common tear-jerkers. But it didn't seem to me that there existed an unerring correlation between a low socioeconomic level and a low cultural level. The situation was more complex and not at all symmetrical. So I told McCormick that we should cut out the nonsense about the cultural level and pay exclusive attention to the economic level.

"He who has spends," I affirmed, "and he who doesn't have doesn't spend, even if he's one of the seven sages of Greece."

McCormick seemed doubtful. So, as an example of great buying power accompanied by semi-illiteracy, I cited, appropriately, the case of the industrialist Luke Spettanza.

"There's also the opposite case," I added modestly. "There's nothing I don't know, and yet you pay me a very low salary."

Without acknowledging this remark, McCormick said that, to be on the safe side, he would employ the services of an agency that specialized in conducting surveys of all kinds. In time, these scientific people proved me right. According to the survey, executives—worn out by the arduous mental effort exerted during business hours—were inclined toward the film versions of American best sellers. Since our duty was to sell bathroom fixtures, the film on the Northampton line was assigned to the movie houses where such versions were being shown.

A second, parallel problem arose. What were we to do—I shudder to tell of it—about the chain of phony intellectual movie houses along the arty stretch of Corrientes Avenue? What was the cultural level of the types who went there? What was their economic level? Big nosed and disheveled, wearing beards and large glasses, always with books under their arms, they were evidently leftist young people, without any doubt, who struggled unceasingly in behalf of the revolution, now seated in the La Paz or the El Foro café, now viewing Buñuel, Fellini, or Bergman.

Now then, what did they understand as the left? In the correct answer to this question would be found the way to the most appropriate toilet for them. Would a Buckingham be representative of the left?

"No," said McCormick. "They'll see it as a sample of Peronist Populism."

"Majestic?" I proposed.

"Conformist middle class," he declared sententiously.

"Royal?"

"Petite bourgeoisie, filthy reactionaries."

"Well then?"

"The Northampton represents perfectly the aspirations of the Argentine left," McCormick solemnly pontificated.

So it came to pass. No sooner did these gilded intellectuals set aside Marcuse, Sartre, or Lévi-Strauss, when Northampton issued a peremptory summons to their mental energies. Subsequent surveys showed that, in general, executives' children assiduously frequented the movie houses of the aforementioned phony intellectual chain. It's true that sons as well as fathers paid their admission religiously, but there was an abysmal difference: the executives did so with "money that was the product of exploitation and economic dependency," while their offspring paid with money belonging to their fathers.

We perpetrated the same tricks on television, *mutatis mutandis*. But we soon resigned ourselves to distributing the films at random because we discovered, a bit late, that *Homo televidens* watches absolutely everything. (The best-laid plans of mice and men often go astray.) Televised classes in home economics or in cooking were quite compatible with Wild West series or detective adventures, and the latter, in turn, were not at variance with interviews of politicians, boxers, or movie starlets. Nevertheless, these apparent anomalies also weighed in favor of Spettanza Bathroom Fixtures: the positive result was an increase in envy and the spirit of emulation. After getting ecstatic over the sight of a Northampton, who would be satisfied with a mere Buckingham?

Thus it was that Spettanza Bathroom Fixtures became the protagonists of many important aspects of national life. To round out this stage of the campaign, McCormick proposed to the Spettanzas the creation of a catchy, idolizing *jingle*, which they accepted with delight. It was to be dinned unceasingly over radio and television and in the movies; in the latter two media, the verses were to be underscored by a kind of artistic ballet, the choreography of which would extol and glorify the four lines of Spettanza Bathroom Fixtures in their entirety.

The *jingle*—of whose verses I am proud to be the bard—began with a rather sad, wistful melody, which gradually became more and more cheerful until it culminated in a jubilant, triumphal explosion of the full orchestra. To come up with a choreography that would *impact*—not my word—McCormick contracted the services of the celebrated dancer and choreographer Fairyfoot de l'Antoinette, in whose disturbing company I worked for several hours. Insensitive to his drooping eyelids, I limited myself to making sure, in this case also, that the spirit and letter of my creation were being respected. Here it is:

JINGLE: "SPRINGTIME IN THE BATHROOM"
Words: by Hernando Genovese.
Music and Choreography: by Fairyfoot de l'Antoinette.
© Persuasive Conviction Advertising Agency.
Total or Partial Reproduction Prohibited.
All Rights Reserved.

Adagio
That gloomy old bathroom,
so cold and so gray,
should be spruced up
in a totally new way.

(Pale old witches dressed in long dark robes dance mournfully to the beat of sad sounds in a dismal forest thicket whose vegetation is made up of cracked washbowls, grayish bidets, rusty bathtubs, and lugubrious toilets.)

Allegro, ma non troppo
Put Spettanza fixtures
in your bathroom today;
some color in your john
will drive the blues away.

(The harpies, now transformed into vaguely beautiful girls who, with cautiously optimistic movements, gradually enter a somewhat more illuminated area. In the midst of the wretchedness of the ancient bathroom fixtures, there stands out here, there, and even yonder, like beautiful, exotic, hothouse flowers, an occasional Spettanza fixture. There is now felt a presentiment of something spectacular about to happen.)

Allegro molto	*Fixtures by Spettanza*
vivace	*to live it up and be gay.*
	They put joy in your bath
	and always make your day!

(With their alluring shapes all clothed in white and in the fullness of their youthful vitality and beauty, accompanied by cheerful, jubilant music, the girls now glide in like water nymphs, leaping springlike from a toilet to a washbowl, from a bidet to a bathtub. In Panic exaltation, all of nature now participates in the rejoicing; the sun pours its light down upon the scene.)

| **Maestoso,** | *For a marvelous bonanza,* |
| **ma divoto** | *Bathroom fixtures by Spettanza!!!* |

(The girls now form a solemn, liturgical ring and, as though in ecstasy, raise their young alabaster arms in unison to heaven.)

The trumpets of fame and success greeted my creations. And, I confess, I felt proud of them. I would even say very proud. When I would run into some acquaintance or other, I enjoyed dazzling him with the revelation that I—yes, I, just as you see me standing here— had authored the texts of the commercials, the film scripts, and the lines of the jingle. I never wearied of spreading the news.

IV. McCormick, the Invincible

I think I mentioned it before, but everything was now going full speed ahead for Spettanza Bathroom Fixtures. And, hence, for Persuasive Conviction. And, therefore, for me. For a certain time they left me in peace, idle, with nothing to do. That's how it was at the agency; sometimes weeks and weeks went by without the paltriest job turning up; then, suddenly, so much work would rain down on us that you didn't even have time to breathe.

I made use of this fair weather period by chatting, reading novels, working out literary puzzles in magazines, and asking in vain for Irene's hand. I'm tired of begging her to marry me; based on who knows what ridiculous reasoning, she thinks I'm kidding. She's a woman who's hard to understand, but a real beauty.

I had a literary vocation. I had already published a couple of books of short stories—without much success, it's true. Now, since I had a lot of time on my hands those days, I should have dedicated it to writing something. But, no, that's just the way I am. When the situation is favorable for writing, nothing occurs to me; then, when I'm overwhelmed with obligations and annoyances, my mind is inhabited by the most brilliant ideas.

The fact of the matter was that one Thursday my peace was disturbed. I was going to say one "ill-fated" Thursday, but that's due to my habit of abusing adjectives. Let's just say, then, one Thursday. We'll see later on whether or not it was ill-fated.

That Thursday McCormick asked me a favor. The moment he came into my office I noticed a strange look on his face. He sat on the edge of my desk and started beating around the bush: he asked me how things were going; he told me a joke that I thought was funny, but which I no longer remember; he told me there were more and more idiotic people in the world every day; he told me: "Look, Hernando," he began to play with a little pencil and a rubber band. "It so happens that the Spettanzas," he let go of the pencil and the rubber band and waved a piece of paper; I immediately recognized the unforgettable coat of arms, "it so happens that the Spettanzas are very pleased, really delighted with the results of the campaign. Just imagine, their sales have increased at a figure around . . ."

I wondered what was going to happen. I watched him suspiciously, intuited that he was cooking up something unpleasant for me, and got ready to defend myself.

". . . and it so happens that they've invited me to dinner," he was now saying while folding in four the piece of paper (which I hadn't read).

He smiled a smile that translated as: "Isn't it wonderful that this has happened to me?" He arched his eyebrows and I again translated: "How enviable my situation is! How many people would love to be in my position!" Terrified, I proceeded to put on a face that would refuse everything. McCormick noticed it instantly—what didn't McCormick notice?—and considered it advantageous to back away from the sticking point a bit to be able to come at it more efficiently from another angle.

"The invitation is for Saturday," he added in a neutral voice, like someone saying, "The Weather Bureau announces increasing cloudiness." "For this Saturday, the day after tomorrow. What do you think?"

I had no reason to think about it. I shrugged my shoulders slightly and limited myself to taking mental note of the information, without uttering any judgment.

"I don't know if I'm making myself clear," he added, picking up the pencil and rubber band again. "The truth is I'd very much like to go. Spettanza Bathroom Fixtures is an account that's done us a lot of good . . . I don't know if I'm making myself clear . . . I'd very much like to go."

"So, go," I answered, playing dumb.

"Yes, of course; no . . . I'd very much like to go, it's true . . . but the fact is that . . . the truth is . . . I don't know if I'm making myself clear . . . , the fact is I can't go . . . I don't know if I'm making myself clear . . ."

He always said "I don't know if I'm making myself clear" whenever he left his sentences unfinished. That gave him room not to be clear and thus to correct himself at any point. He sat looking at me, waiting for my answer. I, turning a deaf ear to everything, drew an almost perfect circle on a piece of paper.

"You see, Hernando? It just so happens that I can't go."

"Well, then," inside the circle I drew a vertical line and another horizontal one, "don't go."

"But we've got to go," he smiled as if resigned to fate. "It'll look bad if we don't go."

McCormick had subtly gone from the first person, singular, to the first person, plural. I was filling my circle with lines, waiting for the decisive assault. It wasn't long in coming.

"I had thought you might like to go . . . ," and now, from first person, plural, to second person, singular.

"Why should I want to go?" I replied.

"Yes, I know . . ." he smiled and playfully aimed the rubber band at my eyes. "I know it's a drag to go to these gatherings. I don't like to go either."

"But before you said you'd very much like to go," I objected, uselessly; I was not unaware that McCormick would ultimately achieve his goal.

"Of course," he corrected himself, without losing his composure. "I expressed myself badly. I meant to say: I'd very much like to go, but . . . How shall I put it?—in other, . . . under other circumstances . . . So I thought you could go, representing the agency."

From the outset I knew that McCormick was going to ask such an absurd thing of me, and from the outset I knew that McCormick would defeat me. But I would sell my defeat dearly. I shook my head vigorously: "Look, McCormick, so as not to waste time in useless conversation, I'm answering you right up front: I-do-not-in-tend-to-go. Period. Period. Let's change the subject."

"But why shouldn't you go? It's no trouble for you," he patted me on the shoulder.

"I already said it: I'm-not-go-ing. Now, just out of simple curiosity (and this will have no influence on my decision), I ask: if you can't go, why doesn't Arrambide or Violini go?"

Why did I say that? McCormick found there the argument he needed: "But I'm in charge of the account. Well, not in charge. Rather, both of us are in charge; you and I."

"I don't know," I persisted in my obstinacy. "Be that as it may, I'm not going, I'm not going, I'm not going, I'm not going." I noticed that my arguments had taken on a childlike stubborness, so I tried to regain lost ground by adding: "I'm not going to waste a Saturday night on those nitwits."

That was another tactical error. Quick as a flash, McCormick retorted: "But it's just *one* Saturday. A single one. Not ten Saturdays. Just *one* Saturday."

"All the same, I'm not going. Period and new paragraph."

"If you go, I'll give you tomorrow off."

"I'm not going."

McCormick thought for a moment, realized that I was a man with grit, and backed down: "If you go, I'll give you tomorrow and all next week off."

"You always win," I pretended to be resigned. "O.K., I'll go, but a condemned man doesn't go willingly to the gallows."

McCormick smiled: "Attaboy!!" and he shot the rubber band at me gently.

I didn't applaud his little trick. On the contrary, I sat there scowling to let him see that I still wasn't satisfied with his deal. But the truth is that I was pleased; six days off—I estimated—would compensate for the three or four hours I would suffer on Saturday.

"I'll make good use of the time and see if I can write a short story," I resolved to myself.

V. Spettanzas in Their Own Juice

*I*n short, I went to the dinner. It was at Luke Spettanza's home. I put on my best clothes, took a humble number 67 bus, got off at a place filled with trees and noises of cars, walked a little way along Libertador Avenue, and rang the bell to an eighth-floor apartment.

In the same motion with which he shook my hand, Luke Spettanza literally dragged me inside. At first I didn't see anything, but I promptly learned it was early. Later on, I met a series of smiling, fawning, unknown individuals dressed in presumptuously bad taste, with unintelligible names immediately forgotten, who were introduced to me as managers, directors, and heads of the various departments at Spettanza Bathroom Fixtures. Luke lugged me around here and there like a rag doll. All I wanted was for those useless introductions to end. But no, such was not my fate.

There now came an additional series made up of the five remaining Spettanzas, their wives, and their children. It was a series with a chaotic system, since I never did manage to get clear in my mind the respective couples and their children. I had scarcely arrived and I was already wishing I were far away from there. Fortunately, the introductions were now culminating with a crowning touch. In a sort of rocking chair was seated old Carmelo Spettanza, with his lumbago, his arthritis, his rheumatism, his 103 years, his parchmentlike mummy skin, and his glasses; he was tiny, wizened, bald, bony, and absentminded, but with soft flesh. It felt eerie to shake that cadaverous hand covered with dark age spots. I thought to myself: "This guy's clock is ready to stop."

"It's an honor to meet you, Mr. Spettanza," I said.

"Make yourself comfortable," Luke told me, and by leaving me alone he facilitated my following this advice.

I was then able to look around a bit and ascertain where I really was. I confess that I liked the place. But I would have liked it better if there hadn't been so many people there and so much commotion. And if the great coat of arms of Spettanza Bathroom Fixtures weren't immodestly glittering on one wall over the false fireplace, intruding unpleasantly upon the warm atmosphere aglow with reddish carpeting and fine woodwork. I don't know what time the dinner began. I do know that I had previously been sitting in a big armchair in the living room for a long time. I was in the company of others, yet alone; sometimes I admire my ability to abstract myself completely from what surrounds me. There was my body; there was my face. But my thoughts were spinning around the heraldic device; I was truly engrossed in it.

Someone penetrated my armor. At my side had seated himself a gray-haired man who, with pipe in hand, told me that Argentina possessed great natural beauties—with which I agreed; he told me that sometimes it was necessary to sacrifice personal interests on the altar of the sacred requirements of society—with which I agreed; "We must, above all things," he told me, "preserve honesty and the immutable ethical and moral values"—with which I agreed. Then he declared that he felt deeply satisfied with the outstanding business record of Spettanza Bathroom Fixtures. He confessed, in all modesty, that he was the one who had sponsored the introduction into the Spettanza lines of the first toilet tanks with a push-button flusher in place of the old ones with a pull chain, "a revolutionary innovation for its era, which, because it was ahead of its time, encountered difficult obstacles until it succeeded in catching on." I kept replying tactfully, more or less, and to this day I think that man has positive thoughts about me.

At a given moment, the visionary of the toilet tank with a push button disappeared and was replaced by a girl some twenty years old, with a rather round face, short hair—I don't care for women with short hair—and suntanned legs, who smoked as though she were officiating at some esoteric rite. Now it was I who initiated the conversation, which soon drifted into unexpected channels: astrology, rebellious youth, the hippie movement, progressive music, the tamed male,[4] women's liberation, and other subjects as novel as they are thrilling.

May I confess that, at times, I'm a snob? What I liked most about this girl—Patricia Spettanza, Luke's daughter—was the style and intonation of her sentences. She would say (for example): "I don't *buhleeeve* it." She'd say, "*Reeuhly?*" She'd say, "How gross!" She'd say, "How *embaaaarrassing!*" She'd say, "That's incredible!" She'd say, "I was just a wreck, y' know?" And the way she'd say all this! Ah, there was the charm! She spoke with that affected, breathy, mumbling tone of voice which, having possibly originated in the swanky Barrio Norte of the city, had spread into the daily usage of the girls—always suntanned, of course!—of the more or less elegant neighborhoods of Palermo, Belgrano, and Caballito. Any day now, it could reach as far as the poorer quarters of Villa Soldati or Nueva Pompeya, a democratization process that I shall not fail to applaud. At any rate, that's what I liked about her. What can I say? Every man has his weakness.

That's what I was thinking about, thereby distracting myself a bit from Patricia's chatter, when two or three words brought me back to reality. Patricia had just affirmed that "she was crazy" about novels. I now expected to hear, poor deluded me(!), beloved names; instead, I heard horrid names. I don't recall how I answered; I do know that I didn't contradict her. A considerable amount of demagoguery was called for to achieve the precise goal I had just set for myself: the seduction of Patricia Spettanza.

Suddenly I was caught in a crossfire:

"Talking about books?" asked Luke, as he seated himself on the arm of my chair.

This position was extremely uncomfortable for me, since I was obliged to raise my head quite a bit to be able to look at him.

"I, too, had a pure, amateur *vacation* to be a writer. When I was young, of course. But then life hit me hard and I had to dedicate myself fully to work and to trading blow for blow with life." (The Spettanzas obviously had boxing in their blood.) "So, you see, I had to set that *vacation* a bit aside."

"What else could you do?" I said fatalistically.

But he hadn't completed his thought. "Even so" (upon looking up, I could see into his nostrils as into two dark tunnels garnished with little hairs), "even so, to the degree that my profession allows me, to the degree that bathroom fixtures leave me a bit of free time, I take a little fling at it, as they say. An occasional thought or two, a poem, an article on economics, a short business news item. By the way, I was never able to ask you before, what did you think about my history of Spettanza Bathroom Fixtures?"

"Quite good."

He was expecting a less succinct opinion. "Perhaps too . . . ?" he began to criticize himself so that I would reject his criticism. "Perhaps too . . . , how shall I put it . . . ? too rhetorical or flowery, too literary, too artistic?"

"No. On the contrary."

"On the contrary?" he asked, frightened.

"I mean, it's always nice to make a show of an occasional rhetorical device . . . a metaphor, a comparison, a play on words, a joke."

"Did the *acnedote* about the marbleworker strike you as funny?"

"Extremely funny," I laughed. "I'm constantly remembering it; every time I go by a cemetery, I burst right out laughing."

Encouraged, he said: "I have an unpublished book of thoughts, aphorisms, celebrated sayings."

"How, 'celebrated'?"

"Huh? Well, uh . . . I didn't mean that. Sayings that I hope will become celebrated. They're written in a fast, bruising, aggressive style. They hit hard."

"Do you like boxing?"

He looked at me, astonished and maybe offended. "More or less. Why?"

"Oh, no reason," I apologized. "Is the style similar to that of the history?"

"Exactly; like two peas in a pod."

"Well, in that ca . . ."

"Although maybe not." He now tried to phrase his judgment more precisely. "In reality, my thoughts are written with more . . . with more . . . more poetry . . . I don't know if that's the right term or not. One of these days I'd like to show you those poems, those adages. To see what you think."

"Fine, with pleasure. But I'm not qualified to . . ."

"It doesn't matter that you don't understand anything about literature"—with total insensitivity he was insulting me. "If you find something there not to your liking, tell me so frankly. Two heads are better than one. I'm a lover of grammar, of precision, of a richness in vocabulary. I have a dictionary of synonyms and everything. Do you have a dictionary of synonyms?"

"No."

He was horrified. "You don't have a dictionary of synonyms? But when you have to write, how do you manage?"

"I write the first words that come to mind. Those are the best."

"But a dictionary of synonyms is indispensable in order not to repeat words, which is so unseemly."

"Sometimes you can't help repeating words."

"Allow me to tell you, you're mistaken. All words have synonyms and they must all be used. For example, in order not to repeat the word *street*, I would say: 'So-and-so went out into the street, walked along the lane as far as the next roadway, and finally took another thoroughfare that would lead him to Such-and-such's house.' How's that?"

"I don't mean to argue, but that's a waste of time."

"It's a matter of styles," he concluded, somewhat resentful. "I like a richness in vocabulary—or lexicon. What can I say?"

VI. Toasts, Toasts, and More Toasts

*W*hy is it that, for some time now, all the girls in the Argentine Republic are named Patricia? I don't know what this proliferation is due to, but the fact is I had cast my eye on one of those many Patricias and I had contrived a way to sit beside her at dinner. Not because Patricia Spettanza had some irresistible magnetism. Not at all. But she was undoubtedly far superior, for example, to the fellow with the pipe in his hand who even now, and with a table between us, continued uttering pompous clichés before the admiring approval of an elderly lady with bluish hair and chubby arms threaded through several bracelets.

I'm not used to eating at crowded dinner parties. The interval between one course and the next ends up taking away my appetite before I've eaten enough. I was thinking it would still be a long time before that meal ended when I felt the urge to smoke. But I didn't have the nerve to do so and devoted myself to watching how the food passed from Patricia's dish to Patricia's mouth. I determined that it was a most interesting spectacle, observing it properly, you understand. The key lay in concentrating on details and abstracting oneself from the context in which they were produced. "If one could plot the trajectory of the fork's movements," I said to myself, "what a complicated tangle would be woven!"

"Why don't you eat?" Patricia startled me with a fast, whiplashing voice.

"I have almost no appetite."

"You don't like the food," she averred.

"Yes, I do like it."

"Then why don't you eat?"

"Because I have almost no appetite."

"Then you don't like the food."

I thought it prudent not to reply "Yes, I do like it," and I was on the verge of uttering some inanity in the form of a flirtatious remark, but the man with the pipe—with which, whether lit or extinguished, he accompanied all his gestures—came involuntarily to my aid. When our glances met by chance, he thought I was being attentive to his words and he sought my opinion, which he assumed to be in accord with his own: "Although it may hurt us as Argentines; I speak the truth, don't you think?"

Instantly I found an appropriate phrase: "Of course. We've got to cut out this false patriotism."

"And, you, what do you say, Patricia?"

"What are you two talking about?"

The man with the pipe arched his eyebrows and sort of winked at me, thus exhorting me to bring Patricia up to date.

"The gentleman," I explained to her in a whisper, "is talking about something that hurts us Argentines."

But the man with the pipe was already proceeding on, casting definitive light on the mystery: "In Germany, after the war, all the workers put in one or two hours extra per day, without wages, to rebuild the country. And that's how Germany lifted herself up again. And look at her now. But we, by contrast, what did we do? We have all the natural resources, and . . . ? We're the same as we were thirty years ago. Or even worse. The trouble is that people here don't want to work. That's the pure truth."

He went on haranguing with pompous gestures. Aside from the fact that the subject didn't interest me in the least and that when I hear an opinion over a hundred times it begins to weary me, it was impossible for me to hear him clearly because the hubbub became deafening at times. "If I can't hear the others, nobody will hear me," I reasoned. In the midst of the noise, I felt safe, immune. Every so often I aimed glances of support at the man with the pipe, who received them willingly. But just glances. In body and soul, I was given over to the delightful task of making myself appealing to Patricia Spettanza. My words, my gestures, my smiles all sought out Patricia's approval. I felt so sure of myself that I took advantage of the situation to slip my arm nonchalantly over the back of her chair and touch her right shoulder every now and then. "What will happen now?" I wondered.

Nothing bad happened. Patricia made a movement of withdrawal two or three times, inviting me to back off. But it was obvious it was all just a matter of insisting a bit. In effect, in a little while my fingers were exerting a slight pressure on her shoulder, which I, in my vanity, judged irresistible. Finally, Patricia seemed to consider the presence of my hand in that place as the most natural thing in the world. Incidents like this give me an optimistic—though fleetingly optimistic—vision of the universe, and I began to forget my initial annoyance. I now gave free rein to my imagination: I thought that I could get to marry Patricia; I thought I could be rich; I thought I could succeed in heading a department at Spettanza Bathroom Fixtures; I thought . . .

I was frightened by a stentorian voice: "I propose a toast," declared Paul Spettanza.

At this incantation, we all stood up. Paul Spettanza raised his glass. I thought: "Now, without anyone being able to prevent it, he's going to make some grammatical mistake."

Sure enough: "I drink to all o' you what makes up this company that, more than a company, is one, big, happy family called—Spettanza Bathroom Fixtures."

We all toasted that great enterprise which was one, big, happy family. Some had already begun to sit down—I among them—when the man with the pipe (you could see he loved being in the limelight) called for silence with exaggerated, windmill movements of his arms.

"That's Rodríguez," Patricia informed me. "A real brown-nose. Daddy can't stand him."

Confiding this to me, though nothing romantic, did represent an act of trust, like it or not, and it was promising that Patricia should confide in me.

"I want to second Paul's toast," said Rodríguez, blushing a little, "by wishing each of you the best of luck."

He had talked just to hear himself talk, because the idea was, more or less, the same one expressed in the previous toast. Anyway, we all wished each other the best of personal fortune. Then Rodríguez didn't quite know what to do and he just stood there looking at the others who, in turn, looked back at him, as if waiting for something else. So, to disengage himself from the situation, Rodríguez began to light his pipe laboriously. Many of us again began to sit down.

"And I should like to add a third toast," put in Luke Spettanza, obliging us to stand up once more. "Yes, ladies and gentlemen. A third toast. A third toast in honor of that great, creative agency with so much creativity, with a great, dynamic, aggressive spirit, with faith in the future, with enterprising vision, which, with so much ability, with such grit, with such vigor, has carried our publicity campaign through so well to its well-deserved success . . ."

There was a certain amount of confusion; many didn't know what it was all about.

"I refer," Luke clarified, "to . . . Persuasive Conviction!"

He paused opportunely, and everybody—including those who seconds before were ignorant of the mere existence of Persuasive Conviction—burst out in cordial, uproarious applause, approving by acclamation our unknown merits.

But Luke's countenance had clouded over and he called for silence with solemn gestures. "Its managing director, Mr. McCormick," he said sternly, "is absent due to a very painful reason"—his voice turned completely gloomy—"due to a very painful reason, I repeat. His dear mother, a noble, old Scottish lady, passed away yesterday in Glasgow. For this reason Mr. McCormick is now in Scotland, fulfilling his filial duty as a son."

Everyone was seized with grief.

"But Mr. McCormick wanted to be present here among us in spirit if not in body. And he wanted the advertising agency to be represented at this amiable gathering by another of its proprietors . . ."

What an incredible liar McCormick was!

". . . by another of its proprietors," he pointed me out with his glass, everyone stared at me through a mortal silence, and now it was I who blushed, "that is to say, by Mr. Hernando Genovese who is," he raised his voice, "nothing more and nothing less, and this is saying it all . . . , than the author of the texts of our successful campaign!"

The throng now toasted me, and I had no place to hide. In my innermost heart I bitterly cursed McCormick and his lies. At that point I noticed expectant looks; I was supposed to say something.

I said: "I propose a toast to Northampton."

A suggestion that was received with hurrahs and applause. I regained my composure. Feeling elated, I proposed successive toasts to Royal, to Majestic, and even to Buckingham; they were all met with tumultuous success.

With this I thought the chapter on the toasts could be considered closed. But no, Rodríguez—he never wearied—got up and made us all get up.

"One final toast, please," he said. But he seemed to be suggesting "Before it's too late." "One last toast. I wish to drink to that noble gentleman of finance, that champion of bathroom fixtures, that strategist of products for the bathroom, whose name is . . . Don Carmelo Spettanza!"

I observed that almost all the toasts contained a note of suspense and that only at the end was the enigma of who would be the recipient of the testimonial cleared up. But everyone was now remembering once again the existence of the old man. In a mad, headlong rush—as if they were going to lynch him—they yanked Don Carmelo out of his rocker, paying no attention to his stiff joints, almost lifted him into the air, and obliged him to drink a toast. He turned very pale, so they put a glass to his lips but withdrew it before he could even touch it. Two of them were holding him up and I was afraid he would drop dead right on the spot. Luckily, that didn't happen. On the other hand, the chaos, which was already considerable, now increased. They all seemed ready to compete over who was capable of showing greater love of that mummified patriarch. A kind of tumult originated around his rocking chair, caused by the crowd struggling to shake his hand, embrace, or kiss him, or all three at once.

I declare the following with pride. During moments of wholesale distraction, I usually keep a cool head. I slyly worked out a way not to pay homage to Don Carmelo Spettanza.

VII. The Fall of Patricia Spettanza

*M*eanwhile, with so many toasts, I had been obliged to let go of Patricia's shoulder. So I took advantage of those moments of confusion with which the dinner culminated to take hold of her hand. It felt slightly moist. Sweat? Grease? Could she have touched her food with her hands? I'm so ridiculously apprehensive in questions of hygiene that I was on the point of letting go of it. Luckily, I was able to reflect on the matter; it seemed a pity to waste all that progress, so I tried to steer us gradually away from the large groups of people.

In this way, when there was a general dispersal and similar clusters formed in the living room, discussing the advantages and disadvantages of bathtubs and washbowls, I—now transformed into a real man of the world, with a glass of whiskey in one hand and Patricia's hand in the other—found myself, as though unintentionally, first in the above-mentioned living room, then in a hallway smelling of floor wax, then seated in a little armchair in Patricia's carpeted bedroom.

In her window were delineated little squares of light from other windows of buildings on Libertador Avenue. I knew that, outside, the cool, clear night was a sea of stars; leaning back a bit in my chair, I discerned a round, full moon high in the heavens. Inside, the warmth, perfume, and bliss of Patricia's room invited one to . . .

I began to feel a pleasant restlessness, a fidgety anxiety. From Patricia's hair, from Patricia's skin came aromatic inducements. To drive away the demon it seemed best, for the moment, to observe the room. Its decor zealously respected the norms advocated by business. The walls sprouted little pennants of different educational institutions—some with names in English—and various posters. At the sight of the latter, I instantly regained my negative frame of mind; I judged absolutely all their mottoes as equally stupid. For example: *Bugging me prohibited from midnight to midnight; Make love, not war; Come with me.* Although I deemed the last two appropriate—so to speak—to the present circumstances, I wondered how anyone could live amidst the unavoidable, repeated reading of those telegraphic slogans. There were also great poems—I mean, poems written in great, large letters—printed on placards in full color; poems that she who paid for them had not selected from a beloved book, but out of some store window. My negative frame of mind was intensifying by the second.

There were still other posters, more pictorial than literary. One of them brusquely reminded me that I was still in the domains of Spettanza Bathroom Fixtures: seated on a toilet, a chimpanzee was holding in his right hand a banana and in his left hand the pull chain of the toilet's water tank (and this, it seems, was considered funny).

"Is it a Northampton?" I asked, singling it out with my chin.

Patricia's reply did not answer my question: "You sure do like to mock people, don't you?"

Why this gratuitous accusation? I thought it wise to change the subject. "Those are the Beatles, aren't they?" I indicated a chaotic, hairy mass of figures.

"No, they're the abominable snowmen!" she retorted sarcastically.

In any verbal duel, I always like to get in the last clever remark. But before I could think of something to say, Patricia was already reflecting, bitter and disappointed: "How sad that they broke up. The most fantastic music in the world. Isn't that sad, man? A little while ago I read that they might get back together again. Hey, wouldn't that be *faaabulous?*"

"God, I hope they get back together again!" I warmly approved. "You just can't imagine how worried I am about the breakup of the Beatles. I've lost my appetite, I often spend sleepless nights, just thinking about the breakup of the Beatles. What a tremendous misfortune! Sometimes I'm afraid their breakup is going to cause me an ulcer."

"Oh, sure, how funny. Tickle me, so I can laugh."

I would've liked to tickle her, all right, but she was already going on: "I'm going to play you a record, so you'll know what real music is."

To my left there was a little low table on which lay a pandemonium of magazines and records. Patricia had to bend over me a bit—or maybe she didn't have to, since she could have gone a short way around—to look for a record on the table. Her chestnut hair's feminine fragrance made me lose control of myself. I tripped her with my right foot, caught her around the waist, and let her drop into my lap. I did it well; there was no resistance. I felt her go limp and could smell her perfume more than ever. Putting on my actor's face, I embraced her, kissed her on the cheeks and, immediately, on the mouth. (Afterward, it occurred to me that we hadn't brushed our teeth. But only afterward.)

Now I lost my proverbial prudence, because Patricia's breathing was quickening, becoming heavy. My poise went up in smoke, I felt nervous, my heart was a galloping horse, my hands were trembling. In the midst of this vertigo, I managed to ask myself, confusedly, what might happen. At once I felt the soft coarseness of the carpet to which we had tumbled. I don't know at what point I found myself—flush, hot, sweaty—on top of Patricia. I saw my frantic hands all over her body; I saw a button pop off her dress and I stupidly followed its roll with my gaze until it disappeared under an armchair. I remember her knee, her thigh, I remember touching—but not seeing—a fine mesh fabric and . . .

Patricia suddenly went taut all over: "Get up, someone's coming," and she hurriedly pushed me off.

I hadn't heard anything, but I was on my feet in a second. Immediately we were seated in two little armchairs more or less distant from each other. With a studious countenance, I was reading, without seeing it, a record jacket.

"What are these young folks doing in here, all alone?" asked Luke Spettanza's face, peering in through the barely open door, with a smile which he probably considered sly: "Ah, you little rascals . . ."

The torso followed the face, and following the torso came the whole body, which seated itself on Patricia's charming bed. He leaned his hands heavily on two violet-colored throw pillows as if he wanted to prevent them from taking flight.

"Hi, Daddy," said Patricia. "Come on in," even though Luke had already come in. "We were listening to records," even though the silence and closed record player contradicted this affirmation.

"That's fine," responded Luke distractedly, without verifying things; it was evident he was concentrating on what he had come to say. "That's fine. That's the way to get away from the hubbub. These gatherings tire me out. I have them because it can't be helped. It's just as I always say: there's nothing like peace and tranquility for meditating."

I saw with alarm that there had appeared in Luke Spettanza's hands, as if out of nowhere, a brown ring binder notebook.

"Can you believe it, Daddy?" asked Patricia; "Hernando says he doesn't like the Beatles and that he prefers the Rolling Stones. Did you ever hear anything more weird?"

That clumsy anxiety to fill the silence with words would have made anyone suspicious. But Luke Spettanza, oblivious, was poking around in his ring binder to the sharp snapping of the rings. The sleeves of his jacket looked like two vipers among some white leaves, but leaves of paper.

Paying no attention to her, he noted: "Every man to his own taste."

The vipers had captured a leaf and handed it to me; Luke's voice said: "Let's see what you think of this."

VIII. The Dreamer and His Faith

"*T*he poems and aphorisms," I thought. "I didn't think he'd show them to me this very day; he had said *one of these days.*"

I must have made some unconscious gesture, because he added: "It's very short. As Gracián said, right?"[5]

"Of course." ("Of course, *what?*")

Luckily, the above-mentioned brevity turned out to be true. In the first place, I noticed that the paper was just a regular sheet, without the coat of arms; this seemed to me a good sign. In the second place, I suspected that the typist was not Luke himself, but someone— perhaps a company employee—who possessed some notion of spelling and punctuation. But the author was, unremediably, Luke. It said:

THE DREAMER AND HIS FAITH

The dreamer is an early riser who gets up bright and early at dawn.

His dreams of a vision of the future are left behind him on the pillow.

His faith in tomorrow, appearing like the sun on the horizon.

At his side are men without faith, dragging out a mediocre existence, without a vision of the future, without vigor.

For them there actually exists only actuality, life being mediocre like the weeds that obstruct the passage of the farmer's plow.

And the farmer symbolizes the Dreamer who, dreaming of the progress of his ideal, his ideal being his commercial enterprise, the dreamer putting his shoulder to the wheel with faith in the future so that his enterprise will be the leading enterprise in its area.

Inasmuch as the Dreamer sets his visionary prow toward progress.

Not being mediocre like mediocre men, inasmuch as José Ingenieros already said it.[6]

Because the Dreamer is the eagle, mediocre men being simple hens with henlike flight, which feed on worms.

The Dreamer soars . . .

The Dreamer has faith . . .

The typist's skills hadn't succeeded in modifying the unmistakable style of Luke Spettanza to whom it was linked, moreover, by the incorruptible conviction that *inasmuch* means *therefore*. From a conceptual point of view, it seemed to me the poem had a poor beginning: there was a certain contradiction in the idea that a dreamer should get up early. However, in comparison with what followed, such a beginning was a true master stroke.

And the truth of the matter is, what did I care whether it began well or badly? My thoughts were all for Patricia, who, during all of this, tried two or three times to speak and was energetically shushed up by her father. That's how he demanded quiet for my perusal of his writing.

"Now he's going to ask, *What's your opinion?*," I thought.

To put off that moment, I undertook a second reading. And I would have started and finished a third, but I thought it might seem too long a time to read something so short.

I looked up.

"What's your opinion?

I didn't know what to say. I said: "Who wrote it?

I thought: "Now he'll say, *I did.*"

He said: "I'll bet you can't guess."

Fine; this riddle gave me a breather.

"Well, let's see now, let's see. Give me a little hint. Is the author . . . ?" I was going to say *contemporary*, but to please him I said: "Is the author actual?"

"Yes."

"Is he Argentine?"

"What are you two playing?" asked Patricia disdainfully. "You're cold, you're getting warm, you're hot, you're on fire?"

"Yes, he's Argentine," confirmed Luke, throwing a furious look at Patricia.

"Hmmm . . . Is he over fifty?"

"Yes," he stipulated. "But I won't tell you any more."

"Hmmm . . . Let's see . . . This is a tough one. Maybe I can get it by process of elimination." I made a fist and successively stuck out the fingers of my left hand. "It doesn't seem to be Borges."

"No, it's not," he said, acquiescent, as if giving me to understand that I had erred by a close margin.

"I don't think it's Mujica Láinez either. It's not Denevi."[7] Discouraged, I shook my three outstretched fingers. "Is it a man or a woman?"

"It's a boy, as the midwife said."

"The trouble is that there are so many famous people who write like this." I saw he was smiling, flattered. "I don't know; I give up. Who is it?"

With Spartan simplicity, he said: "Me."

"No! Well, I congratulate you, sir!" I shook his hand and wondered, at the same time, if I wasn't going too far; nevertheless, I added: "This poem is a real lesson to our young people."

"Yeah, but there's a generation gap," Patricia pointed out for some reason.

"Youth has always been the same, it's always been young," retorted Luke. "In my day, too, we boys were leftists, we had noble ideals. Just as Patty has photos of those modern, long-haired singers in her room, I had a picture of Alfredo Palacios in mine. Are you old enough to remember Palacios?"[8]

"Yes, he was a guy with long hair."

"Exactly. He was a great man, a man of integrity." He looked at me suspiciously, as if expecting me to contradict him. "He was the embodiment of true socialism."

"I'm not interested in politics," declared Patricia. "What I'd like to do is study interior decorating and executive secretaryship."

Could the two of them be trying to drive me crazy?

"Young people," Patricia now added, "demand to be given their rightful place in present society. The other day I read in a magazine that we live in a gerontology."

"Gerontocracy," I corrected her.

"I'll give you an example," she went on without paying any attention to me. "In Ethiopia the Negrus is still . . ."

"What Negrus?" I again corrected her. "You must mean the Negus or Emperor."

"How silly!" she replied. "In Africa they're all Negroes."

There were just too many mistakes strung together for me to handle alone, so I decided to ignore them. Besides, now it was Luke who was holding forth on anthropology: "For example," he was saying, "the Pygmies are short in stature, but they're still happy. I saw it in a movie on television."

"I'll give you another example," said Patricia. "In Japan, Hirohito is still ruling, and he was already in power during the war."

"That has nothing to do with it," denied Luke, "because the Japanese respect traditions. That's why they cultivate flowers. They're great floriculturists. Remember when we went to see the flower exhibition in the village of Escobar? You have to admit I'm right on that one."

I sat there, entranced, for a few moments. What capricious wind was playing with the ideas of father and daughter? But Patricia had already forgotten about gerontocracy: "What about Sylvia Martucci who had a fight with her mother and took off to live in an apartment, alone?"

"Yes, and she's probably doing cute things in that apartment," Luke declared sternly.

"So what? At least she's liberated and is fulfilling herself, couple-wise, in a meaningful relationship. Do you know Sylvia Martucci?" she asked me, like someone making an accusation.

"How could I know her?" I answered, still reeling under the painful effects of the words *liberated, fulfilling, couple-wise,* and *meaningful relationship.*

"She's a very intelligent girl. She knows English and bookkeeping. Her father gave her a job in his company."

"What kind of company does her father have?" Luke was now getting interested.

"A laboratory specializing in pharmaceutics. They're the ones who produce the antidiarrhetic Constipex."

"Humph" grumbled Luke. "I don't like that business. They may look very innocent, very philanthropical, but beneath it all they're conspiring against the bathroom fixtures business."

"You're too materialistic," replied Patricia. "We have to have a little idealism, too. Well, as I was saying, Sylvia Martucci left the company and went to live with a guy who's studying economics and plays the guitar. In addition, he paints and sings protest songs against the consumer society."

"Instead of protesting, he should've done as I did, become a *self-made* man by fighting, by working hard and steady."

"But he works too!" adduced Patricia.

"What does he work at?" Luke asked, almost with repugnance.

"Singing protest songs against the consumer society. He earns a lot; the more he protests, they more they pay him."

"I don't know or care about that," Luke had now gotten hard-headed. "You two should have seen me when I was a boy," he half-closed his eyes with an evocative air. "At night I used to run around the streets, sticking up posters for the Socialist Party; bright and early the next morning, I'd be on the job at my father's office, watching over the personnel to make sure they were working as they should. In those days people had more grit, more dynamism," he turned toward me, as if looking for a contrast. "That's why I always inculcate in the lads, the young people who work in the company, that they should work and save and know how to invest their money. Pesos are like seeds: you've got to know where to put them. If you sow a seed in the sand, you can be sure a tree isn't going to grow there. The same things goes for money. Besides, there's another factor. Not just hard, steady work. To achieve a solid financial position, you've got to have faith in the future."

Then Luke stared at me reprovingly. Doubtlessly, he was expecting something from me. I said: "How I wish I had that faith in the future," and I sighed. I was amazed by the moaning intonation I had managed to give the phrase.

It was so sad that Luke thought it worthwhile to console me. "But my good man!" he dealt me a hard wallop on the back. "Don't say that! You're still a young man. You have your whole life before you. Why shouldn't you have faith in the future? Don't just stand still! Don't let down your guard! Work with faith and you'll get to be something in life!"

"I'm already something," I declared weakly.

"Yes, I know, I know. I didn't say that intending to offend you." (I wasn't offended in the least.) "Are you saying you're already something because of your position at Persuasive Conviction?"

"No, I didn't say it just because of that. I think there's been some misunderstanding; I'm not one of the owners of the agency."

"I already knew that. I said that in my toast to impress the guests and to make you look good, so they'd think you're a capable person. Mr. McCormick advised me to do it."

That made me mad. I said: "In view of that, I should inform you it's a lie that McCormick's mother is Scottish and that she has passed away in Scotland. In reality she was born in La Coruña, Spain, and is now living, in perfect health, at the corner of Artigas and Yerbal streets in Buenos Aires."

"I knew that too."

This revelation made me even angrier. "And you said it on McCormick's advice."

"No. I said it on my own initiative. A spontaneous notion, as they say. Where were we?" he changed his tone, anxious to take up again a subject dear to him.

"That boring stuff about faith in the future," Patricia reminded him.

"You're the bore. As I was saying, work with faith, with a will, don't let down your guard, let 'em have it with both fists, if necessary. Life is a jungle and you've got to hack your way through somehow. Knock down trees, cut through the thicket, uproot vines, cross rivers. . . ."

I was distracted for a moment, thinking about the adventures of Tarzan.

". . . we mustn't live tied to the present. My motto is: *Our experience in the past; our feet in the present; our eyes on the future.* At the office I have a little poster with that axiom on it. The main part, and get this firmly into your head, is the vision of the future, planning for tomorrow. If you'll allow me, I'm going to ask you a question that may sound rather naïve. Will you allow me?"

I made a gesture of acquiescence.

"The question is this: have you got next year planned?"

I had to make an effort not to laugh right out loud: "But, Mr. Spettanza, I don't know what I'll be doing five minutes from now. How can I even imagine what I'll be doing next year?"

"You see?" he tapped his knee with his index finger. "There's your mistake."

(Where? On his knee?)

"The lack of a vision of the future. You're thinking now like a young bachelor. But tomorrow, for example, you might get married. Wouldn't you like to give your loved ones, your immediate family, the maximum comfort, the greatest advantages, a beautiful life full of nice things?"

"Of course," I answered, languishing; this conversation was making me sick.

"Consider Patricia, for example," he continued. "Born with a silver spoon in her mouth, private schools, the best education possible. I gave her a Fiat when she turned eighteen."

"Is she your only daughter?" I asked.

"Yes, sir, my only daughter. But even if I had twenty children, I'd give them all the same, yes, sir."

I hadn't intended to express a doubt, but rather a simple curiosity. But Luke felt offended. "And, like Patricia, you too are a lad who apparently was lucky enough to receive an education," he pointed at me accusingly with his index finger. "Life is opening its boundless horizons to you," he was getting poetic again. "I didn't have the good fortune to study," now his tone was melancholy, almost tearful. "I was tripped up."

I didn't ask him how he had been tripped up. So, in view of that, after waiting a few seconds, he continued: "It so happened that I had to repeat the second year of high school. The teachers had it in for me because of my independent spirit. I was examined in eight subjects and I couldn't pass them."

"There's always been unfairness," I observed.

"I had a lot of talent for all that grammar and composition stuff. I like writing a lot. But writing conceptually, you understand; that is, formulating thoughts, inferring morals, setting forth rules of conduct, writing speeches. I hadn't yet reached the age of twenty-three when Don Salvador Fazzolari, who was a member of the soccer subcommittee of the Atlanta Athletic Club,[9] invited me to the Lions' Club of Villa Crespo to give a speech I had written on the virtues of saving money and perseverance. You can imagine how nervous I was; there was assembled the cream of the business and cultural world of Villa Crespo.[10] You should have heard how they applauded me."

To make him get back to his bad memories, I said: "You were telling me you had to repeat the second year of high school."

"Yes, I took it over, unfortunately. Then my father, with good reason, I recognize it now, took me out of school and put me to work in the business. And don't think I had a soft job either, eh? No, sir, not at all; I worked as a common laborer. These hands," he showed them to me as irrefutable proof, but I could see nothing special about them, "these hands are the hands of a working man," he said it in an anguished tone of voice that reminded me of the tear-jerker films of Luis Sandrini. "Boy, have these hands shined faucets!"

I'm insensitive at times; instead of being moved, I felt like kicking him in the head!

"Anyone but me would have felt frustrated," his optimism was returning. "Not me. I never let down my guard. Besides, to tell the truth, I like shining faucets better than studying botany, history, and all that other junk that's of no use at all. Nevertheless, and I tell you now just as frankly, and it ain't just braggin', but I've read a lot. I'm a true self-educated person, a *self-made man*, as the Americans say. I've even read more than a lotta Ph.D.s with a degree hangin' on their wall. Do you like to read?"

"I think reading is just *fantaaastic*, just *faaabulous*," said Patricia, in a burst of f's and elongated vowels. "Right now I'm reading *Airport*."

"I respect all opinions," Luke interrupted her, forgetting that I owed him a reply, "but all those little novels and stories are drivel. No, I'm referring to serious books, books that leave something. . ."

I was about to ask him what that *something* was, but I felt lazy.

". . . books that can educate me on the professional level. Therefore, my young friend Hernando (you don't mind if I call you by your first name, do you?), you commit a *crass* error in not reading."

I hadn't said I didn't read.

"One must read, read untiringly," he was gradually raising his voice more and more, "one must read to improve himself, so as not to be out of place in any social situation. For example, I'm at a gathering and people are talking about travel and tourism. Great; I shine there, because I know the names of all the capitals of Europe."

"Oh, Daddy, anybody knows that," said Patricia.

("You took the words right out of my mouth," I thought.)

"It's just an example," replied Luke, miffed, as if, because it was merely an example, it wasn't erroneous. "Anyway, we've got to read, but not just on the professional level. Although it's true I do read a lot in my area of specialization: magazines of finance, economics, business, architecture, interior decorating. A manufacturer of bathroom fixtures is like a doctor: he must, without rest, remain current, be up-to-date with the latest innovations in his art. Both these professions are really two high priesthoods. Moreover, I'm a subscriber to the ARASOMANBAFIXNLIK."

"To the what?"

"To the ARASOMANBAFIXNLIK," he responded, quite naturally.

"What's that?" I asked, without a trace of irony. "Something Swedish? One of those sauna things that are in vogue?"

"No, no," he laughed. "It's the journal of the society we all belong to: the Argentine Association of Manufacturers of Bathroom Fixtures and the Like. It's an acronym: ARASOMANBAFIXNLIK. I sometimes contribute an article or something. My brother Paul does too, but he's too impulsive. Last year he wrote an article criticizing the urinals at the municipal airport, and the government closed down our magazine. And then they say there's freedom of the press."

"If I remember correctly, your father was the president of that association."

"By no means," he specified. "You must be careful not to confuse things. My father was president of the Democratic Society of Manufacturers of Bathroom Fixtures and the Like. Later on there was a schism," his face became sad and gloomy. "There was elements in the Society with ideas that were too totalitarian; they wanted to push the square toilet monopolistically. At that point, many of us separated and founded the Association. A few nitwits remained in the society. In short, there was other problems too. It's a very delicate subject and I don't want to get into it. You'll forgive me this reticence."

He thought I was stoically respecting his silence, but another thought was flitting around in my head. "What did you say was the name of the association's journal?"

"ARASOMANBAFIXNLIK."

"You sure need a good memory to remember it, eh?"

"Well," he smiled, giving me to understand that no talent was denied the manufacturers of bathroom fixtures. "As I was telling you, I read a lot. Did you read *How to Win Friends and Influence People?*"

"To tell you the truth, no."

"That's a pity."

"Really."

"I'm going to lend it to you."

"Fine. Thank you very much."

"It's probably a bore," exhaled Patricia.

"You keep quiet, scatterbrain. Why, you never get beyond your silly little novels. By the way," he added, looking at me, "Mr. McCormick mentioned that you was into all that stuff about publishing companies."

To take revenge for that association of ideas, I prepared not to understand such outlandish phrasing. "Into all that stuff about publishing companies?" I repeated, as if analyzing a sentence of an unknown language.

"Yes, that is, he told me you had published some books. I dunno. Somethin' like that. What're they about?"

"They're short stories," I said, resigned.

"Oh," he replied, like someone saying *What shit.* "I'd like to read them." (I thought: "You would *not* like to read them.")

"How can I go about getting them? I don't suppose you could . . .?"

(I thought: "Not even in my wildest dreams.") I said: "They're on sale in any bookstore."

"Oh, I see," he felt cheated; not because he couldn't read the books, but because he hadn't managed to get them free. "Well, later on, you jot down the titles on a little slip of paper for me. Now, getting to the point" (that is to say: "Let's stop talking about your inanities and let's get to what's really important; let's get to my interests"), "I'd like to publish a book I have here."

He pointed alternately at the spring binder and at his head; I assumed the book had a partially real existence and a partially potential existence.

I didn't say anything. Patricia started to speak: "But . . ."

"How do I do it?" added Luke.

"What's the book you want to publish about?"

"Well, it's not easy to *difine* it. The content is varied, a potpourri, as they say. Things like 'The Dreamer and His Faith.'"

I wrinkled up my nose: "I don't mean to disillusion you," I said, in order to disillusion him, "but it's very unlikely they'll publish it for you."

He looked at me with a stern frown. "Why not?" and there was unjustly wounded dignity in his voice.

"You write with too much lyrical flare. That's not for these times without ideals. You yourself say it when you speak of the eagle and the hens that eat earthworms."

"Worms," he corrected.

"The hens that eat worms," I repeated. "Although they also eat earthworms. So, as I was telling you . . ."

"Do you think so? Are people so materialistic now?" he half-closed his eyes, as if seeking a spiritual oasis in the happy past.

"Publishing companies are businesses, like Spettanza Bathroom Fixtures. And, in a certain way, they even complement each other."

"What do you mean, 'they complement each other'?" he seemed to be bitten by a snake.

Now you may not believe it, but I was flustered and extremely angry. My germinating but confused thought went something like this: "Some of the shit that's published would deserve being thrown into the toilet." Instead, I said: "I mean, the essential thing is the human being. And, just as the book acquires all its value in contact with the reader, in like manner does the toilet attain its lofty civilizing significance upon being used by Man, with a capital letter."

I thought I was making fun of him, but might it not be the opposite? I noticed a spark of anger in Patricia's eyes.

"What a beautiful thought!" Luke exclaimed, delighted; yes, without a doubt, he was making fun of me. "If you don't mind, I'd like to include it in my book. May I?" he was even playing the clown. "Or will you sue me for plagiarism?"

"I relinquish it to you with great pleasure," O.K. Fine; I'd go along with his little joke.

"Thank you very much. I'm going to make a note of it right now. Patricia, have you got a pencil around here?"

Patricia handed him a ball point pen all chewed up and Luke started to write on the edge of a newspaper. "How did it go? 'The lofty, civilizing significance of the toilet ennobles Man, with a capital letter.'"

It wasn't exactly like that, but I recognized his phrase as superior to mine.

"So," he added, tearing off the piece of paper, "you're of the opinion they won't want to publish it for me? What kind of works do the publishing houses put out?"

He carefully tucked away in a pocket the thought he had jotted down; he was probably serious about what he had said.

"Anything that sells big. Pornographic stuff, with swear words, drugs, and violence. You know what I mean?"

"Do you write like that?" he looked at me with the face of a Juan B. Justo socialist.[11]

"Of course," I answered, pleased as Punch.

"You surprise me, my young friend," he now put on the face of a severe teacher. "And, I'm being sincere, you surprise me unpleasantly. Do you mean, then, that you don't believe in the ethical and moral values?"

"I used to believe, before, in the ethical values, but not in the moral ones. Later on, I believed in the moral values, but not in the ethical ones. And now I don't believe in either the ethical or the moral values."

"Which seem to you the most essential? The ethical or the moral ones?"

"Both seem equally contemptible to me. Besides, *ethical* and *moral* mean the same thing. You, who are fond of synonyms, should . . ."

I saw that he hadn't understood, or even heard me.

"The fact," he said slowly, "is that you are a leftist, isn't that so?"

"How did you notice? As you can see, I'm a co-partisan of yours, since you used to go around pasting up Socialist Party posters."

"Yes, but you can't compare. That was a healthy socialism, a socialism clearly understood, a socialism that embodied ethical and moral values."

"Times change."

"Fine, but let's get off this subject, since it's beside the point," he made a gesture as if shooing away a fly. "To sum up, you really advise me not to try to publish it?"

"I don't advise you anything. I'm not the last word on the subject," I suddenly felt horribly tired and pessimistic, like denying the whole universe. "You can do something: grab your manuscripts and, without letting down your guard, with faith in the future, go around to the publishing houses and pound on doors and desks with your fists. If you do it that way, maybe they'll publish it for you."

Like so many other times, I failed to restrain myself. He looked at me reproachfully. "Young man, I seem to detect in your words a certain mocking intention toward convictions of mine that I consider quite respectable."

"I categorically deny any mocking intention," I replied.

"Well," he answered dryly, "you two will have to excuse me if I leave you alone. I must attend to my other guests."

IX. How to Win Friends

I excused him with great pleasure. He had scarcely closed the door when I tried to embrace Patricia again; but I had a surprise waiting for me:

"Get away from me," she said angrily. "You're rotten . . ."

What was that for?

". . . you made Daddy angry. With his heart condition, you don't know the harm these fits of anger do him."

"But what did I say?" I wasn't about to admit an accusation of homicide.

"You know very well what you said to him. Don't play innocent. You know very well what you said to him: that stuff about faith in the future."

"And so? Is faith in the future sacred? Besides, I said it without any malice," there was no point in Patricia and me getting into a debate. "Anyway, your father gets angry about any silly, little thing." I took her hand again.

She gave it a yank and pulled loose.

"The trouble with you is you think you can make fun of everybody. As soon as I saw you, the minute I spoke to you a little bit, I realized you were a contemptuous person. You can see it even in . . . , even in . . ."

"Even in my ears," I suggested.

"How funny. Tickle me, so I can laugh," this was doubtlessly a leitmotif of hers. "I don't know why you think you're so exceptional."

"I never said that I thought I was exceptional."

"But it's just the same. It's as if you had said it. You can see it even in . . . , even in the way you look at people."

"You're quite mistaken."

"And, anyway, what the hell are you after all? A sorry, insignificant little employee of a publicity agency nobody ever heard of."

Anyone else would have been offended; I took solace in thinking of the ominous effect her remark would have had on McCormick. I insisted, once again, in holding her hand. Patricia was now talking like a magpie and, attentive mainly to her own words, she made only slight movements of unwillingness. And, without faith in the future, she failed to get loose. In the midst of her supersonic paragraphs, every once in a while I managed to slip in an occasional conciliatory remark: "Don't be mad" was one of them; "Come on, don't be so moody" was another; "Forgive me, I didn't mean to." These were my words, but I wasn't interested in airing a question of personal honor, so, consequently, my intentions did not belong to the realm of the synonymous ethical and moral values. When I did try to get hold of myself, we were already frolicking about once again on the rug, my hands more active than ever. A modest confession: I was aroused. Some extenuating circumstances: the cold outside; the whiskey; the soft carpet; that general warmth; Patricia's fragrance. I had an insane idea. Luckily, other ideas, those belonging to a sane individual, came to my aid: I thought there would be other occasions in the future; I thought someone might open the door; I thought that, if I locked it, they could kick it down. I then noticed that a familiar feeling was beginning to come over me: I foresaw the danger, the embarrassment, the ridiculousness, the discomfort of . . . Sweaty and flushed, I made a superhuman effort and pulled away from Patricia before the irreparable could happen.

I was more than timely. An instant later, in came Luke Spettanza. He was brandishing a book.

"A promise is binding," he declared sententiously. "Here's *How to Win Friends and Influence People.*"

"Thank you very much," I responded, trying to calm down, not to pant.

"In spite of the fact," he added, "that you didn't want to lend me your books."

"It's not that I don't want to," I lied. "It's that I don't have a single copy left."

"Well, that's O.K. Don't worry. One of these days, I'll send the office boy out to buy them."

He didn't ask me what the titles were. That really made me angry.

X. Oh, My Elusive Muse, You Who Speak Only When You Want To . . .

*T*hat night I fell asleep immediately, machinating all kinds of ambitious plans related to Patricia. Incredibly enough, Sunday morning I forgot about Patricia. I had been favored with a most interesting, confused, unapprehensible dream; I awoke with the idea that there was material there for a good fantastic story. When I did recall it, however, it didn't seem as beautiful to me then as I thought it was when I was dreaming it. I noticed inconsistent elements, unexplainable facts, blurry actions. It went something like this (but not *exactly* like this; exceedingly more vivid): a very ugly, very poor, very ignorant woman had fallen deeply in love with a successful man of our times; a rich, elegant, I want to suppose, cultured man. Now then, I—I am sure—was not that man. Since I like to write in first person, that already presented a difficulty. And there were other bothersome details. For example, how was I aware of that situation? How was it that I seemed to live it from within? Then it happened that the woman, with the mere strength of her thought, a thought of prodigious power, succeeded in getting the man to become gradually interested in her, and she ended up instilling into her beloved's brain a series of imaginary qualities possessed by her. He saw her as beautiful, distinguished, seductive. And then . . . And then . . . How did she do it? There was the elusive key. In the dream there were so many and such sharp details that everything was perfectly plausible. But now it wasn't.

At six o'clock in the morning, awake but tired, I resolved to get up and start to write at eight. Then I fell into a light sleep. At eight-thirty I ascertained that the sky was gloriously blue and that the joy of a radiant sun was inundating the yellow streets of autumn. It was a pity to stay shut in like a rat, so I went to play soccer. I might as well have stayed at home. I couldn't pay attention to the game, which, under normal circumstances, really excites me. The dimly outlined—or perhaps now already lost—plot of the dream kept fluttering around in my mind.

I returned home with my strength drained. "As soon as I finish eating," I told myself, "I'll sit down and write it all at once." But that wasn't true; I knew I wouldn't be able to write it, yet I was prepared to struggle. As was foreseeable, when I finished lunch I neither sat down nor wrote a single word. Between the hustle and bustle of the Spettanzas' dinner party, the hustle and bustle in Patricia's room, and the hustle and bustle at the soccer game, I was done in. I gave up and stretched out to take a nap. "Just until three o'clock," I vowed stoically, and I set the alarm clock. When it went off, I silenced it and went on sleeping. I got up after six.

I brewed some *maté*,[12] and set out my cigarettes, some blank sheets of paper, and a fountain pen filled with black ink. (In case there's someone who doesn't know it, I hereby inform him that good stories cannot be written with a ballpoint pen or with blue ink.) I drank a few *matés* while I meditated on the first words. I lit a cigarette. I finished it. I drank another round of *matés*. I lit a second cigarette. I kept searching for the initial words, which are the most important ones, those which shape the whole story and give it its proper tone. Without exception, those that occurred to me were inappropriate. The sheet of paper remained candidly virginal. Now fearful, I exhorted myself: "You've got to write something; otherwise, the story's not going to materialize." In the upper-right-hand corner I wrote firmly: 1. O.K., fine. I already had the first page of the story; now all I had to do was write it. "I'm going to begin just any way I can. I'll rewrite it later, in any case." I wrote:

That a powerful feeling should engender a powerful thought. . .

That technique of starting a story with the word *that* looks like— is—an imitation—a poor imitation—of Borges. I corrected:

At times, a powerful feeling can engender a thought so powerful that . . .

I thought the *at times* and *can* contaminated the whole sentence with trivial potentiality. I corrected:

A powerful feeling engenders a powerful thought . . .

"Worse than ever," I told myself disconsolately. "That assertive and irrefutable tone seems suited to a chemistry treatise. Besides, I don't like that verb *engender* at all." I read it again. I now noticed an unjustifiable rhythmic parallelism. To punish myself, I sang in a low voice, to the rhythm of a train:

"Pow-er-ful feel-ing! Pow-er-ful thought!"

"Pow-er-ful feel-ing! Pow-er-ful thought!"

It was truly horrible.

"Damn!" I exclaimed. "What lousy luck!"

In anger and rage, I grabbed the paper and tore it into tiny, little pieces. I took another sheet and stubbornly wrote again in the upper-right-hand corner: 1. I decided to devote myself to thinking and resolved not to write a single word until I had the whole story mentally constructed. To steady myself in this ideal, I put the top on the ink pen, a possible source of temptation. But it was all useless; if I don't have the initial words, I can't go on. And I couldn't manage to hit upon them. Superfluous or missing circumstances always came to me; uselessly detailed or uselessly fuzzy events always kept turning up. Moreover, as I thought about it, the fantastic treacherously transformed itself on me, in a gradual way, into the grotesque and even into the ridiculous. And, as if these misfortunes were not enough, at every moment there occurred to me scores of funny sentences or episodes. I stood my ground; I would not accept them. Was I forever condemned to write stories that provoke laughter? Could I never be pathetic in fiction, as I am, intimately, in reality? Could I never stir the heart of the reader? Not thousands of readers who are moved by things that make me laugh. No; even if it were just *one* reader.

In short, I *knew* the story was denied me. But I persisted in my whim. I didn't shrink from the well-known superstitions and appealed to the usual ruses. I got a pad of graph paper and filled another fountain pen with green ink. Of course, it didn't work. I resolved—and this produced one more defeat—to forget writing the story, but not to forget its conception.

Because of the time off that McCormick had granted me, the following week was to be all mine. More than anything else, I made use of it by continuing to think fruitlessly about the story. That is, I made use of it for nothing. I imagined details, dialogues, particulars, places, and colors. Then I cast them all aside as ineffective or, what is infinitely worse, because they were completely unusable, because they were vain paragraphs worthy of oblivion.

XI. A Drama of Our Time

*I*t's superfluous to say that, although discouraged by the recalcitrant story, I didn't let that stop me from going out with Patricia. I got to know her friends, her manner of being, her hobbies (girls like Patricia always need to have hobbies). I also got to know other things about her. However, aside from the main point, that they are irrelevant, a gentleman just doesn't talk about such things.

In a word, that girl was not for me. Of course, in certain periods of scarcity, one doesn't go around making excessive demands about character, spiritual values, and—if you will—about "the elective affinities."[13]

Sometimes I contradict myself. I just said I wouldn't speak of certain irrelevant matters, because this is not the story of my adventures but, rather, the story of precise events in which the leading roles are played by proud, extraordinary people. And yet, I'm now going to tell about a ridiculous incident that happened to me at noon on that Friday, my last day off. I hasten to point out that it has nothing to do with our story; it will take up only this chapter and may be omitted without any loss whatsoever.

I shall begin by highlighting a praiseworthy feature of my personality: I have no calling to be a Don Juan. I do, however, place a limit on the range of this virtue: my asceticism does not go so far as to pass up worthwhile opportunities. I shall exemplify this with my anecdote.

The episode began around eleven o'clock. I was sitting on my balcony, drinking *maté* for the second time that morning. After ten years, I was rereading with great pleasure the fascinating adventures of *King Solomon's Mines*. Nevertheless—I noted with sadness—I had enjoyed them much more when I was a boy.

At a given moment, I became aware that someone was watching me.

I looked up. On the balcony of the apartment building across the street I spied, somewhat diffuse among railings and flower pots, the presence of a girl. The fact of being master of my own time made me feel happy and enterprising; I raised my hand and sent her a greeting. She said "Hi" with a wave of her arm and withdrew from the balcony.

Now interested in the possible derivations, I stayed out on mine. I furtively tried—she was doubtlessly peeking at me through the cracks in the louvers—to glimpse the interior of her apartment, but I couldn't see anything. Since the sun was shining in my eyes, windows and doors appeared to me to be like dark rectangles.

Meanwhile, I distracted myself with the idea that I had never noticed the existence of that building, which was ridiculous since, evidently, the construction dated from . . . "She isn't coming out any more," I told myself, and went back to my reading. I couldn't have read ten lines when she reappeared. Perhaps her clothing registered some changes.

I began to lavish facial expressions and gestures on her, but in vain. Now seated in a big wrought-iron chair, the girl was reading—or pretending to read—a magazine. "It's a trick," I thought. "She must see me, and now she has put herself on display." I couldn't distinguish her features very well, but I could see her body: tall and slender. And her lank, dark hair, which fell straight to her shoulders. "Who can she be?" I wondered. "I've probably seen her many times in the bakery."

I had a felicitous idea. I left the balcony, went into my bedroom, and peeked at her through the shutters: in all innocence she was looking toward my building. Then I went running back out and, oh, propitious fates(!), I surprised her in that revealing posture.

Bursting with pride over my ingeniousness, I triumphantly greeted her with a broad wave of my hand, which indisputably demanded reciprocation. In effect, she returned my greeting. The normal thing, after greetings, is to initiate a conversation, but, of course, we weren't going to yell at each other back and forth across the street. Then, with my right index finger, I made a dialing movement, which, as everyone knows, meant could I call her on the telephone. Shrugging her shoulders and opening her hands out wide, palms up, the girl answered me again and again, and even once again, that she didn't understand. Wretch! How could she not understand?

I went back inside, unplugged the telephone, and returned to the balcony with it. I raised it with both hands over my head, exhibiting it like a sporting trophy. ("And now, you little moron, do you understand or not?") Yes, she understood; her face lit up in a lightning flash of a smile of large white teeth, and she responded with an affirmative gesture.

All well and good; I now had authorization to call her, but I didn't know her number. I would have to use mimicry to ask her.

I now resorted to very strange facial expressions and gestures; anybody seeing me would have thought I was crazy. It was hard to formulate the question, but it was up to her to guess what I needed to know. I think there was ill will on her part; in her flirtatiousness, she wanted to amuse herself a bit with me. In doing so, she stretched the cord of my patience as far as she could, and, at the very instant it was about to break, that is, when I was on the brink of discouragement and was getting ready to give up, she understood.

She sketched some numbers in the air with her index finger. Some numbers? But, what numbers were these? Did they belong to some exotic, perhaps already extinct civilization? Or were they in code? Or were they letters? Yes, they were, in fact, letters, because the last two figures looked like two capital Fs. What message was she transmitting to me? A Russian last name?

Ah! I then realized she was writing facing me. The double final F must, therefore, be interpreted as an initial 77.[14] Satisfied with my shrewdness, I worked out the complete translation and got the coveted seven numbers that would put me in communication with my charming, unknown neighbor.

I was very pleased. I plugged in the telephone and dialed. Someone picked up the receiver on the first ring:

"Yeeess!" a deep, masculine voice thundered in my ear.

Surprised by this turn of events, I hesitated a moment, searching for the words I would use.

"Who is it?" the harsh, loud voice added, now with a trace of anger and impatience.

"Uh . . . Uh . . ." I mumbled, frightened. "Is this 771 . . . ?"

"Talk louder, sir!" he interrupted me in an extremely annoying way. "I can't hear you at all, sir! Who do you want to talk to, sir?"

He said *who* instead of *whom,* and he said *sir* in a tone normally used to say *imbecile.* Scared to death, I babbled: "Uh . . . To the young lady."

"What young lady, sir? What young lady are you talking about, sir?" a definite threat was now lurking in the gruff voice.

How do you explain something to someone who doesn't want to understand?

"Uh . . . to the young lady on the balcony," my voice was a thin, little thread of spun glass.

But he wouldn't take pity even on this. On the contrary, he became more infuriated: "Please, sir, don't bother us! We're working people here!"

An angry *click* cut off the connection. Disconcerted, burned up, red in the face, I stood there for a moment, drained of strength. Then—as if it might do me some good—I glared at the telephone and cursed at it between my clenched teeth: "You can go straight to hell, you dirty, rotten son of a bitch."

Then I aimed some harsh mental epithets at that foolish girl who hadn't taken the precaution of answering the phone herself. But, immediately, I thought I was to blame for having called so quickly. From the speed with which the man with the gruff voice answered, I deduced that the instrument was probably within reach of his hand, perhaps on his desk. I tried to imagine that man, attributing hateful characteristics to him: I thought of him as fat, potbellied, red-faced, and sweaty. "We're working people here," he had said. So what do I care? Everyone works; there was no special merit in that. Did I perhaps live on a private income? That's what I should have answered him. Yes, sir. That very thing. Or perhaps something more devious, more subtle, more baroque. The undeniable fact, however, was that that loud-mouth had inflicted upon me a definitive telephonic defeat. I felt a little depressed and desirous of revenge.

Just to do something, I drank a glass of water. Then I went back out on the balcony, resolved, however it might be, to ask the girl her name. But she wasn't there. "Of course," I inferred, with reckless vanity, "she would be in by the telephone, waiting anxiously for my call."

Now full of renewed spirit, but still smarting a bit, I dialed the seven numbers. I heard one ring, and then heard: "Yeeesss . . . !!!"

I hung up, terrified. "Sonofa . . ." I mumbled with sadness and rancor, and, at the pronouncement of this phrase, there occurred to me an idea that I deemed brilliant.

I thought: "That abominable troglodyte across the street gets away with tyrannizing me simply because I'm lacking one thing: the name of the person I want to speak to. Hence, it's essential to get it."

Then I thought: "Last names appear in the Green Directory.[15] I don't have a Green Directory. Large businesses have a Green Directory. Banks are large business enterprises. Banks have a Green Directory. My friend, Balbón, works in a bank. The banks open at twelve o'clock."

I waited until 12:05, and called Balbón:

"Oh, my dear friend, Hernando," he answered, scarcely did he hear one word from me. "I am extremely joyful, contented, and comforted to hear your voice again . . ."

"Thanks, Balbón. But, listen . . ."

". . . your voice of a carefree, cheerful young man free of obligations, duties, and responsibilities. Oh, happy you, dear friend Hernando, for you are a stranger to all kinds of woes. Happy you, who take life as a fortunate becoming and allow no external matter to perturb the peace of your ordered existence. Happy you, for you swim in financial abundance, working only three or four hours a day. Happy you. . . ."

Now some skeptic, and there's always one around, will probably consider as impossible the existence of people who talk like Balbón. I have no way to prove it, but I beg to be believed; I swear, swear again, and swear once more that Balbón exists and that he really talks that way.

After adorning me with all the imaginary pieces of good fortune he could think of, he continued on—without letting me speak—to the second stage, which consisted of attributing to himself—by way of tragic contrast—all the calamities of the visible and invisible universe.

"On the other hand, I, the humble, the modest, the abject Horace Henry Balbón, continue today, as yesterday and tomorrow, as the day before yesterday and the day after tomorrow, dragging a heavy, onerous, and burdensome wagonload of miseries, misfortunes, and sadness through this distressing, tempestuous, and horrid vale of tears which, in the manner of an inferno, a Hades, an Avernus . . ."

I had heard this story thousands of times. "But didn't you tell me they had promoted you and that now you're earning quite a good salary?"

"Yes, that's true," he admitted. "I now earn three times more than before, I have a high-placed job of importance, and they have even given me a personalized stamp with my signature on it."

The word *personalized*, drawn out and with every letter clearly pronounced, made me let out a guffaw.

"And yet," he went on, without being offended, "the heavy, onerous, and burdensome wagonload of miseries, misfortunes, and sadness still exists. And I go on dragging it, languishing, ill, and perhaps with one foot already in the grave, across the face of this perfidious, cruel, and malign planet . . ."

I became a bit distracted, waiting for him to finish his complaints. Suddenly, I heard: "Well, I've really enjoyed talking to you. Until the next time."

And he hung up. Indignant, I called him back: "Hey, Balbón!" I reproached him. "Why did you hang up?"

"Oh," he said. "Did you want to tell me something?"

"Well, of course I did! What would I call you for if I didn't? I need you to look in the Green Directory for me and see what last name corresponds to the following telephone number."

"Wait a minute. I'm going to look for my fountain pen, since you know how I hate, detest, and abhor writing with pencils, ballpoint pens, or markers."

I had to wait for him.

"That number," he said, after one or two minutes, "corresponds to a family with the last name of Castellucci. But, what do you want it for?"

"Thanks a lot, Balbón. I'll explain it to you some other day. *Ciao.*"

"Good-by," he replied, with a trace of resentment in his voice.

Now I was ready; now I was in possession of a powerful weapon. With a jovial spirit and a firm finger, I again dialed the girl's number.

"Yeeesss . . . !!!" thundered the caveman.

Without hesitating, in a sonorous, well-modulated voice, which did not exclude a certain peremptory tint, I articulated: "Will you please connect me with Miss Castellucci?"

"Who's calling, please?"

Asking "Who's calling, please?" is a custom I don't like. To confuse him a little bit, I said: "George Arasomanbafixnlik."

"But, sir!" he exploded. "The Castellucci family hasn't lived here for about four years, sir! We're always being bothered with calls for the Castelluccis!"

"Well, if they don't live there anymore, why did you ask me who's call . . . ?"

His furious *click* interrupted me in the middle of the sentence; he hadn't even let me express that minimal protest against his despotism. Ah, but it wasn't going to end up like this! I lunged at the telephone like someone grabbing for a revolver.

"Yeeesss . . . !!!"

With the pronunciation of a mentally retarded individual, I asked: "Iz diz da Casdewoodzy fabwy?"

"No, *sir*! The Castellucci family hasn't lived here for over five years, sir!"

"Ah . . . how dice; I'b speakig to mizduh Casdewoodzy . . . How'z id goid', mizduh Casdewoodzy?"

"No, please! Now, get this straight, sir!" he was a powder keg ready to explode. "The Castellucci family hasn't lived here for about seven years, man!"

"How a' yoo, mizduh Casdewoodzy?" I insisted, cordially. "Ad yoouh wive? And de two gids? Don'd yoo wemembuh me, mizduh Casdewoodzy?"

"Hey, who is this?" besides being ill-tempered, the monster was curious.

"Diz iz Dom speakig, mizduh Casdewoodzy."

"Tom?" he repeated, with revulsion. "What Tom?"

"Dom, mizduh Casdewoodzy, Dom, Dom, da piber's sod, da one who stod a pig ad away he wun."

"What . . . !?" he hadn't understood me very well, since I was choking with laughter.

"Dom, mizduh Casdewoodzy, Dom Sudder."

"Tom Sutter? Which Tom Sutter?"

"Dom Sudder, mizduh Casdewoodzy, da one oo'z bwind id one eye, ad gan'd see ouda de udder."

That was a kind of atomic bomb: "Quit pestering me, do you mind, you Mongolian idiot! Why don't you put a bullet in your brain, you poor devil?"

He hung up with a violent slam. That was a pity; I wanted him to go on insulting me. It was delightful to imagine my enemy: red in the face, all in a sweat, apoplectic, with his telephone instrument perhaps damaged by the slam.

I felt very pleased with myself, and not being able to talk to the girl on the balcony no longer mattered to me.

XII. The New Metaphysics

That week turned out to be so unproductive and insipid that the most positive thing that happened to me was the one I've just related. Hence, you can imagine what the others must have been like; they simply didn't exist. I won't even speak of the short story that was denied me; all my efforts proved useless, and I decided to give it up definitively.

Those five days off passed by, then, like a gray gust of wind, and the moment came to return to the agency. Without any apparent cause, I entered into a prolonged somber mood, a period during which I could make no sense of my actions. As a kind of irregular routine, carried out at unequal intervals, I found myself every so often with Patricia Spettanza. The only incentive I saw in these encounters was their erotic dimension. If it weren't for that, it would have proven impossible to unravel the meaning of our relationship. Patricia had a unique aptitude for being ignorant or disdainful of all the things that were dear to me and, in turn, for being profoundly interested in aspects of the visible universe whose right to exist I flatly denied. When I was with Patricia, I felt desolately empty at times. Occasionally, I recalled fleeting conversations I had had with other women. I remembered them with nostalgia; with unexplainable nostalgia, of course, because I well knew that, if they were repeated enough, in the long run they too would have ended up wearying me. Just as Patricia wearied me with her insubstantial chatter made up of elements of the most rigorous—and already dead—current subject matter. Patricia belonged to the immense class of people who are lacking in memory, so that all oblivion was always novelty for her.[16] In addition, she would take it into her head to relate long anecdotes to me, full of inaccuracies but peopled with characters whose names she cited punctiliously, as if I knew them; that is, she informed me what their names were but not what they were like. Or, when she wasn't doing this, she was reproducing arguments she had had with ex-girlfriends—now irreconcilable enemies—in which not only was Patricia always—but always, always, always—right, but her rightness was also recognized with total humility by her antagonist of the moment.

In this way, two or three months must have passed.

Meanwhile, it seems that the world, insensitive to my misfortunes, continued on its merry way and, so as to make no change in its customary routine, it introduced several modifications into the course of universal history.[17] I found out about some of them on a certain Monday at the agency when McCormick said to me: "Here, read this, and see what a cute little surprise is in store for you."

He slipped under my nose the latest issue of the magazine *Anthropoids*. A shadow of annoyance darkened my countenance; I abhor the mere existence of magazines. And, within this species, I abhor, above all, magazines about current events. And, within this subspecies, above all, the magazine *Anthropoids*, that indefatigable machine for fomenting and perfecting the already congenital and incurable stupidity of the human race.

Besides—I already mentioned it—I was in a bad mood and wasn't of a mind to decipher enigmas. I wanted to ask McCormick what it was, specifically, that I was supposed to read. But he had already disappeared, and I felt too lazy to get up and go ask him. With a scowling face, mumbling muted curses under my breath, I quickly leafed through those multicolored pages. So much imbecility was housed in such excellent paper, in such perfect print, and in such beautiful photographs. Issue after issue repeated the same faces, the same smiles, the same clichés, the same comments, the same commonplaces, and all with a similar destiny: immediate oblivion. And then in the next issue one had to commence relearning the same, unvarying catalogue of idiocy. And let nobody tell me there can be intelligence without memory, because I won't believe him.

I at once found the article that had awakened McCormick's interest. But first I wanted to see what its companions were: "the other parts of the system that support the whole."[18]

Between pages 58 and 63, it had been considered worthwhile to record, for the benefit of civilization and the sake of posterity, the vital thought of a group of taxi drivers. These rolling peripatetic philosophers, far from limiting their opinions to the mysteries of their profession, extended their meditations into other fields of knowledge, from the state of the world economy to ironclad interpretations and vindications of the Argentine woman. To lighten the reader's burden of such profound concepts, *Anthropoids* repeated here and there a pleasant, even chummy note, which consisted of referring to the taxi drivers as "cabbies." Oh, well, what can I say?

Pages 67–70 informed us that a Famous Television Star had just gotten married, because of which *he was news*, and, accordingly, it became necessary *to do a piece on him*. But *the trick wasn't so easy* for the Clever Reporter and the Ubiquitous Photographer, since the Famous Star *had wanted to keep the ceremony secret*, to the point of *having gotten involved in a heated argument with the doorman at the Civil Registry,*[19] since, *due to a possible indiscretion on the part of said doorman*, the Famous Star *was identified by over fifty persons who fought to get near him*. These grave antecedents explain why, when the Clever Reporter and the Ubiquitous Photographer ring the doorbell at *a luxurious chalet in the Los Troncos quarter* of Mar del Plata,[20] the Famous Star answers the Clever Reporter and the Ubiquitous Photographer in a dignified manner, as follows: *"I know why you've come, but I don't wish to make a big production out of something so personal."* But the Clever Reporter is a resourceful man. He makes it clear that *he doesn't intend to invade the star's privacy and that he's not interested in the trivial details of the marriage, but rather in* the Famous Star's *thoughts following that act of responsibility which the marriage contract entails*. He adds that *it's the basic, legitimate aspiration of* Anthropoids' *readers to know thoroughly the thinking* of the Famous Star, who still seems doubtful and undecided. But then the Clever Reporter presents a decisive argument: *A man becomes someone else when he marries*, he says. *He sees life in a different way*, he adds. And then he underscores: *He assumes a different point of view toward love, work, and everything that really matters*.

"Everything that really matters," I mused, interrupting my reading, "everything that really matters."

But while I was thinking about what might be the meaning of the words "everything," "really," and "matters," the Famous Star, although grudgingly, was already recognizing the truth contained in the Clever Reporter's words: *Yes, that's true*, he states with Spartan moderation. Now holding the winning cards, the Clever Reporter strikes the definitive blow: *That's why we're interested in talking to you*, he declares. To be more precise, he specifies with Cartesian rigor, *to the new man you surely are since marrying the Beautiful Advertising Model*. In the face of the irrefutable force of this axiom, the Famous Star, with a sigh and without losing his reticence, says: *All right, come on in*. From this point on, the Famous Star, opening his heart to the Clever Reporter and exposing his captivating face to the Ubiquitous Photographer's camera, declares (example no. 1): *It's essential for a man to know where he's standing on the face of this earth. To reveal himself through the things he loves, whether beings or dreams.* Or (example no. 2): *I do things essentially to be true to myself, because I'm true to what I say and to what I do.* At once he pontificates (example no. 3), *above all, the essential thing is to be a human being as a man,* and, as such, what the Famous Star desires (example no. 4) *is essentially to have a vital witness in my life,* which vital witness would be—it's superfluous to point out—his brand-new wife, that is to say, the Beautiful Advertising Model who would become (example no. 5) *essentially a witness to my dreams, to my ambitions, to my aspirations, and to my daily struggles in what is my essential form of self-expression: my art.*

"Nothing is contingent," I said to myself, "nothing is secondary; everything is essential."

But then the Clever Reporter thinks *he won't be violating any agreement* not to ask questions about the private life of the Famous Star *if he asks him to define for him the meaning of the married couple.* In effect, the Clever Reporter is not violating any agreement, because the Famous Star hastens to formulate the requested definition: *the couple has been, since the beginning of time . . .*

I stopped, perplexed: "since the beginning of time." I experienced a kind of metaphysical vertigo. "Since the beginning of time . . . ," I stammered. "But, has anyone, even including *the arduous students of Pythagoras,*[21] ever known when time began?"

I went on reading: *Since the beginning of time (and not just chronological time, but also psychological time, which is the one that matters most), the couple has been the basis of a society.*

This parenthesis, which established a severe distinction between chronological time and psychological time, with the stipulation that the latter was more important than the former, finally baffled me. I then attempted to grasp the concept by means of a reworking of the sentence, just as I used to do when I was a student and was confronted with texts of chaotic style: "Since the beginning of the existence of psychological time predominantly and since the beginning of the existence of chronological time in less measure, the couple has been the basis of a society." It certainly was understandable now; but it still didn't mean anything.

"Well . . . ?" inquired McCormick, reappearing. "Did you read the article on page 64?"

XIII. A Moving Story

*M*cCormick went away, and I was left alone with the article on pages 64 and following, which I read. It said: *"You don't know this man, but he knows you intimately. He is 103 years old and feels younger than ever. The business enterprise founded by his grandfather is now celebrating a century of existence. Almost the same age as the nation. He is full of memories. His name is Carmelo Spettanza and he is news. Doesn't the name sound familiar to you?"* These were just the general titles and subtitles which—in the manner of the chapter headings of *Gulliver's Travels*—constituted a sort of summary of the text that followed. *Anthropoids* and Swift were similar to that extent.

In line with the multicolored tradition of *Anthropoids*, no less than ten photographs in full color illustrated the essay. Seated invariably in his rocking chair, the living mummy of Don Carmelo was multiplied tenfold from different angles. Observing closely, I noticed that they had placed a large cushion beneath his buttocks. Observing even more closely, I saw that the cushion displayed the luxuriously embroidered coat of arms of Spettanza Bathroom Fixtures. I tried to remember whether he had such a cushion at the dinner at Luke's house, and wasted several moments of my life thinking about this foolishness.

One gathered, from the photos and their captions, that, instead of retiring to the Riviera, the Isle of Capri, or the mountains of Switzerland, Don Carmelo had continued to live modestly in the Chacarita quarter of the city, a decision that, in the magazine's judgment, seemed to be a touch worthy of infinite praise and veneration. Now I have good eyesight and I'm an attentive observer; I am quite familiar with the various districts of Buenos Aires and I know that their boundaries are vague. There are people who don't know whether they live in Núñez or Saavedra; there are people who don't know whether they live in Flores or Floresta; there are people who don't know whether they live in

Chacarita or Colegiales, in Colegiales or in Belgrano. In a word, it's all a matter of *moving the boundary markers to gain a few acres.*[22] Therefore, I affirm that there's no house in Chacarita like the one shown in the photos; it was one of those superb mansions in Belgrano, with three floors, balconies, diamond-shaped leaded windowpanes, slate roof, and gardens.

I devoted myself to an examination of the photographs. Almost all of them were monopolized by Don Carmelo, who had, as scenic background, the walls, pictures, fireplace, and bookshelves filled with thick, uniformly bound books. In several of these photos, the patriarch appeared with pen and paper in hand, in a meditative pose, as if about to make some momentous decision. Each photo had a caption. For example: *He always managed his business personally. Now, although retired, his passion for bathroom fixtures remains keen, and he likes to "have a go at the paper work," as he himself says.* Or, this one: *Don Carmelo looking over the new toilet designs. "There are different architectural ideas now," he points out. "We think about the esthetic features, but without sacrificing comfort."*

Another photo was taken in the rear garden of the house. Don Carmelo was patting a huge, very beautiful German shepherd. I would have liked to have a dog and a garden like those and, in my pettiness, I felt a bit of envy. The caption read: *"Hot Sauce," his favorite dog. "The day will come," Don Carmelo predicts, "when even animals will have their own bathroom fixtures."*

But the most interesting was the largest photo, because of its apparently glorifying purpose. Arranged like a complete soccer team—with the first team, substitute players, the coach, physical trainer, team physician, and other assistants—all the direct and lateral descendants of Don Carmelo were disposed around his rocking chair. To take the photo, they had evidently had to erect some bleachers since the crowd occupied four different levels. Don Carmelo was below and right in the middle, like a kind of center forward. To Don Carmelo's right and left, with three on each side, I saw Luke Spettanza, Matthew, Mark, John, Peter, and Paul. I again saw the semiforgotten faces of their six wives. I saw the mob of grandchildren and discovered that there were also some great-grandchildren. Down below, at one end, in the position of right wing smiled Patricia Spettanza. Even though the photograph was gigantic, there were too many people in it and, of course, on a very reduced scale. Patricia looked a little different to me, and also more attractive (Oh, the mirages of publicity!). *The Spettanza clan en masse,* declared the caption sententiously. *Ever united in affection and in bathroom fixtures.* I reexamined Patricia. She was wearing a kind of blue overalls for two-year-olds. Some fellow had his right arm over her shoulders.

I'm like the dog in the manger. Patricia mattered little or nothing to me, and I showed an interest in her only occasionally, depending upon the time I had at my disposal, the mood I was in, and how I felt. However, I didn't like the presence of that smirking individual who doubtlessly had more money and more free time than I did. "Maybe I'll call her later," I thought.

What a coincidence; it happened just as in the soap operas. In came Irene: "Hernando, there's a call for you on my line."

"When are you going to marry me, Irene?"

She bit her lower lip and shook her head in despair: "Don't you ever weary of uttering the same drivel all the time?"

"It's not drivel. It's a question asked in all seriousness. You just tell me, 'tomorrow,' and I'll marry you tomorrow for sure. Will you?"

"Quit the nonsense and go answer the phone!" (Sometimes I can drive the most angelic creature to distraction; it's just a matter of perseverance.)

To be more comfortable while talking, I tried to sit in Irene's chair, but she beat me to it, and I had to remain standing. Though I don't know through what perversity, that instrument is fastened to her desk and it has a very short cord, so I had to converse by bending down like the hunchback of Notre Dame. I expected to hear the voice of Luke Spettanza, who was constantly bothering us with different questions and suggestions. Instead, I heard Patricia's voice.

"I was just thinking about calling you," I said. "I just saw you in *Anthropoids.* Congratulations."

"Oh, shut up. I'm so mad about that picture. I didn't turn out cute at all."

That wasn't my opinion, but I went along. "You look a hundred times better in person. When will I see you again, it's been so long?"

"Oh, sure. It's obvious how interested you are. I haven't seen hide or hair of you in about a month."

"What can I do about it? Blame it on your father and your uncles. Day and night, Saturdays and Sundays, I'm a slave to their campaign."

"Do you want me to pick you up when you get out of work?"

"That's what I was going to ask you to do. I'll wait for you."

"But not today, eh? Tomorrow."

"Why not today?" I noticed suspicion in my voice and regretted it.

"I've got something to do today. I'll be there tomorrow."

"O.K. *Ciao.* See you tomorrow."

When I hung up, Irene disappeared hastily, without letting me ask her if she wanted to marry me.

I went back to my reading. *Anthropoids* was a never-ending box of surprises. Incredibly, the article began by imitating the marvelous style of a best-selling novel translated from English. But the first chapter had a rather tangolike title:

Eighteen sixty-something . . .
Through the streets of San Telmo[23]

It read as follows:

· M. S. wound the green wool muffler nice and tight around his neck, tucked the ends into his jacket, leaned his ruddy hand on the freezing cement of the levee, and vaulted over. The river was low and quiet. He dropped onto the dirty sand and began to walk along the riverbank. A short time before, with the last few coins he had left, he had drunk a very strong, very black cup of coffee and then had wandered through the narrow streets of that still unknown quarter of the city. It was three in the afternoon, it was overcast, and M. S. had no place to sleep that night, but he wasn't worried. Ever since he arrived from that village in Italy, he always faced up to the same challenge and he always won out, as if he were one of those comic strip heroes.

Later, he went up along Independence Street. Suddenly, on a rubbish heap, among the cans, pieces of cork, and empty bottles, he saw something white and shiny. He bent down, picked it up, and looked at it as if it were a diamond or the body of an unknown bird. He ran his rough, immigrant's fingers over the polished object. Where had he seen *that* before? There were some blue letters on it, but M. S. didn't know how to read or write. He was still torn by the memory of hunger back there in his village. Then, later on, the hope of America. That's it! Now he remembered. During the long crossing on the *Princess Appicciafuoca*, had once passed by the officers' lavatory. It was open. He was curious and went in. A brutal hand grabbed him by the neck and threw him out of the place. It was an Irish sailor. *"Be off with ye, ye scalawag!"* he told him. *"Ye've no business*

around here! Git back down to yer filthy hold!" But M. S. couldn't
understand, and his immigrant's eyes opened wide in anger and
pain. He was Italian, and the sailor had spoken in an English contaminated by a Celtic dialect. However, upon receiving a violent
kick, he was able to translate into Neapolitan what the other man
was saying to him. Now he remembered. The white, shiny object he
held in his rough, immigrant's fingers was made of the same material
as *something* that had been there in the officers' lavatory on the
Princess Appicciafuoca.

Massimo Spettanza had found his destiny. The white object (a diamond? an unknown bird?) was a fragment of an old toilet. But he
didn't know that, since in his village in Italy there were no toilets,
except in the home of the *signor podestà.* But Massimo Spettanza
had never been in that *palazzo*, let alone used the bathroom. He
closed his eyes dreamily. The *signor podestà* had a daughter. Massimo
had been in love with her. He still was. *Ah, quanto bella era Enza
Quasimoda!*[24] He pushed those thoughts away. He must think now of
where he would sleep that night. He shrugged his shoulders, tossed
the shiny, white object back onto the rubbish heap, and continued
walking with his immigrant's steps through the streets of San Telmo.
Behind him, bathed in the gaslight of a street lamp, remained the
shiny, white object (a diamond? an unknown bird?). The blue letters
said *Pescadas.* And it was as if the sun of a bright, promising future
were already lighting the way of Massimo Spettanza . . .

Thus ended the first chapter, with those pathetic touches that
moved my heart and amidst the suspense and uncertainty created by
those three suspension points. The second chapter, with appropriate
symmetry, was titled:

*Nineteen sixty-something . . .
Through the streets of Chacarita*[25]

I felt that my strength was insufficient to read it completely. So I
leafed through it, skimming over the top, and managed to find out
something incredible. When Massimo Spettanza became rich, he
made a trip back to Italy where he asked for—and received—the
hand of Enza Quasimoda, the *podestà*'s daughter. Massimo remained
there for over a year and, when Pietro was born, the three of them
came definitively to Argentina. And then they say Espronceda wrote
preposterous things![26]

But it all didn't end there. There was still a third section in which was reproduced a series of questions and old Don Carmelo's corresponding answers. To my surprise and disbelief, he answered with precision, with a certain ingeniousness, with a sense of humor, and even with a polemical tone. I remembered him as having one foot in the grave and the other on a banana peel; hence, I felt absolutely certain that the interview was a complete fake, forged in the editorial room of *Anthropoids*. They probably just sent a photographer to Don Carmelo's house and afterward, from Luke's tangled verbal thread, they must have unraveled the ball of yarn of the history of Spettanza Bathroom Fixtures. Yes, the journalists at *Anthropoids* payed homage to the Goddess Idiocy, but—and we must recognize it—with what ability!

The gist of the article was this. "Thanks to an outstanding, productive business record, marked—naturally—by honesty, faith in the future, and good business sense, Spettanza Bathroom Fixtures had established itself as a leading firm in its area, an example to and the pride of all Argentine industry. Don Carmelo Spettanza, a unique, noble, and patriarchal figure, from his modest residence in the Chacarita quarter, radiated the light of his wisdom and experience over the above-mentioned firm of Spettanza Bathroom Fixtures, surrounded by the affection of his relatives and friends and with the respect of all the personnel of the aforesaid firm of Spettanza Bathroom Fixtures, that great, big, happy family which . . ."

XIV. Apotheosis of Spettanza Bathroom Fixtures

*M*eanwhile, the graphic advertisements, films, and jingles continued singing tirelessly the praises of Spettanza Bathroom Fixtures. Our lack of sleep was yielding fruit. And what fruit! Thanks to the creativity of the Persuasive Conviction Advertising Agency—to which my contribution was not inconsiderable—the Northamptons and the Royals, the Majestics and the Buckinghams, and all of them together had increased their sales by some very high percentage. McCormick's prediction was being fully realized; the Spettanza brothers were already sick of counting their money.

The demand for the products was so immense that—despite enlarging the manufacturing facilities and multiplying hundredfold the number of workmen—the Spettanza Bathroom Fixtures company was inadequate to satisfy the urgent orders even minimally fast. The industrial plant and the delivery department were working without letup, in round-the-clock workdays.

Some irregularities and instances of special privilege were reported; certain very influential persons in banking, politics, sports, or art managed to get their Northamptons, it was indignantly whispered about, without respecting the strict sequence of their orders. This provoked widespread misgiving, and some civil servants had to resign.

But these merely anecdotal incidents did not manage to sully the sparkling image of Spettanza Bathroom Fixtures. So true was this that, as a matter of national priority, Congress enacted a law authorizing Spettanza Bathroom Fixtures trucks to use powerful, bloodcurdling sirens; in this way they were able to make their way swiftly through the most fiendish traffic in order to deliver the greatest possible number of fixtures. At any hour of the day or night, the speedy green-and-yellow hot rods of Spettanza Bathroom Fixtures went howling through the streets, highways, and byways of the great cities and tiny towns of the entire nation, screeching to the four winds their message of hygiene and cleanliness.

In spite of the permanent night schedule and the multiplication of machines, workers, and trucks, Spettanza Bathroom Fixtures accepted orders only three years in advance. Even so, it was necessary to stipulate that, in case the customer couldn't be located at the time of delivery, *ipso facto*, he lost his turn and, consequently, he had to wait three more years and so on. There then sprung up a new source of employment: the profession of the *waiters*—as they were popularly called—whose job it was to wait for the possible—but never certain—arrival of the bathroom fixtures during hours when the owner of the house was away. These *waiters* received very high salaries, but any sacrifice was preferable to being deprived of the Spettanza fixtures for three more years. It was also common to see, at four or five o'clock in the morning, a bleary-eyed but satisfied man in pajamas, signing with a trembling hand a receipt for the brand-new, eagerly desired bathroom fixtures that had just been delivered to him.

There then spread among the populace a kind of fanaticism, a sort of blind adoration for the Spettanza bathroom fixtures. Until then, the favorite topic of conversation among Argentines had been comments on the performance, the qualities, or the defects of their respective automobiles. It was fascinating, and it allowed them to go into other, extremely interesting aspects of the subject: how many kilometers they could get to a liter of gasoline; how much mechanics and body and fender repairmen charged; how one safely navigated the shoals of intricate insurance transactions; how high the price of garage rentals had gone; and so on. Although it may seem incredible, people now forgot these matters and everywhere you went—whether it was the Boca Juniors soccer stadium or the dining room of the Alvear Palace Hotel—the only thing you heard were conversations about the Northamptons, the Royals, the Majestics, or the Buckinghams.

In parallel fashion, fabulous legends were woven about Don Carmelo Spettanza and his sons; thus was born a new, complex, heroic mythology. Supernatural virtues and sublime characteristics were attributed to each Spettanza. This also produced certain consequences. When he was recognized on the Avenida de Mayo, John Spettanza nearly lost his life as a group of admirers almost crushed him in seeking his autograph; from then on, he always went about surrounded by a stern police bodyguard. Paul, the youngest, was inundated with steamy love letters from impetuous adolescent girls and even from mature women; people even began to hint at a love affair with a European princess. The most important publishing houses disputed the publication rights to Luke Spettanza's vital philosophical thought which—with the title *Reflections of a Bathroom Fixtures Manufacturer*—tumultuously saw the light of day in Buenos Aires, became a best seller, the object of fascinating polemics, and was translated into all the languages of the civilized world. It got the National Prize for Literature and was, of course, nominated for the Nobel Prize (which it didn't win, since that year it was the turn of a representative from the African Republic of Zambombia).

Since it couldn't be otherwise, the fame of Spettanza Bathroom Fixtures transcended the borders of Argentina, and the products began to be massively exported to the most remote points of the globe. In these circumstances, there occurred a grave political crisis, which had its origin in the so-called Popular Manifesto of the Argentine Communist Party. In this patriotic document, Spettanza Bathroom Fixtures was zealously denied any right to export even the most humble washbasin until it had entirely satisfied the legitimate aspirations, cherished by every Argentine household, of having its own Spettanza fixtures. Nevertheless, for elementary reasons of universal brotherhood, the fixtures destined for the Soviet Union and other neighboring countries of the latter were excluded from this prohibition. There then ensued a colossal debate in which all political sectors participated. The liberal view, which demanded the most absolute freedom of trade, finally prevailed. The port of Buenos Aires took on an unusual appearance. As far as the eye could reach, well out into the Río de la Plata estuary, one could discern hundreds of freighters, flying the most varied flags, which were patiently waiting in line to fill their holds with Spettanza bathroom fixtures.

I felt justified national pride upon thinking that, perhaps at that very moment, in Pakistan or in the Sudan, in Afghanistan or in Chad, some exotic, inscrutable, turbaned,[27] citizen was enjoying the advantages of a Northampton, a Royal, a Majestic, or a Buckingham. The culmination of this string of successes took the form of a letter from NASA, an agency that ordered five complete Northampton lines to be installed on the moon, so that the astronauts might make use of them during the welcome breaks in their scientific labors. In a magnanimous gesture, the Spettanza corporation decided to donate, free of charge, the five lines "in honor of progress," as read a phrase of a lengthy public statement—also composed by me.

And now, a modest confession. But not too modest. I—humble little fellow that I am—included myself among those who, at the crack of dawn, interrupted their sleep to take delivery on a complete line of Northampton fixtures. Yes, Northampton. Why shouldn't I count myself among the number of the exquisite? What the hell! Besides, the Spettanza brothers exempted me from the obligatory three-year waiting period and favored me with a 5 percent discount. After all, one is entitled to certain privileges.

XV. An Untimely Act

I have always led a life divided into internal and external domains, I have never been able to get the two of them to harmonize in my daily existence. To put it another way, one has to work at something, but I worked only in activities that didn't interest me. Oh, blissful happiness of the grocer whose heart beats to the precise rhythm of the lunch meat slicer!

It was then, precisely during the period of the great successes of the publicity campaign, that my internal domains clouded over in a kind of extended parenthesis during which no activity I began ever reached fruition. I went back to my old tricks, trying again and again to write that story which faded a bit more from my memory with each passing day. Again and again I failed. Later on I limited my ambitions and attempted to write whatever I could; I got tired of tearing up paper. Time passed, and it drove me to despair not to be able to create a simple story. Of course, I lack the slightest perseverance and I'm incapable of striving for anything seriously; so my strength was far from being drained.

During all of this, my external domains were impetuously bubbling over. The date of the triumphal celebration of the Spettanza Bathroom Fixtures centennial was approaching, and the work at the agency again intensified. I had to compose an insipid invitation to be sent to various categories of lowlifes and phonies: merchants, industrialists, fashionable painters, fashionable writers, fashionable boxers, fashionable soccer players, dieticians, plastic surgeons, fashion designers, interior decorators, stars and starlets of stage, screen, and television, advertising models, and so on. In short, the same old faces as usual, which, in turn, would be reproduced in the magazine *Anthropoids*, with the caption "The Party of the Year" or something along that line, so that office employees and elementary schoolteachers could admire and identify with them. Wasn't it wonderful to partake in "The Party of the Year," even if only through the multicolored pages of *Anthropoids?* Wasn't it beautiful to be in the know about the unforgettable conversation between the fashionable boxer and his wife, the fashionable starlet, and the fashionable dietician and his wife, the fashionable tennis player? Why it was almost as if one were right there, amidst all that splendor, and not just reading *Anthropoids* on the crowded, 6:00 P.M. subway.

The invitation—a large card made of fine, heavy paper—was a gem in its class:

Spettanza Bathroom Fixtures is celebrating its one hundredth birthday.

One hundred years at the service of the nation and the community.
We want to celebrate it with those who make this country great.
With all the beautiful people.
With you, for example.
We'll be expecting you. Saturday, the 27th. At the Bow-Wow Club,
of course.
When you arrive, the Spettanzas will greet you with a smile and a
drink.
Later on, you'll dine sumptuously,
Dance,
Have a good time, and
Enjoy the evening's entertainment.
Make the night yours.
Participate in the raffle of a complete Northampton line.
Watch a parade of beautiful girls,
And, from among them, help elect Miss Toilet.
We're counting on you.

Everyone was extremely pleased. McCormick was dancing up and down; I was fed up. Gradually, but with greater and greater intensity, a blind rage was slowly taking possession of me, an utterly disproportionate hatred toward the Spettanzas, the guests, the lovely girls, Miss Toilet, the advertising agency—toward the whole universe.

But that didn't prevent the unavoidable Saturday from rolling around, the day on which the apotheosis of Spettanza Bathroom Fixtures would be celebrated. In the morning, McCormick and I were at the deserted agency for a while to wind up some last-minute details that would put the master touch on the whole affair. From there we went to the Bow-Wow Club to make sure that everything was in perfect order and that nothing was left to chance or improvisation. We ascertained, in effect, that the centennial show would have the grandiose framework it deserved: the stage was set; the kitchen service ready; the china and silverware sparkling; the master of ceremonies, musicians, and comedians hired and in good health; the invitations sent; and the press bribed.

"From this point on," commented McCormick, "we'll become the most important advertising agency in the country."

"Thanks to whom?" I intimated.

"I'm going to give you a nice salary increase after it's over."

"I won't turn it down."

When we got back to the agency, there awaited us an angry letter signed by a member of the Argentine Academy of Letters. The echoes of Spettanza Bathroom Fixtures had even reached as far as that learned body! In the letter we were reprimanded for having failed to mention, in some advertisement or other, the "indubitable" Latin etymology of the word *inodoro*, made up, he stated, of the negative prefix *in* (meaning "non" or "without") and a derivative of the third-declension noun *odor-odoris* ("odor"), whose meaning, in short, was . . . [28]

I made a paper airplane out of the letter, and we were already getting ready to leave when something awful happened. I had a hand on the doorknob and McCormick, a bit behind me, was finishing putting some documents in his brief case. Suddenly I saw the six Spettanzas standing there, as if they had materialized out of nowhere. Perhaps the fact that the office was deserted, the shutters down, curtains drawn, desks unoccupied, and the typewriters covered increased the ghostly quality of that apparition.

They came toward me in a mad rush. Frightened, I backed up a few steps. But when they saw McCormick a bit farther on, behind me, they ran toward him and huddled tightly around him, like baby chicks around a mother hen. Pale, excited, and confused, the Spettanzas were all talking at the same time. To regain his freedom of movement, McCormick retreated and barricaded himself behind his desk in his office. Jostling each other, the six Spettanzas tumultuously invaded the office. Not wanting to go in, I remained in the doorway and found out what had happened.

A catastrophe. Old Don Carmelo, although he apparently had no serious ailments, had just passed away about an hour before. No one could accuse him of having died on purpose, but one would have to agree that the moment he chose was not the most opportune.

At that instant, I thought only of myself. I was afraid McCormick would call me in to ask my opinion, so I took refuge in the bathroom for a little while. When I stopped hearing voices, I came out.

McCormick was alone and absorbed in thought. He didn't explain to me what their reasoning had been, but he did tell me the decision they had reached: "At this stage of events, it's impossible to turn back."

"And so?"

."Everything will go ahead as planned," he said laconically.

And then he added a few ideas. The fact that Don Carmelo's death had coincided with the firm's centennial celebration should even be considered one of those timely instances of potential symmetry that constitute an energetic challenge to the imagination of the talented advertising copywriter. Consequently, the festivities would be carried through exactly as planned. Of course, it was also essential not to neglect Don Carmelo's funeral rites. Despite their never-denied capacity for work, the Spettanza brothers were naturally not going to be able to be in two places at once: now at the party to receive congratulations; now at the wake to accept condolences. Hence, it had been resolved that the funeral chapel was to be set up on the premises of the Bow-Wow Club, so that the wake and the party might unfold simultaneously, in harmonious, eighteenth-century, neoclassic unity of time, place, and action.

XVI. Sanitary Centennial

$\mathcal{S}$o it came to pass. As secret jack-of-all-trades of the advertising campaign, I included myself, of course, among the number of those invited to the Bow-Wow Club. Up until that moment I had planned not to go. But when I learned that to the natural attractions of a triumphal celebration there were being added those of a wake, my curiosity was aroused and I changed my mind.

Just as the invitation had foreseen, the Spettanzas received me with a smile and a drink. I shook hands with them and congratulated them on their jubilant first century; they thanked me with smiles from ear to ear. At once I conveyed to them my heartfelt condolences; they thanked me with grieving faces.

McCormick summoned me with a wave of an arm from a table where he was sitting with his partners, Arrambide and Violini. I had a place reserved next to them.

"You could have invited Irene," I said to them by way of greeting.

McCormick had other worries: "Look up there," he said, pointing at the stage. "We had to do things at breakneck speed, but we were able to manage quite nicely, I think. It's a pity we had to reduce the size of the stage a bit to make room for the coffin and all that other junk. This will probably dull the splendor of the show and the coronation of Miss Toilet."

"What could we do?" I comforted him. "It was an act of God."

I didn't share his annoyance. The stage was quite ample. Three-fourths of it, from left to a little beyond center, was carpeted in red and decorated with colored balloons, crepe paper, and various other party items; it was equipped with microphones, amplifiers, and other things necessary for the master of ceremonies to liven up the gathering, the musicians to play their instruments, and the comedians to tell their jokes.

On the other hand, the extreme right, austerely carpeted in severe black, was filled with numerous floral offerings, so many that the candles and coffin could barely be seen. The latter piece of furniture conformed to a model especially designed in homage to the corpse in question and had, therefore, the shape of a bathtub; in this way, the reposing figure of Don Carmelo appeared to be serenely stretched out in his bath.

On the basis of an initial, unperceiving glance at the stage, a negative spirit might criticize certain discordant elements, but, after just a very short time, one's sight became accustomed to it and the funeral chapel seemed like the most natural thing in the world there.

A bit later, the modern Fathers of the Nation were now assembled at the Bow-Wow Club: merchants, industrialists, fashionable painters, fashionable writers, fashionable boxers, fashionable soccer players, dieticians, plastic surgeons, fashion designers, interior decorators, stars and starlets of stage, screen, and television, advertising models, and so on. They all knew each other and saw each other continually, but their greetings were as spectacular and effusive as though they had been separated from each other for centuries. Here and there, there were frequent, repeated kisses and hugs, showy exclamations, and hysterical little shrieks. Adorned with tape recorders, the reporters from *Anthropoids* were scampering from one place to another to register the testimony of the guests. Photographers were capturing now-grief-stricken faces next to the casket, now-jovial countenances on the dance floor.

Suddenly I noticed that some fellow wearing big glasses, from *Anthropoids*, was talking to Violini: "I've already got the title of the piece," he was telling him. *The Red and the Black*. Just like the novel by Stendhal."

"And like the team colors on Newell's Old Boys' soccer jerseys," I butted in, just to put in my two cents' worth.

The program went forward in the manner foreseen in the invitation and without a single hitch, except, perhaps, for the fact that deliverymen from different florist shops were constantly crossing the dance floor, carrying huge funeral wreaths. To sum up, I mean that in fact I did dine sumptuously; in fact I did dance wildly with Patricia Spettanza (a pity Irene wasn't there); in fact I did guffaw boisterously at the nonsense that several comedians, each one cruder than the last, uttered from the stage; and in fact I did participate in the raffling off of a complete line of Northampton bathroom fixtures (a pity I didn't win the prize).

The election ceremony of Miss Toilet, the Queen of Argentine Bathroom Fixtures, merits a separate paragraph. It was undeniably exciting to watch the parade of thirty beautiful girls in tiny tight bikinis, who aspired to be selected as queen and thus achieve fame and stardom. The valuable prize included not only being crowned but also receiving a vacation in Miami and a tempting contract to play the leading role in a film musical in technicolor. As a member of the panel of judges—all of us were—I had to vote. Every man to his own taste, as the philosopher said; I, unfortunately, did not vote for the winner. But she, too, was a magnificent beauty, and with impartial spirit I applauded her until my hands hurt. To the triumphant sounds of bronze trumpets, visibly moved, and with a certain majestic air befitting her new-found royalty, the lovely creature ascended to the stage where, in the red sector, the coveted throne, spotlighted by multicolored light projectors, now awaited her; it was a huge, fabulous Northampton toilet adorned with laurels, olive branches, and different allegorical motifs. Her eyes brimming with tears of happiness, the Queen took her seat on the toilet, and the photographers' cameras flashed again and again. Luke, Peter, and Paul Spettanza were the ones charged with conferring upon the sovereign, with trembling hand, the royal attributes, which were three in number. First Luke covered her graceful body with a dazzling, iridescent cape, the fabric of which—in a soft print—displayed a series of microscopic bathroom fixtures. Then Peter encircled her white brow with a golden, showerhead-shaped crown. Finally, Paul, kneeling on one knee, tendered her a scepter made of fine ebony and topped with a plunger made of the same wood. There's no need to point out that, in very prominent places, cape, crown, and scepter featured the omnipresent coat of arms of Spettanza Bathroom Fixtures. At the culmination of the ceremony, the cheers and ovations rose to a deafening crescendo. Then we all went up onto the stage—I was not among the last—to congratulate, embrace, and kiss the award-winning young lady.

This must have been around two o'clock in the morning. Then came the vertigo of the dancing, the drinking, the nearness and fragrance of feminine bodies, the intermittent multicolored lights, and the ear-splitting, frenzied music. Every now and then balloons would explode, and there were showers of confetti, streamers, and flowers, which some oddball had lifted from the funeral wreaths. Microphone in hand, the master of ceremonies—all one great big smile—was howling out things like: "Shake it up, gang! We're gonna have a real blowout tonight!"

And we shook it up, trying, according to his instructions, to make it a real blowout. In the midst of the semidarkness and the blinding lights, Patricia and I pressed against each other and kissed without letup. Thus, in this fever pitch, it became broad daylight.

Suddenly the music stopped and all the lights came on. Smiling, Miss Toilet was still seated on her throne like a high priestess, flanked to right and left by the two Princesses positioned on respective bidets. In contrast to the abruptly stifled din, there was now a dense silence. There, in the full light, we could finally see each other's faces, and it was like waking up from a dream.

"My dear friends," announced the master of ceremonies, now with a gloomy countenance, "after the joyous celebration that has brought us together at this delightful party, there now comes the painful moment of accompanying to their final abode the mortal remains of him who in life was the undisputed pioneer of the Argentine bathroom fixtures industry: Don Carmelo Spettanza."

And with a reverent bow of his head, he indicated the casket. Some schlemiel, and there's always one around, applauded. The rest of us looked at each other a bit astonished; by now we had almost forgotten the wake. At that instant I felt horribly tired. From so much smoking, drinking, and dancing, my head ached, my eyes were burning, and my mouth tasted as if it had a handful of sawdust in it.

The hearse and other cars were waiting in the street. The doors of the Bow-Wow Club opened wide and the funeral procession emerged. First the undertaking establishment's employees carried out the wreaths and, by mistake, a balloon or two. Then out came the six Spettanza brothers carrying the bathtub in which Don Carmelo was forever reposing. The relatives followed behind. And then we, the guests: the merchants, the industrialists, the fashionable painters, the fashionable writers, the fashionable boxers, the fashionable soccer players, the dieticians, the plastic surgeons, the fashion designers, the interior decorators, the stars and starlets of stage, screen, and television, and the advertising models. And me. Yes, me, too.

We set about distributing ourselves in the cars. Since it was so hot, the Princesses and the other girls did so right in their bikinis. Only the Queen kept on her royal cloak and crown and held on to her regal scepter; it was obvious she felt very proud. I noticed at once that people with similar interests were forming into groups. For example, the master of ceremonies, the comedians, and the musicians—with their electric guitars and long red dinner jackets—formed one nucleus in three consecutive cars. I rejected an invitation from McCormick and got in another car with Patricia. We were all—some more, some less—somewhat inebriated, and we had streamers, confetti, and flower petals on our clothes and in our hair.

The caravan started out. After two or three winding curves, it took the Avenida del Libertador, heading west.[29] Patricia squeezed up against me, enveloping me in such an intensely alcoholic exhalation of breath that it forced me to turn away my face and make me think my own breath probably wasn't any better. I put a stick of chewing gum in my mouth and offered her one.

"I don't want any," she said.

"Your breath is so putrid, it would turn someone's stomach," I pointed out.

"Why don't you go straight to hell?" she replied. (Oh, well, I guess that's the thanks you get for worrying about your fellow man!)

It was now a little after ten; it was oppressively hot and a blazing sun was beating down on the city. I took off my tie and put it in a pocket. Later on I had to take off my jacket. Then I unbuttoned three or four buttons of my shirt. The lucky ones were the girls from the beauty contest; they had spread canvas beach mats and towels on the hoods and trunks of their cars and had stretched out on them during the funeral procession to get a bit of a suntan. Just a bit though, because it immediately clouded over, and a dark overcast sky forebode one of those sudden storms the summer often unleashes. I saw the first flash of lightning and heard the first thunderclap. From the musicians' car there came to me the strains of *It's raining, it's pouring, the old man is snoring*. I began to worry about the impending rain. I was fidgeting with impatience and would have liked to ask the drivers to hurry up.

We were now heading south. But bad luck pursued me. There was yet another five-minute delay on Maure Street, in front of the Spettanza Bathroom Fixtures place of business, so Don Carmelo could bid a symbolic farewell to his firm, which was closed at the time because it was Sunday.

And, finally, at the cemetery, so many speeches and funeral orations were delivered that not even Bossuet could have written so many.[30] There were five orators: one spoke in the name of Don Carmelo's friends; another, in the name of the ARASOMANBAFIXNLIK; another, in the name of the Rotary Club; another, in the name of the Social-Democratic Party; and, finally, the ubiquitous Rodríguez spoke in the name of the personnel at Spettanza Bathroom Fixtures.

He displayed an alarmingly copious sheaf of typewritten pages. What I can't figure out is how he could write so much in so little time; it's evident he was a man of fruitful inspiration. He began to read; seldom have I known anyone who read worse than Rodríguez. He would read in one sudden, spirited rush and paused only when he ran out of breath. Consequently, you couldn't understand anything he said. What an interminable speech! To the rhythm of each turn of a page, I would look at the sky, calculating whether I could make it home before the rain let loose. This anxiety wouldn't allow me to pay any attention to the oration, but every now and then I caught such terms as *inevitable, life beyond the grave, resignation, painful loss, journey of no return, his spirit will live on, this great big happy family, period of bereavement and foundering*. With the word *foundering*, the first big heavy drops struck my face. And, immediately, another lightning bolt zigzagged through the huge black storm clouds. And then, in the midst of thunder and flashes of light, there was unleashed, now irrepressible, the second universal deluge.

I felt a desire to flee, to run through the cemetery, reach the street, and jump on any bus that would take me to more sheltered places, because Rodríguez still had five or six pages left to read. But then this

cloying man surprised me—he surprised me pleasantly, I admit it—
as he now demonstrated a laudable presence of mind and a remarkable facility for improvisation.

"What more can I, a mere mortal, add," he said, "when my words
pale, when heaven itself is wailing in torrents over the death of our
beloved Don Carmelo Spettanza?"

If he had said *weeping* instead of *wailing* and had omitted one
when, I think I would have hugged him. At any rate, I here pay
homage to Rodríguez, who, interpreting the general feeling, hastily
put away his papers, thereby regarding his address as concluded.
This was correctly interpreted as the signal for total dispersal. The
bathtub was literally tossed into the grave, and we all ran like madmen
to take refuge in the cars. That was not an orderly retreat but, rather,
a shameful rout; each one of us just ended up in any car whatsoever.

I was lucky. I found myself seated between two of the bathing beauties—one a blonde, the other a brunette—both of them soaked like
mermaids that had just come out of the ocean. This felicitous simile
inspired me, so I offered them chewing gum, which they accepted.
I felt talkative, and we began to converse pleasantly. They seemed to
me like a pair of imbeciles, and it crossed my mind to tell them that I
was nobody less than the owner of the Persuasive Conviction Advertising Agency. I got the blonde to give me her telephone number,
which I jotted down with great difficulty on a damp one-peso bill.

This probably took place somewhere around the La Paternal station
of the Urquiza Railway. When the car reached Federico Lacroze Avenue, I informed the driver I preferred to get out there. I ran swiftly
through the heavy rain, crossed Corrientes Avenue on the run, and—
soaked to the skin and panting—took shelter under the marquee of
the Empire Pizzeria. When a number 42 bus showed up, I got on and
collapsed into a seat. To relax better, I leaned my back against the
side and stretched my legs out into the aisle. The heat, rain, and fa-
tigue had turned me into a pathetic figure.

At home, I submerged myself in my Northampton bathtub for a long
time, dried off, spread some talcum powder on, and combed my hair;
each one of these operations was a farewell to that long captivity.
Then I had a huge lunch, ate voraciously, went to bed, and lost con-
sciousness immediately.

I woke up well after six P.M., very contented, and in possession of
an admirable mental clarity. Because now I knew what story I should

write, and I also knew I would do it with extraordinary ease.

It's true that the story about the powerful thought had been definitively denied me, and I acknowledged it. But it no longer mattered to me, since each man writes what he has to write. I set out my cigarettes, an ashtray, and the *maté*. I brewed one, found it delicious, brewed another, lit a cigarette, put on my glasses, and, on a blank sheet of paper, in very dark black ink, I printed, in firm block letters, the title of my new work:

SANITARY CENTENNIAL

March – October 1975
Buenos Aires: Editorial Plus Ultra, 1979

SHORT STORIES

A LIFESTYLE

*I*n my youth, before becoming a farmer and cattleman, I was a bank employee. This is how it all came about:

I was twenty-four years old at the time and had no close relatives. I was living in this same little apartment on Santa Fe Avenue, between Canning and Aráoz.

Now, it's well known that accidents can happen even in such a small space. In my case, it was a tiny accident; when I tried to open the door to go to work, the key broke off in the lock.

After resorting in vain to screwdrivers and pliers, I decided to call a locksmith shop. While waiting for the locksmith, I informed the bank I would be coming in a bit late.

Fortunately, the locksmith arrived quite promptly. Concerning this man, I remember only that, although he looked young, his hair was completely white. Through the peephole I said to him: "My key broke off in the lock."

He sketched a quick gesture of annoyance in the air: "On the inside? In that case, it's already a more difficult matter. It's going to take me at least three hours, and I'll have to charge you about . . ."

He estimated a terribly high price.

"I don't have that much money in the house right now," I replied. "But as soon as I get out, I'll go to the bank and pay you."

He looked at me with reproachful eyes, as if I had suggested something immoral to him: "I'm very sorry, sir," he articulated with instructive courtesy. "But I am not only a charter member of the Argentine Locksmiths' Union, but also one of the principal framers of the Magna Carta of our organization. Nothing has been left to chance in it. If you should have the pleasure of reading this inspiring document, you would learn, in the chapter dedicated to 'Basic Maxims,' that the perfect locksmith is prohibited from collecting subsequent to the conclusion of the work."

I smiled, incredulous: "You're joking, of course."

"My dear sir, the subject of the Magna Carta of the Argentine Lock-smiths' Union is no joking matter. The writing of our Magna Carta, in which no detail has been overlooked and whose various chapters are governed by an underlying moral principle, took us years of arduous study. Of course, not everyone can understand it, since we often employ a symbolic or esoteric language. Nevertheless, I believe you will understand clause 7 of our Introduction: 'Gold shall open doors, and the doors shall adore it.'"

I prepared not to accept such ridiculousness: "Please," I said to him. "Be reasonable. Open the door for me, and I'll pay you at once."

"I'm sorry, sir. There are ethics in every profession, and in the locksmiths' profession they are inflexible. Good day, sir."

And, with that, he left.

I stood there for a few moments, bewildered. Then I called the bank again and informed them I probably wouldn't be able to come in that day. Later on I thought about the white-haired locksmith and said to myself: "That man is a lunatic. I'm going to call another locksmith shop, and, just in case, I'm not going to say I have no money until after they open the door for me."

I searched in the telephone directory and called.

"What address?" a guarded feminine voice asked me.

"3653 Santa Fe, Apartment 10-A."

She hesitated a moment, had me repeat the address, and said: "Impossible, sir. The Magna Carta of the Argentine Locksmiths' Union prohibits us from doing any work at that address."

I lit up in a flame of anger: "Now listen here! Don't be ridic . . ."

She hung up without letting me finish the word.

So I went back to the telephone directory and placed some twenty calls to as many locksmith shops. The instant they heard the address, they all flatly refused to do the job.

"O.K., fine," I said to myself. "I'll find a solution elsewhere."

I called the janitor of the building and described the problem to him.

"Two things," he answered. "In the first place, I don't know how to open locks, and, in the second place, even if I did know how, I wouldn't do it, since my job is cleaning up the place and not letting suspicious birds out of their cages. Furthermore, you've never been too generous with your tips."

I then started to get very nervous and carried out a series of useless, illogical actions: I had a cup of coffee, smoked a cigarette, sat down, stood up, took a few steps, washed my hands, drank a glass of water.

Then I remembered Monica DiChiave; I dialed her number, waited, and heard her voice: "Monica," I said, feigning sweetness and nonchalance. "How's everything? How's it goin', honey?"

Her reply left me trembling: "So, you finally remembered to call? I can tell you really love me. I haven't seen hide or hair of you in almost two weeks."

Arguing with women is beyond my capacity, especially in the state of psychological inferiority in which I then found myself. Nevertheless, I tried to explain to her quickly what was happening to me. I don't know whether she didn't understand me or refused to hear me out. The last thing she said before hanging up was: "I'm nobody's plaything."

I now had to carry out a second series of useless, illogical actions.

Then I called the bank, in the hope that some fellow employee could come and open the door. Bad luck; it fell to my lot to talk to Enzo Paredes, a dimwitted joker whom I detested: "So you can't get out of your house?" he exclaimed abominably. "You just never run out of excuses not to come to work!"

I was seized by something akin to a homicidal urge. I hung up, called again, and asked for Michelangelo Laporta, who was a little brighter. Sure enough, he seemed interested in finding a solution: "Tell me, was it the key or the lock that broke?"

"The key."

"And it was left inside the lock?"

"Half of it was left inside," I replied, already somewhat exasperated by this interrogation, "and the other half outside."

"Didn't you try to get out the little piece that's stuck inside with a screwdriver?"

"Yes, of course I tried, but it's impossible."

"Oh. Well then, you're going to have to call a locksmith."

"I already called," I retorted, suppressing the rage that was choking me, "but they want payment in advance."

"So, pay him and there you are."

"But, don't you see, I haven't got any money."

Then he grew bored: "Man, Skinny, you sure have your problems!"

I couldn't come up with a quick reply. I should have asked him for some money, but his remark left me baffled, and I couldn't think of anything.

And so ended that day.

The next day I got up early to start making more phone calls. But— something quite frequent—I found the telephone out of order. Another insoluble problem: how to request the repair service without a telephone to place the call?

I went out onto the balcony and began to shout to people walking along Santa Fe Avenue. The street noise was deafening; who could hear someone yelling from a tenth floor? At most, an occasional person would raise his head distractedly and then continue on his way.

I next placed five sheets of paper and four carbons in the typewriter and composed the following message: "Madam or Sir: My key has broken off in the lock. I have been locked in for two days. Please, do something to free me. 3653 Santa Fe, Apartment 10-A."

I threw the five sheets over the railing. From such a height, the possibilities of a vertical drop were minimal. Wafted about on a whimsical wind, they fluttered around for a long time. Three fell in the street and were immediately run over and blackened by the incessant vehicles. Another landed on a store awning. But the fifth one dropped on the sidewalk. Immediately, a diminutive gentleman picked it up and read it. He then looked up, shading his eyes with his left hand. I put on a friendly face for him. The gentleman tore the paper up into many little pieces and with an irate gesture hurled them into the gutter.

In short, for many more weeks I continued making all kinds of efforts. I threw hundreds of messages from the balcony; either they weren't read or they were read and weren't taken seriously.

One day I saw an envelope that had been slipped under my apartment door; the telephone company was cutting off my service for nonpayment. Then, in succession, they cut off my gas, electricity, and water.

At first, I used up my provisions in an irrational way, but I realized in time what I was doing. I placed receptacles on the balcony to catch the rain water. I ripped out my flowering plants and in their flowerpots I planted tomatoes, lentils, and other vegetables, which I tend with loving and painstaking care. But I also need animal protein, so I learned to breed insects, spiders, and rodents and to make them reproduce in captivity; sometimes I trap an occasional sparrow or pigeon.

On sunny days I manage to light a fire with a magnifying glass and paper. As fuel, I'm slowly burning the books, the furniture, the floorboards. I discovered that there are always more things in a house than are necessary.

I live quite comfortably, although I lack some things. For example, I don't know what's going on anywhere else; I don't read newspapers, and I can't get the television or radio working.

From the balcony I observe the outside world and I notice some changes. At a certain point the trolleys stopped running. I don't know how long ago that happened. I've lost all notion of time, but the mirror, my baldness, my long white beard, and the pain in my joints tell me that I'm very old.

For entertainment I let my thoughts wander. I have no fear or ambitions.

In a word, I'm relatively happy.

Letras de Buenos Aires 3, no. 10 (September 1983): 73–79

IN SELF-DEFENSE

*I*t was about ten o'clock on a Saturday morning. My eldest son, who's the devil incarnate, thoughtlessly scrawled a curlicue on the door of the neighboring apartment with a piece of wire. Nothing alarming or catastrophic, just a quick little flourish, most likely unnoticeable to anyone who wasn't on the lookout for it.

I confess this with embarrassment: at first I thought about keeping quiet (who hasn't had such moments of weakness?). But then I realized that the right thing was to apologize to my neighbor and offer to pay for the damages. This decision in favor of honesty was supported by my confidence that the costs would be slight.

I gave a quick rap on their door. About my neighbors I knew only that they were new in the building, that there were three of them, and that they were blond. When they spoke, I found out they were foreign. When they spoke a bit more, I assumed them to be German, Austrian, or Swiss.

They laughed good-naturedly and gave no importance whatsoever to the scrawl; it was so insignificant that they even pretended to strain to be able to see it with a magnifying glass.

They firmly and cheerfully rejected my apologies, said that "boys will be boys," and, in short, refused to let me pay for the repair costs.

We took leave of one another with hearty handshakes amidst resounding laughter.

When I returned to my apartment, my wife—who had been watching through the peephole—anxiously asked me: "Will the painting be expensive?"

I calmed her: "They won't take a cent."

"Lucky break," she replied, and squeezed her purse slightly.

No sooner did I turn around when I saw a tiny white envelope by the door. Inside was a calling card. Two names printed in small square letters: WILHELM HOFFER AND BRÜNNEHILDE H. KORNFELD HOFFER. Then, in minute blue handwriting, there was added: "and little Wilhelm Gustav Hoffer send cordial greetings to Mr. and Mrs. Sorrentino and ask a thousand pardons for the unpleasant time they may have had over the supposed mischief—which was no such thing— of little Juan Manuel Sorrentino when he adorned our old door with a cute little sketch."

"Good heavens!" I exclaimed. "Such genteel people. They not only don't get angry, but they offer apologies to boot."

To repay such kindliness in some way, I took a new children's book that I was keeping as a gift for Juan Manuel and asked him to present it to little Wilhelm Gustav Hoffer.

That was my lucky day; Juan Manuel obeyed without imposing any humiliating conditions on me, and he returned bearing the sincerest thanks of the Hoffers and their offspring.

It was about twelve o'clock noon. On Saturdays I usually attempt, unsuccessfully, to get in some reading. I sat down, opened the book, read two words, and the doorbell rang. On these occasions, I'm always the only one at home and I have to get up. I let out a grunt of annoyance and went to open the door. There I found a young man with a mustache, dressed in the uniform of a little tin soldier, eclipsed behind a huge bouquet of roses.

I signed a paper, handed him a tip, received a kind of military salute, counted two dozen roses, and read an ocher-colored card: "Wilhelm Hoffer and Brünnehilde H. Kornfeld Hoffer send cordial greetings to Mr. and Mrs. Sorrentino and to little Juan Manuel Sorrentino, and thank them for the lovely book of children's stories—nourishment for the spirit—with which they have honored little Wilhelm Gustav."

Just at that moment, my wife returned from the market, burdened with shopping bags and stress: "What beautiful roses! Do I ever love flowers! How did it ever occur to you to buy them, you who never think of anything?"

I had to confess they were a gift from the Hoffers.

"We've got to show our appreciation for this," she said, distributing the roses in vases. "We'll invite them to tea."

I had other plans for that Saturday. Weakly, I ventured: "This afternoon?"

"Don't put off till tomorrow what you can do today."

It was about six P.M. Gleaming chinaware and a snow-white tablecloth covered the dining room table. A short time before, obeying orders from my wife—who was seeking a Viennese touch—I had to put in an appearance at a delicatessen on Cabildo Avenue to buy some little tea sandwiches, tiny pastries, sweets, and other dainties. Everything first rate, of course, and the package tied up with a little red-and-white ribbon, so that it all really whet the appetite. As I passed by a hardware store, a mean stinginess drove me to compare the amount of my recent purchases with the price of the most gigantic can of the best paint. I experienced a slight feeling of distress.

The Hoffers didn't come empty-handed. They were encumbered by an enormous cake—white, creamy, baroque—that would have sufficed for a whole regiment of soldiers. My wife was overwhelmed by the excessive generosity of the present. I was, too, but I was now feeling slightly uncomfortable. The Hoffers, whose chatter consisted mainly of apologies and flattery, did not succeed in capturing my interest. Juan Manuel and little Willie, whose games consisted mainly of running, fighting, shouting, and wreaking havoc, did succeed in alarming me.

At eight o'clock it would have seemed to me commendable of them to leave. But in the kitchen my wife whispered in my ear: "They've been so nice. That cake! We've got to invite them to dinner."

"To eat what? There's nothing to eat. Why have dinner when we're not hungry?"

"If there's no food here, there will be at the deli. As far as not being hungry is concerned, who said we have to eat? The important thing is to share a table and spend an enjoyable time together."

Despite the fact that the important thing was not the food, around ten in the evening, loaded down like a mule, I again transported huge, fragrant packages from the delicatessen. Once again, the Hoffers demonstrated that they were not the kind of people who show up empty-handed; they brought thirty bottles of Italian wine and five of French cognac in a chest made of iron and bronze.

It was about two o'clock in the morning. Exhausted by my treks, gorged with an excess of food, intoxicated on the wine and cognac, and giddy with the emotion of friendship, I fell asleep immediately. It was a lucky thing; at six o'clock, the Hoffers, dressed in casual clothes and with their eyes protected by dark glasses, rang the doorbell. We were driving with them to their country house in the neighboring town of Ingeniero Maschwitz.

Anyone who says this town is right near Buenos Aires would be lying. In the car I thought nostalgically about my *maté*, my newspaper, my leisure time. If I kept my eyes open, they burned; if I closed them, I fell asleep. The Hoffers, mysteriously rested, chattered and laughed during the whole trip.

At their country place, which was very pretty, they treated us like kings. We basked in the sun, swam in the pool, had a delicious cookout, and I even took a nap under a tree full of ants. When I woke up, it dawned on me that we had come empty-handed.

"Don't be boorish," my wife whispered. "At least buy something for the kid."

I took Willie for a walk through the town. In front of a toyshop window, I asked him: "What would you like me to buy you?"

"A horse."

I thought he was referring to a little toy horse, but I was mistaken; I returned to the country house on the rump of a spirited bay, holding on to little Wilhelm's waist and without even a small cushion for my aching behind.

Thus passed Sunday.

On Monday, when I got home from work, I found Mr. Hoffer teaching Juan Manuel to ride a motorcycle. "How's it going?" he asked me. "Do you like what I gave the lad?"

"But he's too young to ride a motorcycle," I objected.

"Then I'll give it to you."

Would that he had never said that. Seeing himself stripped of his recent gift, Juan Manuel burst into an ear-splitting conniption fit.

"Poor little guy," Mr. Hoffer sympathized. "Kids are like that. Come on, little fellow, I've got something nice for you."

I got on the motorcycle, and, since I don't know how to ride one, I began to make motorcycle sounds with my mouth.

"Halt, right there, or I'll shoot you!" Juan Manuel was aiming an air rifle at me.

"Never aim at the eyes," Mr. Hoffer advised him.

I made the sound of a motorcycle braking, and Juan Manuel stopped pointing the gun at me. We both went upstairs to our apartment, rather pleased.

"Oh sure, it's all fine and dandy to receive gifts," my wife pointed out. "But you have to know how to reciprocate. Let's see what you can do in that department."

I grasped her meaning. On Tuesday I acquired an imported automobile and a carbine. Mr. Hoffer asked me why I had gone to the trouble; with his first shot, little Willie broke a street light.

On Wednesday there were three gifts. For me, a massive bus used for international travel, equipped with air conditioning, a bathroom, sauna, restaurant, and ballroom. For Juan Manuel, a bazooka manufactured in Asia. For my wife, a luxurious white evening gown.

"Where am I going to wear that gown?" she commented, disappointed. "On the bus? It's your fault for never giving his wife anything. That's why I'm getting handouts now."

A horrendous explosion almost deafened me. To test his bazooka, Juan Manuel had just demolished, with a single shot, the house on the corner, which has fortunately been uninhabited for some time.

But my wife was still going on with her complaints: "Oh, sure, for the gentleman, a bus big enough to travel in as far as Brazil. For the young master of the house, a weapon powerful enough to defend himself against the cannibals of Mato Grosso. But for the maid, a little party dress. Those Hoffers, like the good Europeans they are, are a bunch of cheapskates."

I climbed up into my bus and started the engine. At a solitary spot near the river, I stopped and parked. Lost in the huge seat, enjoying the cool half-light that the drawn window shades afforded me, I there gave myself over to serene meditation.

When I knew exactly what I had to do, I headed for the government ministry to see Pérez. Like all Argentines, I have a friend in a ministry, and this friend's name is Pérez. Now, although I'm quite enterprising, in this case I needed Pérez to intercede with his influence.

And I succeeded.

I live in the district of Las Cañitas, which is now called San Benito de Palermo. To build a railroad from the Lisandro de la Torre station to the doorway of my house, the silent, resourceful, and uninterrupted labor of a multitudinous army of engineers, technicians, and workmen was called for. Using the most specialized and up-to-date international machinery, and after expropriating and demolishing the four blocks of sumptuous buildings that formerly extended along Libertador Avenue between Olleros and Matienzo Streets, they crowned such an intrepid undertaking with resounding success. It's superfluous to point out that the buildings' owners received fair, instantaneous compensation. The fact is that, with a Pérez in a ministry, there's no such word as *impossible*.

This time I wanted to surprise Mr. Hoffer. When he came out at eight o'clock Thursday morning, he found a shiny red-and-yellow diesel locomotive hitched to six railroad cars. Over the door of the locomotive, a little sign read: *Welcome to your train, Mr. Hoffer.*

"A train!" he cried. "A whole train, just for me! It's the dream of my life come true! I've wanted to drive a train ever since I was a little boy!" Mad with joy and without even thanking me, he climbed up into his engine, where a simple instruction manual awaited him to explain how to run it.

"Hey, wait," I said, "don't be so rambunctious. Look what I bought for little Wilhelm." A powerful tank was destroying the sidewalk pavement with its caterpillar treads.

"Neat-o!" shouted little Wilhelm. "And how I've been wanting to blow away the obelisk." [1]

"I didn't forget your wife either," I added. And I handed him the very finest, softest mink coat, recently received from France.

Since the Hoffers were so eager and playful, they wanted to try out their presents at that very instant.

But in each gift I had placed a little trap.

The mink was coated on the inside with a magic evaporating emulsion that a witch doctor from the Congo had given me, so that, scarcely did she wrap herself in it, Madam Brünnehilde was first scorched and then turned into a gossamery little white cloud, which disappeared up into the sky.

No sooner did little Willie take his first cannon shot at the obelisk, when the tank turret, actuated by a special device, was shot off into space, and it deposited the little fellow, safe and sound, on one of the ten moons of the planet Saturn.

When Mr. Hoffer set his train in motion, it swiftly and uncontrollably hurtled along an atomic viaduct, the route of which, after crossing the Atlantic, northwest Africa, and the Strait of Sicily, suddenly ended in the crater of the Mount Etna volcano, which, at that time, was erupting.

So it was that Friday came around, and we received no gifts from the Hoffers. In the evening, as she was preparing dinner, my wife said: "Yeah, that's the way it goes. Be kind to your neighbors. Spend money. A train, a tank, a mink coat. And what do they do? Not even a little thank-you card."

En defensa propia, pp. 117–125
Buenos Aires: Editorial de Belgrano, 1982

*F*or some time now, my book-
shelves have been filled to capacity and overflowing. I should have
had them enlarged, but wood and labor are expensive, and I prefer to
put off these expenses in favor of other, more urgent ones. In the
meantime, I've resorted to a temporary solution: I placed the books in
flat, and in this way I managed to make better use of the little space
available.

Now it's well known that books—whether they're vertical or horizontal—gather dust, bugs, and cobwebs. I haven't the time, the patience, or the dedication to do the periodical cleaning required.

On a certain cloudy Saturday a few months ago, I finally decided to
take all the books out one by one, give them a dusting off, and run a
damp dustcloth over the shelves.

On one of the lower shelves, I found Piccirilli. Despite the dust in
those nooks, his appearance was, as always, impeccable. But I became aware of that only later. At first, he just looked to me like a
piece of shoestring or a bit of cloth. But I was mistaken; it was already
Piccirilli, from head to foot. That is to say, a complete little man five
centimeters in height.

In an absurd way, it struck me as strange that he should be dressed.
Of course, there was no reason for him to be naked, and the fact that
Piccirilli is tiny does not warrant our thinking of him as an animal.
Stated more precisely, then, I was surprised not so much by the fact
that he was dressed as by how he was dressed: a plumed hat, a filmy
shirt with point lace edging, a coat with long tails, leather, floppy-
topped hip boots, and a sword at his waist.

With his bristly mustache and his pointed, little Vandyke beard,
Piccirilli was a tiny living facsimile of D'Artagnan, the hero of *The
Three Musketeers,* just as I remembered him from old illustrations.

So then, why did I name him Piccirilli and not D'Artagnan, as
would seem logical? I think, above all, for two complementary reasons: the first is that his sharp pointed physique literally demands the

small *i*'s of *Piccirilli* and rules out, accordingly, the robust *a*'s of *D'Artagnan;* the second is that, when I spoke to him in French, Piccirilli didn't understand a word, which demonstrated to me that, since he was no Frenchman, neither was he D'Artagnan.

Piccirilli must be fifty years old; there are a few silver threads running through his dark hair. I am thus calculating his age the way we do with human beings of our size. Except that I don't know whether identical amounts of time are meted out to someone of Piccirilli's tininess. Seeing that he is so diminutive, one tends to think—unjustifiably?—that Piccirilli's life is shorter and that his time passes more swiftly than ours, as we understand the case to be in animals or insects.

But who can know that? And even in the event that it is so, how does one explain the fact that Piccirilli wears seventeenth-century clothes? Is it conceivable that Piccirilli is nearly four hundred years old? Can Piccirilli, that being who occupies so little space, hold title to so much time? Piccirilli, that being of such fragile appearance?

I should like to question Piccirilli on these and other matters, and I should like him to respond; and, in fact, I often do put such questions to him and, in effect, Piccirilli answers them. But he can't manage to make himself understood, and I don't even know whether he understands my questions. He does listen to me with an attentive look on his face, and, no sooner do I fall silent, he hastens to answer me. To answer me, yes, but in what language is Piccirilli speaking? Would that he spoke in some language I don't know; the trouble is, he speaks in a language that is nonexistent on earth.

Despite his physique so suitable to the letter *i*, Piccirilli's high-pitched little voice only utters words in which the exclusive vowel is the *o*. Of course, since Piccirilli's voice timbre is so extremely shrill, that *o* sounds almost like an *i*. This, however, is a mere conjecture on my part, since Piccirilli never pronounced the *i*; hence, neither can I guarantee, by way of comparison, that that *o* is really an *o*, nor, as a matter of fact, that it is any other vowel.

With my scanty knowledge I endeavored to determine what language Piccirilli speaks. My attempts proved unfruitful, except that I was able to establish in his speech an invariable succession of consonants and vowels.

This discovery could have some importance if one were sure that, in reality, Piccirilli speaks some language. Because any language, however poor or primitive it may be, will probably be characterized by a certain linguistic scope. But the fact is that all of Piccirilli's speech is reduced to this phrase: "Dolokotoro povosoro kolovoko."

I call it "phrase" for the sake of convenience, for who can know what those three words contain? Whether they really are words, and whether there really are three? I have written them like that because those are the pauses I seem to perceive in Piccirilli's single-stringed diction.

As far as I know, no European language possesses such phonetic characteristics. As for African, American, or Asiatic languages, my ignorance is total. But that doesn't concern me since, on the basis of all evidence, Piccirilli is, like us, of European origin.

For that reason, I addressed him with sentences in Spanish, English, French, Italian; for that reason, I attempted words in German. In all instances, Piccirilli's imperturbable little voice responded: "Dolokotoro povosoro kolovoko."

At times Piccirilli irritates me; other times I feel sorry for him. It's obvious he regrets not being able to make himself understood and thereby initiate a conversation with us.

"Us" includes my wife and me. The intrusion of Piccirilli produced no change in our lives. And the truth is that we esteem and even love Piccirilli, that minuscule musketeer who eats with us in a very mannerly way and who keeps—Lord knows where—an entire wardrobe and personal possessions proportionate to his size.

Although I can't get him to answer my questions, I do know he is aware that we call him Piccirilli, and he has no objection to being called that. On occasion, my wife affectionately calls him *Pichi*. This seems to me like a breach of formality. It's true that Piccirilli's smallness lends itself to affectionate nicknames and loving diminutives. But, on the other hand, he's already a mature man, perhaps four centuries old, and it would be more appropriate to call him *Mr. Piccirilli*, save for the fact that it's very hard to call such a tiny man *Mister*.

In general, Piccirilli is quite proper and demonstrates exemplary behavior. At times, however, he playfully attacks flies or ants with his sword. At other times he sits in a little toy truck, and, pulling it by a string, I take him for long rides around the apartment. These are his meager amusements.

Does Piccirilli get bored? Can he be alone in the world? Are there other creatures of his kind? Where can he have come from? When was he born? Why does he dress like a musketeer? Why does he live with us? What are his intentions?

Useless questions repeated hundreds of times, to which Piccirilli monotonously responds: "Dolokotoro povosoro kolovoko."

There are so many things I would like to know about Piccirilli; there are so many mysteries he will carry with him to the grave.

Because, unfortunately, Piccirilli has been dying for some weeks. We suffered a great deal when he got sick. Seriously ill, we immediately learned. But what treatment could be devised to cure him? Who would dare surrender the tiny body of the being called Piccirilli to a physician's judgment? What explanation would we give? How were we to explain the unexplainable, how speak of something about which we are ignorant?

Yes, Piccirilli is leaving us. And, helpless, we shall let him die. I'm already concerned about knowing what we're to do with his almost intangible corpse. But I'm more concerned, infinitely more concerned, over not having delved deeply into a secret that I held in my hands and that, without my being able to prevent it, will escape me forever.

En defensa propia, pp. 11–15
Buenos Aires: Editorial de Belgrano, 1982

1

$\mathcal{M}$y wife's name is Graciela; mine is Arthur. "They're such a charming couple," our friends are always saying. They're right, we are a bright, young, elegant, cosmopolitan married couple, good conversationalists and financially secure. As a result, a large part of our life is spent at social gatherings. People vie to invite us, and we must frequently choose between one party and another.

The essential feature of our conduct is that we never have to be begged. We hate giving the impression that we're aware of our qualities and, hence, when accepting their invitations, that we are bestowing a great honor upon our hosts. But they do consider it an honor, and this fact also weighs in favor of our reputation as generous, magnanimous people, free of pettiness and suspiciousness.

I swear we make no effort whatsoever to stand out. Nevertheless—and I'm speaking impartially—Graciela and I are always the best looking, the nicest, and the most intelligent. We are the life of the party.

Graciela is surrounded by the gentlemen; I, by the ladies. Naturally, we're strangers to jealousy and distrust; we know that no man, except Arthur, is worthy of Graciela; that no woman, except Graciela, is worthy of Arthur.

How many people must doubtlessly envy our social success! And yet, Graciela and I detest social life, we abhor gatherings, we hate parties. Moreover, we are actually shy, contemplative individuals given to silence and solitude, to reading and intimate conversation; persons who despise crowds, dances, loud music, frivolity, small talk, and forced smiles.

Well then, why the devil are we so urbane? Why can't we turn down even a single invitation to a social gathering?

The truth of the matter is that deep down Graciela and I have no willpower and we don't dare say no. On our way to a party, we're submerged in gloomy thoughts, bitter tribulations, and painful guilt feelings. But once we enter into the noisy whirlwind of the throng, the voices, faces, smiles, and jokes all make us forget the annoyance of being there against our will.

But then, home once again, how it hurts us to consider how fragile our personality is! How painful our feeling of helplessness! How horrible to see ourselves always obliged to be the life of the party!

Burdened by a problem similar to ours, two ordinary people might have fallen into despair. But, far from that, Graciela and I are in the midst of a campaign to avoid further invitations, to cease being the life of the party. We have devised a plan, the purpose of which is to make ourselves unpleasant, obnoxious, abhorrent.

Now, then, when we're at parties, we don't have the courage to appear unpleasant, much less obnoxious or abhorrent; to such a degree are we imbued with our role as the life of the party. But in our own home, where serenity invites contemplation and where the pernicious influence of parties doesn't reach, we are transforming ourselves into pariahs of refined society, turning into the antithesis of the glorious life of the party.

When we put our plan into practice—some two months ago—it still suffered from many shortcomings. Our inexperience, our excitement, our lack of cold-bloodedness at first caused us to make some serious mistakes. But people learn throughout their lives; little by little, Graciela and I were improving. I'd be exaggerating if I said we've achieved perfection; I can state, however, that we feel pleased, satisfied, even proud of our latest performance. We are now awaiting the fruits of our labors.

2

There's always some couple that's especially friendly toward us and wants to be invited to our home. We have no objection to doing so, but we take the liberty of delaying to the maximum the moment of extending the invitation. When it does come, the couple, whether it's a pair of young nonconformists living together or a ripe old married couple, is waiting for nothing else and rushes to accept it.

We made the Vitavers wait a long time, a very long time, before inviting them. The point is that, given their dangerous qualities, with that kind of people one had to be careful. I preferred not to improvise, and I wanted us to be very well prepared.

Beneath his false air of the respectable gentleman, Mr. Vitaver is semi-illiterate. His lack of culture, an unlimited bad faith, a total disregard for his fellow man, and an implacable dishonesty have, of course, led him to make a fortune. After all kinds of marginally legal businesses, he has established himself as a pornographic book publisher. Hence, one of his favorite expressions is, "We, the disseminators of culture . . ." Needless to say, I despise Vitaver: his spiritual emptiness, his greed, his coarse humor, his eagerness to please, his impeccably shaved face, his unscrupulous beady little tradesman's eyes, his exquisite clothes, his manicured fingernails, his suspiciousness, his desperate need to be respected, to make a proper place for himself. For my taste and character, all these wretched features combined to paint an atrocious portrait. And Vitaver sought out my friendship; my supposed connections with what he called "the world of letters" were important to him. He doubtlessly cherished the idea that my frequent contact with novelists, critics, or poets would act by way of osmosis on him, taking the rough edges off his mercantile crudeness. He never suspected that the majority of those writers—as brutish and uncultured as he himself—were concealing what was only stupidity beneath extravagant attitudes that sought to be shocking.

Vitaver's wife is not his wife, but his concubine. This fact, which should be immaterial, irrelevant to approval or reproof, fills the Vitavers with pride. They imagine that such daring covers them with a glorious halo of modernity and open-mindedness; they never miss an opportunity to talk about it. I don't know what her name is; Vitaver calls her *Adidine*, a nickname that, although it evokes shades of prostitution, also sounds like a pharmaceutical product. The latter is an attribute that fits her very badly, however, for there is nothing aseptic about Mrs. Vitaver. On the contrary, her taut, shiny, moist oily skin evokes all the possible humors of the human body. In general, when both dimensions are compatible, she tends more to width than to length: her fingers are short and fat; her hands are short and fat; her face is wide and fat. All of her is broad and fat. And she is obtuse, and she is ignorant, and she is pompous, and she is dyed, and she is daubed, and she is bejeweled, and she is repugnant.

And so, Vitaver and Adidine, based on grossly commercial reasons, sought our friendship, the friendship of the life of the party. And we were sick of being the life of the party, and we were sick of these Vitavers in particular and of the hundreds of Vitavers who tormented

us weekly with their stupidity, their frivolity, their mercantilism.
At that point, we invited the Vitavers to dinner at our home.

3

Graciela and I are neither princes nor paupers. But we live comfortably, we can renew our wardrobes often, and we have a small car
and lots of books. We own our apartment. It takes up the entire second floor of a house on Emilio Ravignani Street, a house built in 1941,
a solid house with very thick walls, fine wood, and very high ceilings,
a house that has not yet succumbed to demolition and the subsequent
construction of a fragile apartment building with apartments heaped
up on top of one another.

On the ground floor there's a hardware store; then there's the entrance to the flat below us and, right next to it, the door to ours. The
door opens directly on a steep stairway made of black marble that
leads up to the second floor, where our home actually begins.

We like the flat. It's larger than we need, so in case of emergency
we can change the furniture from one room to another and carry out
other strategic maneuvers.

The heavy rain that fell the night of the Vitavers' visit was a challenge to my creative spontaneity. Although it wasn't foreseen in my
plans, I knew how to take advantage of it to the maximum.

From behind the closed shutters on the second floor, we peeked out
at the ostentatious arrival of Vitaver's enormous car, we saw how he
parked at the curb across the street (there's no parking on our side);
with delight, we observed the Vitavers get out, encumbered by rain-
coats and umbrellas, and we watched them cross the street on the run
and rush headlong against our door like two fighting bulls. Unfortunately, we have a balcony, and it sheltered them a bit from the rain.

Beside our door there are two doorbells, each with a little card-
board nameplate. The first announces my last name; on the other it
says MR. JABBERWOCKY, a name I took from a poem in *Through the
Looking Glass*. Besieged by the whirlwinds of freezing rain, which
the wind pelted at him every little while, Vitaver rang the doorbell
corresponding to my name once, twice, and once again. That noise,
monotonous, of course, sounded to us like celestial music. Vitaver
rang, and rang, and rang; Graciela and I did not answer.

At last, Vitaver inevitably rang the Jabberwocky's doorbell, from which he received the little electric discharge I had foreseen. Naturally, it's Vitaver's fault; who told him to ring the doorbell of an unknown person?

Our ears pressed to the shutters, Graciela and I listened with glee to the Vitavers' conjectures: "I tell you, the doorbell gave me a shock!"

"It just seemed that way to you."

"You ring, you'll see."

"Ow! Me too!"

"Didjuh see? Can the bell be ringing upstairs?"

"Is the number of the house right?"

"Of course. Besides, there's his last name."

Then I barely stuck my head out through the shutters and, prudently covered with a waterproof hat and an umbrella, I shouted from the second floor: "Vitaver! Vitaver!"

Happy to hear my voice, he ran out to the edge of the sidewalk to try to see me, because of which he got much wetter. He tilted his head back and completely neglected to hold his umbrella up. "How are you, Arthur?" he shouted, squinting his eyes against the rain lashing his face.

"Fine, just fine, thank you," I replied cordially. "And your wife? You can't have come alone, have you?"

"Here I am," said Adidine, obligingly rushing out next to Vitaver. It was wonderful to behold the way the water was running down over her tightly set hairdo and her fur coat.

"Hello, there, Adidine. How are you? Always so pretty, eh . . . ," I said. "What a downpour! And just this morning the weather was beautiful. Who could have imagined that? But . . . Well! Don't just stand there getting soaked! Get up against the wall, and I'll let you in right away."

I closed the window and let ten minutes go by. Finally, I called out again: "Vitaver! Vitaver!"

He was obliged to go back out to the curb.

"Please excuse the delay," I said; "I couldn't find the key to save my life."

With great difficulty, Vitaver etched a woeful smile of understanding on his face.

"Here comes the key," I added. "Catch it and go right ahead and open the door yourself, if you will. Just take it for granted you're in your own home."

I threw it to him with such bad aim that the key ended up falling into the water in the gutter. Vitaver had to squat down and stir around in the dark water for a while with his hand. When he stood up, having now salvaged the key, he was wetter than a mackerel.

He finally opened the door and came in. I already pointed out that the stairway marble is black; so it barely gets dark and you can't see a thing. Vitaver groped around on the wall in the darkness until he found the light switch. From upstairs I heard *click, click, click,* but the light didn't go on. Then I shouted: "Vitaver, it looks like the light bulb burnt out just this minute. Come up very slowly, so you don't fall."

Clutching the two railings with an iron grip and in the uncertain light of short-lived matches, the Vitavers came hesitantly up the stairs. Graciela and I awaited them above, wearing our warmest smiles. "How *are* the charming Vitavers?"

Vitaver was getting ready to shake hands with us when a shriek of horror from Graciela turned him to stone.

"What have you got on your hands?! Oh, my God, look how you're all stained! How awful, your clothes! And Adidine's beautiful coat!"

Huge red stains covered Vitaver's right side and Adidine's left side.

"Damn!" I became indignant, clenching my fists in a rage. "What'll you bet Cecilia took it into her head this very day to paint the stairway railings? What a stupid girl!"

"Cecilia is the maid," sighed Graciela, considering the matter at an end. "She's driving us crazy with her dumb tricks."

"Domestic help is getting worse every day," Adidine said heroically, as she looked out of the corner of her eye at the hairs of her mink coat all stuck together. "I just don't know how we well-to-do families are going to get along!"

She had no idea to what extent this last statement worsened her situation.

"Tomorrow without fail," I insisted with a dire look on my face and an admonishing index finger, "I'm putting Cecilia right out in the street."

"Oh, the poor girl," said Graciela. "Just now, when she was beginning to learn? And she's already like a member of the family."

"Right out in the street!" I repeated with greater emphasis.

"But consider the fact that poor Cecilia is an unwed mother, that she has two babies. Don't be inhuman!"

"I'm not inhuman," I specified. "I'm being just, which is quite different."

"Justice cannot be upheld without a humanitarian foundation," Graciela adduced. "Epictetus said that . . ."

And leaving the Vitavers disdainfully forgotten, Graciela and I engaged in a learned debate, abounding in apocryphal quotations and authors, concerning justice, equity, morals, goodness, and other values remotely applicable to the case of the nonexistent Cecilia.

The Vitavers listened to our conversation, anxious to intervene but—inept as they were—without knowing what to say. Evidently, they were suffering, they were suffering a great deal. But how artfully they concealed it! They too aspired to be as worldly wise and as congenial as we are; they assumed that, in a similar predicament, Graciela and I would not have lost our smiles.

We finally remembered the existence of the Vitavers and helped them rid themselves of their rainwear, umbrellas, and coats. Vitaver was wearing a magnificent, black dinner jacket, a shirt with narrow lace edging, and a bow tie; he was elegant to the extent that such an outfit could refine his rough, underworld nature. Adidine was wearing a long white sparkling evening gown; she was profusely jewelled, finely perfumed.

"Oh, Adidine!" Graciela exclaimed with admiration when the intense dining room light fell fully on those wonders. "How elegant, how lovely you look! What a beautiful gown! And those shoes! What I wouldn't give to have clothes like that! But we're so poor. Look what I had to put on. These are my best clothes."

The Vitavers had already seen our apparel and had already pretended not to notice anything unusual about it. But Graciela and I, implacable, were not about to exempt them from the unpleasant experience of looking over our garb while they, in turn, were attentively observed by us.

"Look, Adidine, just look," Graciela repeated, twirling around like an advertising model. "Look, look." She was all disheveled and had no make-up on. She was wearing a very old mended blouse and a plain skirt covered with big grease spots and with the hem unstitched. She had on silk stockings perforated with big holes and long runs and, over the stockings, a pair of brown anklets that partially disappeared inside some dilapidated slippers. "Look, Adidine, look." Adidine didn't know what to say.

"And I, what am I to say?" I intervened. "I don't even have a shirt!"

In effect, I had put on a grayish municipal street sweeper's smock right over a heavy woolen undershirt full of holes. Around my bare neck I had tied a frayed old necktie. A pair of baggy, dirty-white bricklayer's pants and black hemp sandals rounded out my attire.

"That's life," I said philosophically, as I scratched my five-day beard and chewed on a toothpick. "That's life, friend Vitaver, that's life."

Completely disoriented, Vitaver vaguely nodded his head. "That's life," he repeated like a parrot.

"That's life," I insisted yet once again. "'So goes the world, Don Laguna, / Old pardner, nothin' lasts, / Fortune smiles on us today, / Tomorrow it'll give us a lash.' *Faust*, by Estanislao del Campo. What do you think?"[1]

"Huh? Oh, yeah," he said hurriedly. "I read it. I remember that old Vizcacha . . ."[2]

"You know what Manrique said about the gifts of fortune, don't you?" I interrupted him. "He said: 'For they are gifts of Lady Fortune, / who swiftly spins her wheel . . .'"[3]

Then, with an affected voice and grandiose gestures, I recited five or six stanzas for him, something I love to do. "Do you get it, Vitaver?"

"Yes, yes, how fabulous!" He hadn't understood a word, and that wretched adjective of his was tantamount to making his crimes worse.

"Today you're loaded with money," I added, poking his chest with my index finger. "You have social status. You have intelligence. You're cultured. You have *savoir faire*. You have a beautiful wife. You have everything, right?" I stopped and stared at him, obliging him to answer.

"Well, maybe not everything," he smiled conceitedly; he actually thought he possessed all those endowments!

"Tomorrow you could lose it all," I then said in a gloomy tone, to show him another facet of the drama of life. "You could lose your fortune. You could end up in jail. You could become seriously ill. Your intelligence could atrophy, your culture become watered down. Your *savoir faire* might be scorned. Your wife could be unfaithful to you."

I went on haranguing him for a long time with the vision of an atrocious future made up of imprisonment, illnesses, and misfortune. We were acting out an odd scene: a ragged beggar was solemnly pontificating before a gentleman dressed in strict formal attire. Together, we constituted a kind of allegory on the disillusionments of the world.

While I soliloquized, the Vitavers' fretful little eyes were leaping here and there. How humiliating! To have worn their best clothes and be received by two grimy, woebegone, melancholy tramps! "How can this be?" they seemed to be thinking. "And what about the clothes, the jewelry, and the elegance they always displayed at parties?"

"We've been left with nothing, friend Vitaver," I said, as if responding to their thoughts. "Yesterday we even had to sell the dining room furniture at a loss."

Then—as if it were necessary—the Vitavers cast a stupid glance over the obviously empty dining room.

"*Ubi sunt? Ubi sunt?*" I emphasized. "Tell me, Vitaver: *Ubi sunt? Ubi sunt? Ubi sunt mensa et sellae sex?*"[4]

"And so," said Graciela, "we have no choice but to have dinner in the kitchen."

"Oh please! That's quite all right," said Adidine.

"And we don't have a table in the kitchen, either, so we'll have to eat on the marble counter top. If you'd like to come this way."

I knew the condition the kitchen was in, and I watched the Vitavers' faces as stupefaction, disbelief, and repressed anger swiftly passed over them.

The kitchen was a kind of monument paying homage to disorder, laziness, filth, and abandonment. In the sink, semisubmerged in water so greasy it was thick and on which floated the remains of meals, were heaped dishes, pots, platters, silverware, and sticky saucepans. Thrown here and there on the floor were about ten days of damp old newspapers. There stood against one wall an enormous trash can overflowing with garbage, with swarms of flies, cockroaches, and worms running and wriggling over it. In the air there floated the smell of grease, fried things, wet paper, and stagnant water.

The Vitavers looked very solemn.

"In just a jiffy," said Graciela, trying in vain to give her words an optimistic tone, "in just a jiffy I'll spread the tablecloth"—and she pointed at the marble sink counter, also covered with remains of meals and empty cans of mackerel—"and we'll eat . . . although . . . although . . ."

Graciela burst into loud weeping. Playing the role of humanitarian, Adidine tried to console her. "Oh, poor Graciela! What's the matter? For heaven's sake!"

"It's, it's just that . . . ," Graciela stammered between sobs and hiccups, "it's just that we don't have a tablecloth either."

Indignant over this breach of confidence, I let fly a furious punch against the wall. But Graciela was unrestrainable: "Everything, we've lost everything!" she howled. "We have nothing! Everything, everything sold at a loss! Even my first-communion dress! Everything, everything lost . . . and all through his fault!" And she pointed a tragic, accusing finger at me.

"Graciela!!" I roared melodramatically, giving her to understand that a single word more from her could drive me into committing an irreparable act.

"Yes, yes, yes!" she insisted, wailing louder and louder and looking to the Vitavers, as if calling upon them as witnesses to her misfortunes. "All because of him! I was happy in my parents' home! We were rich, we lived in San Isidro,[5] in a cheerful home with a rose garden. One ominous day, that happiness was cut short. One ominous day, a monster appeared, a monster that was stalking my youth and beauty, a monster that took advantage of my innocence."

"Graciela!!!" I insisted with concentrated rage.

Ignoring me, she continued on, always addressing the Vitavers: "The monster had a human shape and it had a name; its name was . . . Arthur!" And she emphasized this name by pressing her clenched fist against her forehead. "And this monster took me from my home, wrenched me away from the affection of my parents, and carried me off with him. And he put me through a life of privation, and he squandered my entire fortune at the race track and the gambling casino. And when he gets drunk on absinthe and vodka, he scourges my back with barbed wire."

Blind with rage, I hurled myself at Graciela and dealt her a resounding slap across the face: "Silence, thou vile insane woman!" I shouted, addressing her with the archaic form, *thou*, so everything would seem more theatrically tragic. "How dare you reproach me? *Me*, the pitiful victim of your whims, your insolence, and your adulteries? How can you offend in such a way the proud, worthy man who, by pulling you up out of the slime, redeemed you from sin and guilt by marrying you?"

And I, too, began to cry and compete with Graciela over who could scream the loudest. Such weeping! We cried with so much conviction that there came a moment when we really couldn't hold back our tears.

The Vitavers, pale and glum, were completely baffled. They had come to our home—the home of the life of the party—in the hope of enjoying a pleasant evening, and now, dressed in their luxurious outfits, they were like spectators at an incomprehensible fight between a poverty-stricken married couple.

They were saying something to us, but, intent on the pleasure of our weeping, we payed no attention to them. Patting me affectionately on the back, Vitaver dragged me over to the wall, near the garbage can. "Better times lie ahead, man," he said. "The Lord'll test you, but He won't break you."

That *man*, together with his habitual use of *you know* and *I seen*, gave me renewed courage for the struggle.

"You mustn't despair," he insisted, but he was the desperate one; it was quite obvious he wanted to disappear as quickly as possible.

Now Adidine came to my side, holding up the fainting Graciela; now they were urging us to make peace; now we were making up.

Drying her tears and blowing her nose, Graciela cleared the counter top by indifferently shoving aside the cans and dishes with her arm until they fell into the dirty water in the sink. But the counter was still covered anyway with crumbs and the somewhat moist, greasy remains of meals. By way of a tablecloth, she spread over those bulging things one of the newspapers she picked up off the floor. On the newspaper she set out four plates laced with cracks, four yellowish spoons, three everyday glasses of different styles and colors, and a large cup for café au lait.

"We only have three glasses," she explained. "I'll drink out of the cup."

How dirty, how greasy, how sticky everything was! How the flies flitted about over our heads! How the cockroaches ran up and down the walls! How the worms wriggled about on the floor!

The four of us sat up against the sink counter and our knees kept bumping the doors of the cupboards built in below it. We were extremely uncomfortable. Vitaver cut a strange figure, seated in the midst of that sort of garbage dump, with his dinner jacket, his shirt with narrow lace edging, and black bow tie, next to his wife, with her low-cut white evening gown and luxurious jewels. On the other hand, Graciela and I were in complete harmony with that filthy, sordid atmosphere.

"There's just one course," said Graciela, apologizing. "Noodle soup."

"How delicious!" exclaimed Adidine. (As if anyone in the world could consider that fare for sick people as delicious!)

"Yes, it is delicious," Graciela agreed. "It's a pity that, because of the fight, it got a little burned."

And from a pot all oozing over and stained, she began to take out some shapeless tangles of dried out, burnt, and now cold noodles and distributed them onto the plates.

"Adidine," said Graciela, "since you're by the sink, could you please fill the glasses with water? We have no wine."

Adidine stood up submissively and turned on the tap. Just as we had foreseen, the water shot out with extraordinary pressure, bounced off the gelatinous utensils in the sink, and spattered Adidine's white gown with the remains of food.

With what disgusted faces the Vitavers ate! And how they tried to conceal it so as not to offend us! And how bewildered they were! Were we really the life of the party? Might we not be a pair of imposters? Constantly surrounded by the grease, the stench, the cockroaches, and the flies, they finished their dried-up burnt soup as well as they could and drank a little water from the cracked glasses. With their clothing stained, their stomachs upset, and spirits chagrined, they said they had to leave, that they had some commitment or other. Despite our urging them repeatedly to have some more soup, they insisted they had to leave, a discourtesy that grieved us, of course. They put on their coats, covered up with their rainwear, and went down the stairs.

"Don't touch the railing," I warned them. "It's just freshly painted, you know."

Before they got in their car, we bade them an affectionate farewell through the window: "So long, dear friends! It's been a real pleasure! Wish we could have these delightful get-togethers more often! Come back anytime!"

They waved at us quickly and rushed headlong into their car, which pulled away with uncommon speed.

4

Two weeks have now passed. During that interval, we have relied on the Vitavers to slander us enough to dissuade anyone from inviting us to another party. I know Vitaver well and I can foresee his wickedness; I know he will have said awful things about us. However, our reputation is too strong; it won't be easy to bring it down through slander.

So now we find ourselves at another party. We're sporting our best clothes, and we're perfumed with the finest fragrances. We display our most expensive jewelry, wear our most sophisticated smiles, and show the warmest cordiality.

We see the Vitavers, each with a drink and smiling, smiling forced smiles. The Vitavers see us and the smile freezes on their faces. Without letting them react, we shake hands with them very naturally and quickly begin to converse with the Carracedos.

We don't like the Carracedos either, for reasons similar to those which make us reject the Vitavers. On the other hand, the Carracedos are desirous of becoming friendly with us; they admire us and hope to gain material advantage from a relationship with us. He is a prosperous businessman, an expert swindler, adept at defrauding. To strengthen the bonds between us, he believes it the opportune moment to appeal to confidences: he tells me about his financial plans, describes the future expansion of his businesses, and tips me off to some tricks about how to make some illegal money and go unpunished.

Carracedo smiles, he smiles a forced smile, proud of his commercial shrewdness, smug about being so able to multiply his wealth, happy with his possessions, his weekend home, and his foreign car.

The Carracedos are so courteous, so cordial, and so friendly toward us that, well, not to invite them to dinner at our home would be inconceivably rude, an act of blatant discourtesy unworthy of the life of the party. So, we invited them; they're coming on Saturday.

And then we, Graciela and Arthur, now thoroughly caught up in the whirlwind of the party, go flitting from room to room, lavishing smiles, kisses, and handshakes. We dance, we tell and laugh at jokes, we are brilliant and admired, and everyone feels appreciation, but also envy, toward us. "They're such a charming couple," our friends always say. Because Graciela and I are always the best looking, the nicest, the most intelligent. Because Graciela and I are still the life of the party.

El mejor de los mundos posibles, pp. 72–88
Buenos Aires: Editorial Plus Ultra, 1976

THE FETID TALE OF ANTULÍN

I. Introduction

*O*h, how I hate Antulín! I hate that man so much that I have attempted to kill him three times, and three times I have failed.

If I were given to allegory, I would say that Antulín is the personification of uncleanliness. For now I'll just limit myself to the simple declaration that Antulín is the most filthy, grimy creature in the entire universe.

Never in the course of the thirty-five years of his reeking existence has he bathed. Furthermore, I'm certain that he maintains firmly intact his determination to arrive triumphantly at the final day of his life without doing so.

As I have managed to ascertain, Antulín is, to put it quite bluntly, a butcher. Indeed, he is nothing less than the owner of a butcher shop. He leaves his bed at five o'clock in the morning to go and oversee his place of business. Hence, he used to occupy the bathroom before me.

I say "he used to occupy the bathroom before me"—in the days when I got up at seven-thirty. That, however, was a very long time ago. I now rise at 4:00 A.M.

2. The Problem of the Socks

*A*ntulín is, then—like it or not—the personification of uncleanliness.

He possesses a single pair of socks, he wears them every day, and he never washes them. Those socks have lost their flexibility. They are solid and rigid like the foot coverings of a suit of medieval armor so that they eternally retain the shape of Antulín's feet. An inexpert sculptor might begin by making use of them as molds and, by filling them with soft plaster of Paris, get a faithful reproduction of a pair of feet—the feet of Antulín.

Upon returning to the boardinghouse toward evening, Antulín would take the precaution of hanging his sticky socks carefully on the bathroom towel rack. The next morning, with serene spirit and honestly satisfied that his socks were no longer moist, he would thrust his feet back into them. Antulín's hygienic principles with regard to his socks were reduced to this simple practice.

The fact of the matter is that, every time I entered the bathroom during the hours between sunset and dawn, the first objects that regaled my sight were Antulín's rigid socks. They would be spread out in such an unlimited way that they left me not even the humblest of spaces to hang my towel temporarily.

Thus, for months and months I shared many hours of my life with Antulín's socks. Finally, one day I was seized by the rebelliousness of an impotent despair demanding of me the heroic act that we must all carry out at one time or another. Now, destiny can take many shapes. Some men achieve epic stature on the field of battle amidst blood, sweat, and dust, mounted on great horses and armed with sword and lance. Others are granted a bathroom and Antulín's socks hanging on the towel rack.

Without an instant's hesitation, I seized Antulín's socks with the tips of my fingernails and hurled them into the toilet. I passionately pressed down the handle of the flusher, and the toilet bowl filled with water. A clear irresistible tide violently inundated its white cavity and, with the same rushing force, all that watery mass noisily receded. But Antulín's socks stubbornly resisted the unleashed forces of the liquid element. There they were, triumphant, in the bottom of the toilet.

With my forehead beaded in anguished sweat, my spirit buoyed up by the ideal of a just cause, my soul still lacerated by uncertainty, and finally having lost all sense of reason, I waited again and again for the toilet bowl to refill. I frantically continued pressing the handle with the contorted face of a man who repeatedly works the trigger of a gun aimed at a tiger that has just sprung at him and is still writhing in its final death throes. Finally, there was a gigantic gurgling noise, and those stubborn socks were sent to occupy the place that they had deserved by unquestionable right from the very moment Antulín first wore them.

Like the shepherd looking for his lost sheep, like the mother for her child, Antulín went about that entire day searching tenaciously but fruitlessly for his beloved socks, which were, perhaps, his only true love. Defeated and crestfallen, he finally gave up the search and came to the wildly conceited conclusion that they had been stolen. Totally crushed, with the heartbreaking feeling of committing an act of betrayal, Antulín made his way to the store on the corner and bought— another pair of socks!

During the following week he didn't dare leave his new socks in the bathroom. But on Monday, carried away by rash optimism, he did it again. And I, now full of confidence in my own power, again threw them into the toilet. "I'd like to know," he mumbled to himself out in the courtyard, "who's the son of a bitch that's stealing my socks. They've stolen two pairs on me already!"

Never again did he leave his socks unguarded. But eventually he forgot a towel, an undershirt, and a handkerchief, each of them representing the only pieces of their kind in his wardrobe. I had tossed them all into the toilet, and I would likewise have thrown in any other garment or item belonging to Antulín, even an overcoat or an umbrella.

Have I already said that I hate Antulín? Well, if not, I hate Antulín. Because in reality the socks were not the most serious aspect of this matter.

3. The Problem of the Odor

*T*he socks were not the most serious aspect of this matter.

Because of Antulín I have to get up every day at four o'clock in the morning. At four o'clock in the morning, and I don't even begin work until nine! This means that, due to that damnable Antulín, I get up five hours ahead of time just as if, instead of a brief, ten-minute subway trip, I had to make a long journey by oxcart. Antulín is to blame for this.

I've already said that he gets out of bed at five in the morning. From his room he heads straight for the bathroom, but he is not led there for the purpose of bathing, since he doesn't even take a sponge bath. He shaves, that he does, very carefully, and he has a copious bowel movement.

Thus, at seven-thirty, the time I used to get up, the bathroom would be impregnated with an unbearable odor. Or perhaps "unbearable" is not the word. It was the most frightful stench the human imagination can possibly conceive of: a wondrous admixture of the combined stenches of a slaughterhouse, a garbage dump, a pigsty, a tannery, sewer water, a frightened skunk, a hyena cage, a soaking-wet dog, and rotting fish. For this reason I have to get up at four o'clock in the morning despite the fact that I don't begin work until nine. All because of Antulín.

However, in truth, neither is the odor the most serious aspect of this matter.

4. The Problem of the Residue

*T*he odor is not the most serious aspect of this matter.

I confess that I hate Antulín. For some reason that escapes me, he is insensitive to the charms of toilet paper. On the other hand, he is a staunch supporter of the freedom of the press and of the complete "use" of the benefits of our free, independent journalism. At five in the morning Antulín charges into the bathroom, spurred on by two different but not incompatible purposes. First, thanks to the Fourth Estate, he acquires a somewhat general yet exact vision of world events. However, the state of the universe must inspire in Antulín a decidedly unfavorable reaction. The minute he finishes his reading, he imposes upon the newspaper the highly delicate task of substituting, with varying degrees of success, for the more specialized toilet paper. Now, then, Antulín's residue being torrential, it is necessary to sacrifice two entire papers. Consequently, the toilet, already suffering indigestion from the shorts and undershirts that I tossed in whenever I had the chance, was unable to swallow all that paper. Above all, however, it simply could not absorb the generous tribute of Antulín. It may have exerted its bravest efforts to salvage its cause with honor and be worthy of its proud tradition, but it always emerged ignominiously defeated.

Therefore, the truth is that at seven-thirty I found myself not only confronted by the most frightful stench in all the visible and invisible universe but also in personal audience with Antulín's own authentic shit. Flanked to port and starboard by the soaked and decorated newspapers, it would be floating springlike on the brown toilet water, like one of those huge aquatic or "floating" islands seen in the Paraná River.

5. The Plumber

*I*t was a conditioned reflex. Antulín entered the bathroom, and the landlady would telephone the plumber.

The latter, an eminently practical man, after considering the necessity of coming every day, decided just to leave his buckets, snakes, plungers, and toilet brushes at the boardinghouse. Therefore, he transferred his headquarters to our house and had the boardinghouse address printed in the advertisements he published in the classified section of the newspapers.

The plumber spent the greater part of his day with us. During his free moments, which were few and far between, he would leaf through a magazine, watch television, or water the plants in the courtyard. But he never relaxed his zeal because of these activities. Out of the corner of his eye he attentively kept watch over the bathroom door, awaiting— even when it was unlikely—a sudden, sneaky assault by Antulín.

Later on, the plumber had absolutely no rest. At unusual hours of the day and night he could be seen, exhausted, with dark circles under his eyes, standing before the bathroom door on the breezy top of a kind of watchtower built out of empty fruit crates. From this perch, like a medieval knight ever ready for combat, he kept ceaseless vigil over the arms that lay at his feet: buckets and plungers to the right, snakes and toilet brushes to the left.

Although his zeal was exemplary, I have, nevertheless, one complaint to lodge against the plumber. He always cured and never prevented. But I suppose one has to take the bitter with the sweet.

For a time, there was even serious talk of a love affair between the plumber and the landlady, but this was a totally unfounded rumor, as will be seen later. At any rate, since the Spanish woman, that is to say the landlady, was his best customer, the plumber, who knew a thing or two about public relations, gave her a small but significant discount. Instead of charging her two thousand pesos for each surgical procedure, he granted her, as an exception and without setting any precedent, a fixed monthly charge of forty-five thousand pesos, to be paid in advance, of course. For this reason I am convinced that not even on Wall Street are there bowel movements any higher quoted than those of Antulín.

6. Antulín's Imprudence

T hate Antulín, but he never suspected it. Indeed he thought he enjoyed my unconditional admiration, and he, in turn, esteemed me with a certain indulgent air of superiority.

Now then, since I was getting up so early in order to find the bathroom in the same condition created by the plumber's latest effort, I had to kill time until eight-thirty. I had gotten used to spending a good part of the early morning in a café located right next door to the boardinghouse. It was a café of the kind I really enjoy, designed some fifty years ago according to the principles of comfort with which the Spaniards made the famous cafés along the Avenida de Mayo warm and inviting. There was an abundance of varnished wood, bronze, and marble; no plastic, formica, or hardboard, nor any of those selenite materials that the endless progress of the Americans has foisted on us.

I would sit next to the window and order *café au lait*, six crescent rolls, and peach marmalade. The waiter, like me, was a fan of the Rácing Club, one of the two Avellaneda soccer teams.[1] We shared a mutual respect, and in an atmosphere of good fellowship both of us would celebrate the victories and seek extenuating circumstances for the defeats of our team. Moreover, he was quick, polite, and clean. A little ray of sunlight would shine in on my table. I would eat my breakfast leisurely, smoke, read my newspaper, and work the crossword puzzle. That was the perfect moment of my day; at that moment Antulín didn't even exist.

Unfortunately, that perfect moment now belongs to the realm of bygone things. As I've already stated, Antulín did not know that I hated him. One ill-fated day he passed by and saw me sitting in the window, harmlessly having my breakfast. It was already too late to attempt the slightest resistance.

Antulín smiled, Antulín came in, Antulín sat down at my table. Antulín talked: he talked about the weather, he talked about boxing, he talked about auto racing, he talked about the numbers game, he talked about the cost of living. Antulín sneezed like a hurricane; Antulín gagged on his own phlegm; Antulín coughed with saliva and with generosity; Antulín expectorated thick globs of spit on the floor; Antulín smoothed his spittle with his shoe until it took on a smooth, compact appearance; Antulín blew his nose into a handkerchief covered with ancient stalagmites of green, yellow, and black mucus. Antulín pilfered four of my six crescent rolls, daubed them with my marmalade, dunked them in my *café au lait*, and devoured them. Antulín leafed rapidly through my newspaper, wrinkled it up, got the pages all out of order, dripped marmalade on them, and instantly came up with the answers to the most difficult parts of the crossword puzzle. Antulín smoked eight of my cigarettes, blew the smoke in my eyes, and broke my cigarette lighter. Antulín patted me brutally on the back and bid me farewell until tomorrow. I hate Antulín.

7. The Conviction of Antulín

*A*fter such a frightful experience, I could no longer go to my favorite café. I now go to another located five long blocks from my boardinghouse, next to a home where there is a Doberman pinscher that leaps up at the iron-grating fence to devour me.

The waiter at this bar is absent-minded and deaf. He is a dauntless fan of the rival soccer club of Avellaneda, the Independiente. He has rude intimidating manners, takes my orders as a personal affront, and waits on me whenever he pleases with a cigarette butt dangling from his lips. The crescent rolls are stale, the marmalade is bitter, and the *café au lait* has skim floating in it. The tables and chairs, with their green and red formica plastic coverings, are cold and uncomfortable. The prices are higher and the window faces in such a way that the little ray of sunlight I used to enjoy so much doesn't shine in anymore. In short, this is not a café. It's a bar, a bar designed according to the principles of inhumanity with which, for some fifteen years now, the Spaniards have been ruining the cafés along the Avenida de Mayo.

In this bar, harassed by so many adverse circumstances, I meditated upon the death of Antulín. The world wasn't big enough for both of us; it was Antulín or me. Now, some poor, unimaginative soul will perhaps suggest that the simplest and most reasonable solution would be for me to change boardinghouses. With infinite pity I would answer that I was guided not by the mere purpose of personal revenge but by a universal, ethical goal, which, notwithstanding, did not preclude my own vindication. Like Alexander the Great, like Julius Caesar, like Napoleon, through the achievement of my own personal objectives I would also carry out a great universal mission. My action would be unforgettable, and it would change the course of the history of the human spirit, which, after the accomplishment of my feat, would have to be divided into two great eras: the one, unenlightened, backward, unrefined, and wicked, which would take in the time from the Paleolithic Age down to the death of Antulín; the other, luminous, progressive, cultured, and just, which would extend from the death of Antulín on into an unforeseeable future.

I judged Antulín impartially. I performed admirably four separate roles: I was prosecuting attorney, defense counsel, judge, and jury. In his opening statement, the prosecutor outlined the charges of the indictment, detailed Antulín's various crimes, and highlighted many important corroborating circumstances. In the face of the prosecutor's eloquence, counsel for the defense seemed defeated even before he began to speak. There was already discernible an attitude of skepticism and rejection toward his words on the part of the jury. Unable to deny the de facto evidence, defense counsel seized upon de jure matters, adducing weak mitigating arguments for Antulín's conduct: his solid lack of culture, his reckless unawareness, his possible chronic dysentery. When the defense counsel returned stoop-shouldered to his seat, he already bore upon his brow the stigma of defeat. Having listened to both sides of the case, the jury withdrew to deliberate. After one second they returned to the courtroom and, amidst the deathly silence of the spectators, pronounced their verdict: Antulín was declared guilty of crimes against the toilet. Immediately there followed a very brief recess so that the judge, a venerable and patriarchal old man, might consider his sentence. Antulín was condemned to death. Given the overwhelming evidence against him, no one really expected anything else. When sentence was pronounced, the crowded courtroom burst into shouts of joy. The gentlemen tossed their hats into the air and the ladies waved their handkerchiefs. Obeying a stern sign from the judge, the bailiff cleared the courtroom.

Fine! Antulín had been sentenced to death. Now the sentence had to be carried out. I argued over and over with myself about the most fitting way to execute him and go unpunished myself. I had ascertained that Antulín was protected under Argentine law since, contrary to all logic, he was considered a human being. I pondered, argued, and quibbled. However, no matter how I tormented myself with these thoughts, I could find no way to put an end to the fetid existence of Antulín.

8. The Electrocution of Antulín

*F*inally, one Monday morning—oh, kind fates!—I was favored by fortune in the guise of the elements of nature. After a stifling Sunday, a day during which even breathing became difficult, one of those late summer storms that sometimes occur in autumn struck with a fury during the night. There was thunder and lightning, torrential rain and lashing winds. How cozy it is to be nestled snug and warm inside when it's pouring rain outside. Except, that is, when one knows he has to get up at four o'clock in the morning!

When I stepped out into the courtyard—at 4:00 A.M.—it had already cleared up. But on the ground, in addition to a puddle or two, I saw that one of the high-tension wires that supply the entire block with electricity had been blown down by the storm. It was partly coiled up, and it immediately reminded me of a snake, a supple black viper, which could kill Antulín. This brilliant metaphor was confirmed by the sight of a kind of forked tongue sticking out of the broken end of the cable. My whole plan consisted of Antulín stepping on the two deadly little wires with his sweaty bare feet. Yes, then I could once again get into the bathroom at seven-thirty!

I had been a young man imbued with the loftiest ideals; but the unequal struggle against Antulín had dampened my spirits, and now my most cherished ambition was simply to win the right to get into the bathroom at seven-thirty.

I didn't give it a second thought. Unhesitating, but cautiously, I picked up the cable, and after complicated geometric calculations I placed the frayed end in the doorway of Antulín's room. I tried to remember the choreography executed by Antulín as he came waltzing out of his room, but in vain, for it had never occurred to me to observe this dance step with the attention it deserved. I harshly and justifiably reproached myself for this unforgivable laziness. Now Antulín's stepping on the viper's tongue would be left entirely to chance. Nevertheless, a diabolical hunch told me that I would succeed.

I went to bathe. It was a long, peaceful, and enjoyable bath, my last bath at four o'clock in the morning! The last? One minute I was encouraged by the gratifying idea of the most smashing triumph; the next moment I would think about the possibility of failure and that never again would I be given a similar opportunity. "It must be five o'clock," I thought. I had time to dry off and dress completely before anything would happen, but I remained in the bathroom for a while longer with eye and ear to the keyhole, eagerly on the lookout for favorable signs. It would be tragic if he had overslept. Some untimely meddler—and there's always one around—might come out into the courtyard and, in an act of misplaced human kindness, alert Antulín, save Antulín's life, and thus oblige me to continue getting up at four o'clock in the morning.

I stood petrified with emotion. I had just heard Antulín's door open. Immediately my ears were caressed by a stifled cry and a dull thud like that of a sack of potatoes falling off a truck. I turned the doorknob slowly and with infinite caution opened the bathroom door. There was Antulín lying on his back, perfectly horizontal. The jolt of electricity had hurled him more than three yards. He was as rigid as his cursed socks, and the toes of his left foot were opened out like a flower in the fullness of summer.

"You sure stepped off on the wrong foot today, you son of a bitch," I hissed at him through gnashing teeth.

With the satisfaction achieved only through the fulfillment of duty, I went back into the bathroom and locked the door. The image of a winner smiled at me in the mirror; I carefully combed my hair, tied my tie, and admired my smile and intelligence. I had never felt so happy. Then I heard shouts, running, exclamations, laments, moans, and doors slamming.

"How awful!"

"Poor Antulín!"

"Oh, look at his foot!"

"We've got to call the hospital right away!"

"You, Ricardo," the Spanish landlady ordered the numbers-racket man, "you're an expert at using the telephone, go call right away!"

"We should call the fire department, too!"

"And the electric-power company so they can come and turn off the electricity."

Stifling the guffaws of pleasure that were welling up out of my throat, I put on my most appropriate face in front of the mirror. I judged that the opportune moment had now come for making my triumphal entrance, and I brusquely sallied forth from the bathroom, pretending to be just finishing buttoning my shirt.

"What happened?" I asked, feigning pity. "What happened?"

9. Dreams as Theatrical Stage Manager[2]

*S*urrounded by a large crowd of boarders and curious onlookers, two stretcher bearers dressed in snow-white uniforms, totally convinced of the leading role the drama of life had assigned them at that moment, put Antulín into an ambulance. When the vehicle abruptly sped off with its siren wailing as loudly as possible, all the boarders gathered into a kind of learned conclave and gave themselves over to the task of suggesting erroneous hypotheses on the causes of the accident. Mine, of course, were the most preposterous of all. Eight-thirty rolled around on me while engaged in these enjoyable discussions, and, now in possession of an optimistic view of the universe, I went off to work where, something unprecedented, I greeted the doorman with a smile and the elevator operator with another.

When I returned to the boardinghouse that evening, I ran into our Spanish landlady on the sidewalk in front. She was just coming from the hospital with discouraging news: "Poor Antulín," she informed me, "is in a state of coma."

"Oh, how sad!" I lamented. "Such a hard-working man."

"This oughta' happen to some of them bums that hang around the neighborhood here," she concluded, angrily rolling her eyes. I shook my head sadly with the air of confessing my own inadequacy to understand the inscrutable designs of destiny, and thereupon I went into the boardinghouse, rubbing my hands in glee. I ate more voraciously than ever and drank a quart of wine. Reeling with alcohol and happiness, I hurled myself into bed and went to sleep instantly. I slept like an angel and had a beautiful dream.

Like a disciplined army, there came parading by in front of me thousands of pairs of brand-new unworn socks neatly wrapped in transparent perfumed little bags. Behind the socks, magnificent rolls of toilet tissue rolled majestically by: white rolls, blue rolls, pink and yellow rolls. Next came marching a company of bright aromatic bars of toilet soap. The socks, toilet tissue, and soap were heading resolutely toward a great city square where executions were held. In the center of the plaza yawned a deep inscrutable pit. There was to be a public execution, and the condemned was none other than Antulín himself. Stretching out over the pit was a thin plank along which Antulín advanced unsteadily, prodded on by the sword of an executioner wearing the traditional black hood. Finally, Antulín reached the end of the plank and stopped in one last desperate effort, but a sharp jab in the rump made him lose his footing. He plunged headfirst to the bottom of the abyss where tons and tons of his own unmistakable excrement awaited him. It was all mixed together in an indescribable mess with his equally unmistakable newspapers, socks, undershirts, shorts, and towels. At once the pit was filled in with earth; the earth bore fruit in grass, trees, and flowers; and there appeared in that Garden of Eden, as if out of nowhere, a white temple with serene Doric columns. A deep peace pervaded my spirit. I entered the temple wherein a limpid atmosphere emanated from the walls of gleaming marble. I walked piously toward the altar where six beautiful blond virgin priestesses were worshiping before an immaculately white toilet out of which wafted celestial aromas that perfumed the air and transported the senses upward in ecstasy toward ethereal regions.

10. Sentimental Interlude

On Tuesday, as if to confirm my dream, the landlady informed me that Antulín had taken a turn for the worse. Wednesday she came from the hospital with her eyes reddened from crying so much. "He's got one foot in the grave," she mournfully announced, and I figured that it was probably his left foot!

I remember those seven days as the happiest of my life. Taking advantage of the Holy Week holiday, I left for Mar del Plata[3] that very Wednesday evening. On the train I chatted with everyone, bought them soft drinks, and passed around my cigarettes. I was so inspired that I even managed to strike up a lively conversation with a rather ambiguous type and his wife, a young woman with straight, long, blond hair who said "*you know?*" after every sentence. A famous magazine had published an extensive interview with her. Although the issue was dated six months earlier, the girl (her name was Sylvia) always carried it around with her as bedtime reading. When she managed to extract the magazine from amidst a pandemonium of clothes, combs, and cosmetics, it looked to me like it was called *People and Imbecility.* However, when I looked more closely, I realized I was mistaken, and that its title was *People and Reality.* I read the piece with interest. In response to the penetrating questions of the clever reporter, Sylvia explained with the necessary psychotechnical details how there had taken shape in her mind the idea of establishing a boutique on the fashionable Santa Fe Avenue, the decor of which would reproduce, on a more or less reduced scale, the bedroom of the Marquis de Sade. I was so cheerful that day that the idea actually seemed ingenious to me, and I warmly congratulated her on her talent.

At the station I said goodbye to Sylvia and her husband (a well-known monosyllabic poet of questionable sex). They gave me the name of their hotel at Mar del Plata and their telephone number in Buenos Aires.

As a result of Antulín's death, everything was going great for me. The weather at Mar del Plata was superb all four days. I won't expand on the following point, since this is not the exciting story of my countless successes with women but rather the fetid tale of Antulín. To synthesize, then: I arranged to meet Sylvia on Point Mogotes Beach; we went dancing in dark expensive places; we kissed; and we ended up at a hotel. For the first and last time in my life, luck was also with me at the gambling casino.

On Sunday afternoon I made the return trip to Buenos Aires. As the train picked up speed out in the country, keeping time with its clickety-clack rhythm, I hummed softly to myself: "He's dead—the sonofabitch—Antulín—He's dead—the sonofa . . ." What a joyous trip! And how wonderful I felt! Tanned and trim, refreshed and happy, with a whole lifetime of nice, clean toilets before me!

11. The Man Who Returned from the Beyond [4]

*F*rom the taxi I had taken from Constitution Station, I noticed a group of people surrounding a white ambulance in front of our house. A cruel presentiment pierced my heart. With trembling hand, I paid the driver and quickly got out of the car, so quickly that I forgot to get my valises out of the trunk. By the time I realized what had happened, the taxi had already disappeared, and I was never to get my luggage back. This incident was an evil omen; I sensed that an ill-fated era was beginning for me.

With weak, trembling legs, I frantically elbowed my way toward the ambulance until I managed to get into the front row of curious on-lookers. I'll never know why I didn't faint right in front of everyone when I heard one of the stretcher bearers, putting on a stupid and presumptuously professional face, say, "He must have somebody up there watching over him."

"It's just that he's such a big, strong man," emphasized the Spanish landlady, whose face was one immense smile.

The sudden contrast between my Mar del Plata happiness and my Buenos Aires wretchedness must have brought on a serious attack of nerves. Weak and dizzy, I locked myself in my room and gave vent to the most uncontrolled gesticulations of rage and insanity. Tearing my hair in desperation, I at last fell into a fit of hysterical sobbing. With my face contorted, biting on the words as if they were poison, I repeated over and over to myself: "Why, that filthy, mean, rotten, mangy, raunchy, foul son of a bitch!! He didn't die!! That bastardly son of a bitch didn't die!!"

I spent a terrible night. I don't think I slept an hour. No sooner would I close my eyes than there would appear before me, in chilling sharpness and precision of detail, the toilet decorated as it was during the days when Antulín rode the crest of his greatest glory. At that point I would wake up soaked in the cold sweat of atrocious nightmares. And while I was suffering in this unjust way, Antulín was probably peacefully asleep in his room, dirty and stinking like a wild boar. I cannot deny that I hate Antulín.

12. Description of a Struggle[5]

*J*ust as I had foreseen, Antulín's resurrection changed the good luck that had accompanied me during his temporary demise.

Around that time, the first effects of the severe emotional shock I had suffered manifested themselves in my physical system. I went around nervous, ill-tempered, and without any appetite, enduring as well as I could the dreadful idea that Antulín again occupied a place on the face of the earth.

Obviously, I needed an outlet, so I tried to call Sylvia. After many unsuccessful attempts, I spoke to the operator and found out that the number they had given me at Mar del Plata did not belong, never had belonged, and probably never would belong to any telephone in the city of Buenos Aires or in any other city in the Argentine Republic. Surprised and confused, I formulated and accepted, then weighed and rejected the idea that Sylvia and her hermaphrodite were secret agents in the service of Antulín.

Despite everything, my unsuccessful attempt at execution had netted me one benefit: while Antulín's convalescence lasted, I could go back to getting up at seven-thirty. Antulín was now doing his business in an enamel chamber pot. Every morning the heroic Spanish landlady (she was in love with Antulín, not the plumber) would carry it, fragrant and overflowing, from the lair of the beast with the same half-timid, half-proud, and solemn air with which a royal page would present the regal crown to the queen of a European country. Let us say to the queen of England, to use a cultured Anglo-Saxon example.

But good things never last very long. There finally came the fatal day on which Antulín, now completely recovered, went back to getting up at five o'clock, the fatal day on which I went back to getting up at four.

Since I hate Antulín, from that point on I began to spy on all his movements in hope of a second opportunity. What really made me mad was that he didn't notice my hatred. Above and oblivious to my machinations, he would greet me warmly, usually patting me on the back. Luckily, I saw him only in the morning and at night, and, inevitably, Antulín was preceded, accompanied, and followed by his characteristic stench of a carrion-eating jackal.

Meanwhile, I tried to do him as much harm as possible. I tried, but I still hadn't managed to inflict any major injury on him. Autumn and winter came and went, spring passed, and the summer arrived. We were in December, and the heat was so oppressive that it was hard to sleep. One night I finally succeeded in falling asleep at three o'clock in the morning, and when I woke in an ugly mood the clock said ten minutes to five. At five o'clock on the dot, propelled by his chronometric, Swiss-precision sphincter, Antulín knocked on the bathroom door.

"Occupied," I said.

"Will you be long?"

I didn't answer.

"Will you be long?" insisted Antulín, raising his voice.

"Eh?"

"Will you be long, I say?"

"Eh?"

"I said, will you be very long, sir? 'Cause I'm in a hurry!" Antulín's voice had taken on an anguished tone.

"I'll be right out," I answered.

I began to lather up again as slowly as I possibly could. I heard Antulín backing away a few steps, doubtlessly to fortify his spirit for the resistance. His effort would be something like the defense of a besieged city, only in reverse. The motto of the defenders, instead of *"They shall not enter!"* would have to be *"They shall not get out!"* He was soon obliged to summon help.

"Please hurry up, sir! Listen, I can't stand it much longer!"

"You can't stand what much longer?" I asked, as I painstakingly scrubbed my scalp with my fingernails.

"I'll go in my pants, sir!" Now prey to lack of bowel control, Antulín had also completely lost his self-control. Nevertheless, he still tried to allege one more argument to plead cause. "With all that beer I drank last night because of the heat, I've got terrible diarrhea."

"Oh! I'll be right out in just a second," I said in a concerned tone of voice, and I thought, "Shit yourself, you beast, and we'll see if that way you'll wash your drawers, even if it's only once!"

I scratched the bar of soap and began to scrub my fingernails meticulously. Then, to my justified indignation, Antulín, now on the verge of despair, assaulted the door with fist and foot. His attitude was going beyond what my unlimited patience could endure.

"What kind of knock is that?" I shouted angrily. "Now, because you're so ill-mannered, I'm not going to open the door at all."

He withdrew into a suspicious silence, which, for the first time, made me reflect upon the consequences that the warranted penalty I had just inflicted upon him could provoke in a boorish spirit like that of Antulín.

Sure enough, when after another half hour I emerged from the bathroom clean and perfumed like a rosebud, Antulín savagely hurled himself upon me and joined battle without any previous provocation or challenge. Furthermore, to my perfect horror, Antulín did not wage combat as a gentleman would have, in an orthodox manner and according to certain fixed rules. Seized by murderous rage, he used (and obliged me to use) every kind of offensive and defensive weapon.

The fact was that Antulín had—quite literally and without any possible euphemism—shit himself, and his whole body was giving off a stench insurmountably perfect in its putrefaction, some of the ingredients of which I was able to distinguish in spite of my life being in danger: greasy hair; a breath smelling of bread and pork sausage all chewed up and washed down with red wine; rank and persistent sweat; belly-button crud; archaic semen; aged smegma; dried urine; viscous unwashed feet; eternal clothes; and ancient, medieval, modern, and contemporary excrement.

With his stubby fat sticky hands, Antulín had grabbed me by the arms in an ironlike grip, was biting my left shoulder, and . . . Well fancy that! Even though it was a crucial moment, it suddenly occurred to me that Antulín must be of Sicilian descent. His short stature, his dark skin, his Bedouin face, and his dark black curly hair told me so. Hitting Antulín was like hitting a rock. I must have let him have a hundred murderous punches in the face without managing to loosen his jaws from my left shoulder. Half-twisted as I was, my chin was thus resting on Antulín's big dandruffy head. As if each and every one of his hairs were hollow, there emanated from them in concentrated form that dreadful combination of poisonous exhalations. I immediately felt sick to my stomach. Desperate, I exerted a titanic effort and gave him a vicious knee in the groin. Antulín released the pressure of his claws slightly, but before the other boarders could separate us, I vomited all over his black hair in ochers and yellows. It was an authentic nonrepresentational painting worthy of being exhibited at the Di Tella Art Institute.

I don't think the fight could have lasted more than a minute. I managed to see three or four peacemakers holding Antulín, who, with a kind of egg-shampoo solution on his head, was uttering death threats and trying to hurl himself at me. Tottering, with shaky legs and an upset stomach, I was propped up against one of the columns supporting the partial roof of the courtyard. Three or four other men under the command of the plumber were keeping an unnecessary watch over me. Antulín's teeth had torn my shirt and produced a bloody wound on my shoulder. At this point, it will be appropriate to admit that I hate Antulín.

13. Purification by Fire

*T*his was on a Monday. I immediately rushed to the hospital and had myself injected with torrential doses of antitoxic serums—antitetanus, antirabies, antisnake, antituberculosis, antityphoid, antispider, anticholera, antimalaria, and antisyphilis—a treatment that produced good results since I managed to survive the wound inflicted by Antulín.

During that week, my hate increased a hundredfold. There were no further incidents with Antulín, but each time we crossed each other's path he looked at me so fiercely, so criminally, that I realized the only alternatives were kill or be killed. At times, when I most need it, I have a stroke of good luck. That very Saturday, scarcely five days after my battle with Antulín, I was given my second opportunity to put an end to him.

Feeling melancholy, I was sitting in a little wicker chair in the shade of the courtyard. Against the implacable Spanish landlady I was defending my right, even my duty as an Argentine, to drink *maté* there. Since my fight with her protégé, she had taken a profound dislike to me. The landlady accepted my arguments in part but introduced as an amendment my obligation to sweep up afterward even the tiniest particle of sugar that might stain the proverbial cleanliness of her mosaic tiles. A few steps away and wearing a stern frown, the plumber was listening to our polemic. He was ready at any moment, as his sparkling eyes indicated, to intervene with his authority and tip the scales in favor of either debater.

Just then, from the back of the house, issued the odor of Antulín, and a considerable while later out came Antulín in person and as sprightly as you please. He was sporting a natty outfit consisting of his everyday drab pants with patterns of beef, sheep, swine, and goat blood designed at his butcher shop and a checkered shirt decorated with wine, noodles, eggs, vegetables, fodder, and greens. If it weren't for the fact that vegetables and proteins were engaged in a territorial dispute with mucus, drool, and sweat, Antulín could have been mistaken for a walking menu that some restaurant with innovative ideas had launched onto the street as a publicity stunt. From his right claw dangled an old satchel so shapeless and filthy that a medieval beggar would have rejected it with indignation.

"Have a nice time, Antulín," the landlady cooed at him in honeyed tones, thereby suspending our debate.

"Thanks, Doña Encarnación," responded the monster.

"You're the one who deserves thanks," she replied, blushing.

Antulín continued on his merry way with Doña Encarnación accompanying him as far as the door to the street. Antulín seemed bucolic. Where the devil could he be going? I considered it prudent not to ask any questions and canceled all outings that evening. Several hours passed, and it was soon my bedtime. I was kept awake by the presentiment that this was the night I would kill Antulín; it's true, of course, that the heat and mosquitoes helped out. It had been years and years since I had stayed home on a Saturday night. I was burning with anxiety, the heat, the bugs, and my hatred for Antulín.

Gradually, all the boarders came trickling in, but Antulín did not return. For a long time, the house remained in complete silence. Every little while I would turn on the light to see the time, and toward three in the morning I had to shut it off quickly. I had heard voices, and among them the unmistakable voice of Antulín. He was apparently coming in completely drunk, led by some friends. *Who* could possibly be a friend to Antulín? He loudly said good night to them, vowing his eternal friendship and promising to give each one of them a gift.

Antulín was left standing alone in the middle of the courtyard. Alone, absolutely alone! He seemed disoriented, as if he had lost all sense of the whereabouts of his room. He just stood there, reeling under the courtyard light. How easy it would have been to put a bullet through his head from my darkened window! Luckily, common sense and the lack of a weapon dissuaded me from doing so.

He finally seemed to remember the location of his room and headed toward it, thus passing out of the range of my vision. All I could do now was listen. For a long time he struggled getting the key into the lock. Then he went in and slammed the door, but I didn't hear him lock the door from the inside.

I realized there wasn't a moment to lose. I went running out of my room in my underdrawers and barefoot. Stealthily, I approached Antulín's door and found that he hadn't even taken the key out of the lock. The bed creaked, and immediately I heard a deep, hippopotamic snort. With my heart in my mouth, I stood there on pins and needles, attentive for some ten minutes longer, without hearing anything else.

Silently, I opened the door and stuck my head in. I almost fainted; my sense of smell was assaulted by the suffocating odor of a caged tiger. Choking back the nausea, I fled from Antulín's lair, ran to my room, drank a good slug of cognac right from the bottle, and plugged each of my nostrils with little balls of cotton batting. Thus equipped, I returned to Antulín's room. In the semidarkness I could make out a barely grayish white mass—Antulín's bed. He was snoring horribly, and his snores were like the grunts of a hog.

I looked for Antulín's cigarettes and spotted his sweat-soaked checkered shirt tossed carelessly on a chair. In the pocket was a package: some cheap, unsmokable, black-tobacco cigarettes. There was also a train ticket. I lit one of Antulín's cigarettes without inhaling the smoke. He stirred slightly but didn't wake up. By the light of the match I examined the ticket; Antulín had traveled to the small town of San Miguel. What for? Recent beef entrails on his shirt gave me my answer: he had doubtlessly been invited to an old-fashioned country barbecue.

I set the package of cigarettes on the floor next to Antulín's bed, left the burning butt on the bed, and, to be even more certain, I emptied out all the fluid from my lighter on the sheets. With another match I set fire to the mattress. I locked the door from the inside with two turns of the key and left the key in the keyhole. I went out through the window, and once in the courtyard I shut the window as airtightly as possible.

I quickly made my way back to my room, got into bed, and thought: "You will die, Antulín, you'll be burnt to a crisp. You'll end up like one of those black blood sausages you no doubt devoured today and which you planned to donate, once they were changed in appearance, to the cultural heritage of our community toilet." Now the heat, the mosquitoes, and the memory of Antulín no longer bothered me. I slowly drifted off into a sweet dreamy state until, finally, I fell into a deep sleep.

I don't know how long I slept, but I was awakened by shouts and running, and I said to myself, "They've discovered Antulín's corpse!" I went out elated, skipping with joy. All the boarders were swarming, half-dressed, in front of Antulín's room. The Spanish landlady was wearing a very funny nightgown. Clouds of dense black smoke were pouring out of the room. The plumber, as self-appointed chief of our makeshift fire department, was spraying water from the hose used to wash the courtyard. The others were streaming in and out with buckets, old gallon cans, and washbasins. The weakest or the laziest were carrying chamber pots of different sizes, styles, and models, among which I recognized Antulín's own pot.

I don't know how I suppressed my urge to laugh right out loud. There were no empty pails left, so I went to the kitchen and, as a last resort, grabbed the big pot used for cooking spaghetti. I filled it with water, but with half-closed eyes I voluptuously imagined that the harmless liquid coming out of the faucet was gasoline. With pathos and pot I entered Antulín's room. Ricardo, the numbers-game man from the back of the house, was a man like Pythagoras whom contact with the mathematical sciences had endowed with a philosophical character. He patted me on the back and said, "In moments of tragedy such as this, people forget their little differences." I nodded solemnly, rolling my eyes as though crushed beneath the weight of a painful truth.

The fire was already almost completely out, but Antulín's room had a catastrophic appearance. Some shapeless balls of burned wool were all that was left of the mattress. Because it was made of iron, the bed had been saved from destruction, but it was all twisted and deformed. On the other hand, the night table, a chair and—hallelújah!—the wardrobe were totally destroyed. I said to myself in an apocalyptic tone: "Behold, here is a just act: Antulín's impure garments have been purified in the holocaust." However, I observed with disappointment that his socks had been left unharmed. They were hanging, safe and sound, from the rung of another chair, for even in his acute state of intoxication Antulín had given his socks preferential treatment. Blackened with soot, soaked, and motionless, Antulín was lying face up on the floor next to the wall. Of his undershirt and drawers, only a few gray tatters with singed edges had survived.

Feigning profound emotion, I acted shocked and took advantage of the moment to dump the water in the pot on Antulín's rigid socks. "What happened?" I asked. "A fire?" The question was stupid, but at tragic moments everyone likes to be told the obvious. Trembling, her face all contorted, Doña Encarnación pointed with a detectivelike air to the scorched package of cigarettes on the chair with the socks.

"He musta fallen asleep with a cigarette in his mouth," she deduced. "A woman just never knows what to expect from this Antulín."

"Neither does the plumber," I added under my breath.

"Here comes the ambulance!" proclaimed a herald in a thundering voice from the courtyard.

"I suppose they'll be taking him to the morgue," I remarked.

"Whaddya mean, to the morgue?" Doña Encarnación replied, indignant. "To the Burn Clinic, sir!"

"What!" I became irritated. "Isn't he dead?"

"Well, there's fate for you." Doña Encarnación was now giving vent to her true feelings, her love for Antulín. "I never wake up durin' the night, you all know how hard I work in this house. As far as I'm concerned, I was woke by an angel. I never get up at night neither, but I dunno what I coulda drunk today, I woke up havin' to go to the bathroom. I'm crossin' the courtyard, half asleep, y'know, an' whuddo I see? Fire in poor Antulín's room!"[6]

14. Deification of Antulín

*T*wo or three days later I had the most miserable Christmas in my entire life. The plumber, who spent all religious and secular holidays with us, spoke uninterruptedly about Antulín. They had formed a warm friendship. Now, in the light of even the most superficial analysis of the *Wahlverwandtschaften,*[7] there could be nothing apparently more diametrically opposed than an Antulín and a plumber. Nevertheless, just as there are right and left, good and bad, body and soul, heaven and hell, so, too, the rigorous order of the universe dictates the existence of an Antulín who incessantly clogs up sewers and that of a plumber who incessantly unclogs them.

Every day the plumber visited Antulín in the hospital. The patient was apparently in fine fettle, and the plumber deemed the Christmas season an opportune time to repeat for us some of Antulín's witticisms. By overcoming the pain, which thankfully was less intense with each passing day, our hero had uttered these gems to the eternal solace and relief of his hospital roommates. In short, Antulín was faring splendidly, and in a few days we would have him with us once again.

In effect, scarcely a month later Antulín made his divine reappearance. He was received like a hero, with showy demonstrations of popular joy, spontaneous affection, and eternal glorification. He was another person. Having lost his hair, eyebrows, and eyelashes, he looked like a recently plucked chicken. At the same time, paradoxically, he had taken on certain human features. Perhaps it was because for the occasion he was debuting a limpidly clean shirt and unpolluted pants. But the socks—oh, the socks—were the same old ones as always!

As a culmination to the events programmed in honor of Antulín, Doña Encarnación organized a magnificent dinner during the course of which I was obliged to shake hands with Antulín, to become reconciled with Antulín, and, as an envied honor, to sit at the right hand of Antulín. This was preceded by a report concerning my heroic, self-sacrificing action with the spaghetti pot, delivered in the fiery eloquence of the numbers man.

To tell the truth, that dinner was delicious. So delicious that Antulín, eating and drinking like a castaway, didn't allow it sufficient time to settle in his stomach. The vapors from all that wildly devoured food found their natural channel of exit through Antulín's huge mouth in the form of noisy belches. These were seasoned with intestinal odors and fluids, which spread up and down the length and breadth of that hellish table like dew on a meadow.

Not during dessert, but in the middle of the meal, the numbers man asked for the floor. In his capacity as acting *ikebanist*[8] of the Association for Ratification of the Action of Liberating Involution, he was a man with expertise in flowery oratorical skirmishes waged at almost all the tombs of the Recoleta graveyard, where he enjoyed the unconditional admiration of the productive economic sectors of the cemetery. He was prompted by an impulse so irresistible and spontaneous that when he began to speak he was still chewing a piece of meat. Listened to in respectful silence, interrupted at regular intervals only by Antulín's incessant burping, the numbers man first sketched a brief portrait of his subject. He then reviewed Antulín's life and thought, describing with feeling the principles that had guided him along the impeccable path that, thanks to his perseverance and honesty, had led him to assume the management of the butcher shop with the unanimous approval of the democratic citizenry. The numbers man concluded his speech with the phrase *I have spoken.* This was underscored by the sincere applause of his table companions, which was eclipsed only by an especially moist and sonorous belch from Antulín, who thus thanked the speaker for his panegyric.

To make matters worse, that evening I earned the enmity of the plumber. He was seated opposite me, to the left of Antulín who occupied the head of the table. I noticed that the plumber was looking at me with an angry frown, and it didn't take me long to figure out why. The plumber had interpreted my forced reconciliation with Antulín as a reenactment of the gospel parable of the prodigal son. I was the prodigal son, the younger son, who having repented of his pride, disillusioned with the vanities of the world, was now returning to the arms of his father, that is to the arms of Antulín. The latter, forgetting my ingratitude, hath received me magnanimously and, in addition, hath seated me at his right hand, giving me to eat with his own fork the most succulent morsels from his dish. The plumber, in turn, represented the elder son, irritated and offended by the apparent injustice being done to him. And thus it came to pass that I managed to hear him reproach Antulín: "Behold, for so many months do I unclog thy sewers and never hast thou favored me with thy attentions." But Antulín answereth unto him saying: "Thou art always with me and all my excrement is, in reality, more thine than mine; but this one"—and Antulín pointed at me with a fatherly gesture—"was dead for me and now is come back to life again; he shall continue to enjoy my residue."

And lo! There I sat huddled like a guilty man, most abject and silent. How I hate Antulín!

15. Last Attempt

*T*he new year was beginning under the darkest of forebodings. That summer I felt so discouraged by bad luck that for several months I resigned myself to my fate. However, getting up at four o'clock in the morning in winter is not the same as doing so in the summer. Cowed by the July cold, one day I attempted to find out if things had changed. "Antulín," I told myself, "is Antulín and his circumstances; or rather, Antulín is only his circumstances."[9] So I got up at seven-thirty. And there in the toilet, stinking as ever, were Antulín's circumstances.

I have already mentioned that Antulín is a butcher. I am an insignificant office worker. Antulín has an inestimable fortune; I, a tiny little income. Antulín bought himself a gas heater for his room, had a meter installed, and slept nice and warm on those freezing nights while I shivered in my bed like a sick dog, thinking that because of him I would have to bathe at four in the morning.

One Saturday night I was returning home from the movies, numb with cold, enveloped in my overcoat and gloomy thoughts. My attention was attracted to some little rays of light that filtered out from under the door of Antulín's room. Consumed with curiosity, I peeked through the keyhole. Antulín, lying back in his bed with the air of a sultan, was reading some lowbrow magazine. Over against the wall, the heater was glowing with all burners lit. When he finished reading, Antulín would surely shut it off.

At that instant I knew everything I had to do. I ran to the hallway on tiptoe. My hands were trembling, and I had to struggle quite a bit before I was able to open the little door to the gas meter. Pitilessly I shut off the main valve. I waited a minute and then turned it on again. I went back to the keyhole to ascertain that everything was in order. Antulín was still reading with a look of concentration on his face. The stove was off, but undoubtedly the gas was still on. I almost sang my way back to my room. "You won't get out of this one," I said to myself, "you won't get out of this one, you filthy son of a bitch."

In the morning, after a peaceful sleep, I got up at seven-thirty, full of optimism and sure of finding the employees from the funeral home in the courtyard. In the bathroom I shuddered with terror; once again I found the unmistakable signature of Antulín.

When I stepped out into the courtyard, I was a man vanquished by fate. The Spanish landlady was now sweeping out Antulín's room. I could find only one explanation: that cursed man, who in my judgment had made a pact with the devil, must have suddenly felt too warm and decided to turn off the heater just one second before I closed the main valve to the gas. Oh, that despicable Antulín!

16. Constant Odor beyond Death [10]

*F*ive years have now passed. Last month Doña Encarnación and Antulín were married. The plumber gave away the bride at the religious ceremony. [11] Although he is now the owner of the house, Antulín has not neglected his butcher shop and has delegated his executive powers there to the plumber, who having retired from his public duties has taken up residence in the boardinghouse dedicating all his wisdom exclusively to our toilet.

To the present day I still get up at four o'clock in the morning. I don't get much sleep and my health is poor. As you might imagine, I have definitely given up attempting to execute Antulín. I recognize his superiority and I know that he is immortal.

Perhaps our world will be destroyed by some cataclysm. There will appear new civilizations, which will carry out archaeological excavations to learn about the past, but of our twentieth-century culture they will find only two monuments: the indestructible toilet used by Antulín, and his perennial socks. May the people of the future know how to interpret Antulín's secret message, which we, regrettably, have never understood in its full range of implications.

Nevertheless, in spite of these considerations, I cannot deny that I hate Antulín.

Imperios y servidumbres, pp. 147–186
Barcelona: Editorial Seix Barral, 1972

ARS POETICA

A father who gives advice . . .
    —JOSÉ HERNÁNDEZ [1]   1

        It's a beautifully bound book. It has just been published and its author has rushed me a copy. It's entitled *History of Argentine Literature.* On one of the first pages there's a dedication, which reads, "For Miguel Bulocchi, solid, transcendental talent of our letters, with the humble admiration of Mirindo Pigafetti." The final pages consist of an alphabetical index of authors studied; my name appears under the letter B: BULOCCHI, Miguel: pp. 242–251. Ten effusive pages in which this celebrated critic and literary historian heaps praise upon me. The reading of these eulogies has inspired me with some clear ideas.

    The clear idea that in the future my name and work will occupy a vast, unavoidable, enduring place in the history of our literature; the clear idea that by virtue of hard work and the unique quality of my merits I had attained the position that others reach by means extrinsic to the essence of the literary work; the clear idea that my books, successful and triumphant, were being disseminated over the length and breadth of Argentine territory; the clear idea that, having gone beyond this limited arena, they were now being eagerly read and discussed throughout the whole Spanish-speaking world; the clear idea that English, French, German, Italian, and Hottentot translations were appearing; in short, these clear ideas brought a smile of well-deserved justified satisfaction to my lips.

    "It's no wonder," I thought, "that at the age of twenty-five I'm a full-fledged best seller, a writer who, having emerged from the very bosom of the people, keeps his finger on their pulse and is the faithful interpreter of their joys, their sorrows, their most intimate, visceral feelings."

    If I had to determine how I managed to rise to such an enviable height, I could say with complete sincerity that I owe nothing to effort. Everything was easy for me: where there's talent in excess, application is unnecessary. An idea that in turn inspires me to make the following observation in the language of Homer: *Quod non dat Natura non praebet Schola* (*non* means "not" or "no" in Latin).[2]

"But are you innately a writer?" I was once asked at the XXVIIIth Gerontocratic Meeting of Young Argentine Poets (West Lanús chapter).[3]

At that moment I avoided articulating a concrete answer, because I didn't yet know what *innately* meant. But now I can confess that in a certain way, yes, I am innately a writer. I was attracted to literature at an extremely young age. As I developed, my readings and meditations deposited in my spirit a sediment of precocious maturity. I remember that at the age when my friends were reading only comic books and sports magazines I was already delving deep into the *Reader's Digest*. Its latest published treatise, for example, is almost completely lacking in photographs and drawings, which gives it a unique quality of substantiality; well, I read it from beginning to end, duly appreciating the subtlety with which the lowliest American soldier managed to fool, deceive, ridicule, and scoff at the highest-ranking Japanese marshal. I used to love that stuff. At that time, my friends called me Michael, and my most intimate friends, Mike.

2

The laws of heredity are not to be denied so easily. The fact is, there are antecedents in my family, and of the best kind. I'm talking about my father. He's nearly a public auctioneer,[4] he knows accounting, and he's a wizard at business. He was elected several times as municipal alderman for San Isidro county.[5] We've always lived in the area, and in his youth my father wrote the social and obituary columns for *The Sword, the Pen, and the Word*, which was the Fourth Estate in the whistle-stop town of Carapachay.[6] In that way he acquired many valuable friends in political and business circles.

He was the first to notice my aptitude for literature. The scene took place six years ago, but I remember it as if it had happened just yesterday, so indelibly was it etched in my memory and spirit.

I was nineteen years old and, as the proverb says, *je sème à tous vents* ("I seemed tousled and ventose").[7] That day I was seated in front of the television, attentively following a thrilling round-table discussion. The table companions were debating the "Motivational Problematics of the Contemporary Couple." There was an actress, a long-haired singer, a soccer player from the burrough of San Lorenzo de Almagro,[8] a woman sociologist with a face like Woody Woodpecker, and a priest in secular garb. The subject was fascinating and I was glued to the screen.

Meanwhile, my father was furrowing his thoughtful brow over the crossword puzzle in *La Nación*.[9] Perhaps he was confronted with an unsolvable problem; perhaps he was only pretending to be engrossed. The point is that he suddenly seemed to become aware that the younger generation was demanding that he take his compulsory battle station in the cultural crusade.

Then he looked up, and, as if it were an innocent question, without his emotional trembling perturbing the steadiness of his voice, he asked me: "Miguel, give me a five-letter word for 'expose something raw to the fire.'"

I turned off the television, thought for a while, looked through a dictionary of synonyms and related ideas, and before the lengthening of the evening shadows I answered him unhesitatingly: "Roast."

With trembling hand, my father quickly wrote the word into the enigma with which *La Nación* was troubling his internal peace, tilted his head back, and collated the result. A smile lit up his austere face. He leaped to his feet and, embracing me, exclaimed: "Miguel, there's gray matter up there!" and he tapped me lightly on my skull. "The future is yours!"

That's the gospel truth.

3

Two weeks later there appeared *With Cavities in My Teeth*, a book of poems, which, as the trumpets of fame proclaimed, constituted my first original work. I'm basically sentimental, and, although *With Cavities in My Teeth* is a long way from the testimonial maturity and the more developed polished style that characterizes my later works, I feel a very special affection for that little book. A brief work, yet its twelve pages are overflowing with feeling and rebellion, experiment-wise, that is; it's written entirely in lower-case letters, without punctuation marks, and it includes a lot of proper names I got out of a magazine on art and literature, which allowed me to come up with some really novel rhymes. For example, those of this distich, which won me a decoration from the Soviet embassy:

the young rebel chews his Dentyne
while reading the works of Marx and Lenin.

Nevertheless, at that moment the book went unnoticed. Of course, I was ahead of my time; the public wasn't yet ready to accept such audacity. So my collection of poems only merited a laudatory critical review in *Notebooks from Combat and the Azure,* whose editor and only writer, Benjamina Buffattelli, was involved at that time in a relationship, coitus-wise, with this prematurely budding young literary talent.

"It lacks something basic," said my father, concerned when he saw the book wasn't selling. "It needs a prologue. We'll publish a second edition. With a proper prologue, a better designed cover, and a paper strip across the cover that says SECOND EDITION!"

"But," I objected in my innocence, "the first one hasn't even sold out yet."

"What's that got to do with it? The second edition will make the first one sell. All it needs is a proper prologue," replied my father, and he took his checkbook out of a pocket.

He's a whiz. He picked up the telephone, called around here and there, questioned this one and that one, called here and there again, and in a few days the earlier-mentioned critic, poet, essayist, and literary historian, Mirindo Pigafetti, showed up at our house. In his hand he was carrying a folder, and in the folder the prologue to my book. My father handed him a check for 50,000 pesos. I then considered it the opportune moment to inject a poetic note into that business transaction and I offered Pigafetti a copy of the first edition of *With Cavities in My Teeth* autographed with my own fountain pen. But the prolific writer told me jovially: "No, but thank you very much anyway. I never read the books for which I write prologues. It's a magic spell of mine to guarantee their success."

And he left amidst smiles and bows. The instant he closed the door I leaped on his composition. To begin with, I didn't understand the title: "By Way of Preface, or Concerning How the Word Does Not Cease in Youthdom." It consisted of fifteen typed pages—there would be more prologue by someone else than text of my own. I read the beginning of the first page:

Exponent of convulsed Argentine, Latin American, World youth—young above all, before all and after all!—, Miguel Bulocchi tenders us, in this collection of lyrics, verses as iridescent as precious stones, which a Baudelaire, a Heine, an Espronceda, a Joaquín V. González would gladly have undersigned.[10] One intuits, one palpates, one touches in it the limpid, ascending vibration of the human being—that rending flesh, that anguished ensemble of viscera, organs, bones and hair—launching himself into a search for the motivation of the here and the now, or rather, with a Husserlean focus, through the *hic et nunc* of the Platonic mystics, whose denunciation of the system was—why deny it?—incontrovertibly dulcified.

I had to stop here: "What does all this mean?"
"Nothing," replied my father. "Absolutely nothing."
I continued my reading:

A ferocious tide of antiprotocolic life experiences, overflowing with bitter nausea and coruscating rebellion in its hopelessness, is implemented, expression-wise, in a factual writing, in a naked, lean language stripped of the ancient rhetoric customary in the effete XVIIIth century and the obsolete XIXth, until it achieves the raw anguish of these verses of pure Rimbaudean lineage: "/ / / /." The beloved and tormented Verlaine once stated on a certain August 15, 1891 . . .

"And these blank spaces, Pop," I asked, "what are they for?"
"You have to put a line or two from your book in there. You separate each verse with a little slash."
"And how do I know which ones belong to the lineage of that guy, what's his name?"
My father looked at me with pity: "What does it matter? It's all the same. Put in anything. Who's going to notice?"
Gospel truth.

4

In short, the second edition of *With Cavities in My Teeth* now appeared.
"We've got to have a debut," declared my father.
No sooner said than done. We held it at the Galería del Este.[11] My father had anticipated all the organizational details. Like flies attracted to honey, disciplined contingents of intellectuals began to pour in. It's incredible the enormous number of intellectuals that swarm around Buenos Aires. One was immediately aware they were intellectuals because all of them were proudly sporting the obligatory uniform of the intellectual. For those who were men (more or less),

talent and nonconformity had prescribed the wearing of beards, long
hair, glasses, and pipes. Among the apparent women, that is, those
lacking beards, there was a proliferation of glasses, wrinkled skirts,
dirty slacks, and dirty words.

Located on a kind of lecture platform, I was the center of attention,
the reason and occasion for that assembled multitude of privileged
brains. My father was seated to my right; to my left, a famished
ambiguous-looking young fellow was hysterically fiddling with his fingers, which were all entwined in a necklace of beads and trinkets that
hung down on his chest.

An hour after the agreed-upon time, the presentation of my work
commenced. The signal was a jab in the ribs that my father gave the
starving young man by stretching his arm around behind my back. As
if suddenly remembering that he had some duty to perform, the fellow
leaped to his feet. He pretended to recognize several friends among
the audience and greeted them with exaggerated gestures. Actually,
he knew all of them, because the same faces were always present, and
they all wanted to be recognized and greeted. "It's now our turn to be
the spectators," they seemed to be thinking, "but we were once the
main characters and may again be so at any time, because in these
affairs it's a rotating system, and today it's your turn, tomorrow mine."
Still several more minutes went by before my young sponsor got the
silence he needed to make himself heard.

Finally, he began to talk about me and my book. After a few
minutes, I learned that I possessed "a profound Marxist formation."
This information won me the swift sympathy of the intelligentsia. I
was on the verge of formulating a correction, but when I saw the bene-
ficial effect produced, I realized that, in effect, I had always been a
Marxist.

The young man harangued them in an effeminately humorous tone,
which did not, however, preclude a depth of concept. So profound was
it that, at a given moment, I didn't know what the hell he was talking
about. Several times he used the words *beatnik, pop, camp, establishment*, words that sent a ripple of pleasure through the crowd. Afterward, I seemed to catch something like American society had never
forgiven I don't know whom for I don't know what. At one point, he
compared my poetry with that of a writer with the last name of Borges.
That was bad; comparisons are odious, as some television announcer
once said. Luckily, he asserted that that guy's poetry was effete and

that he was going in the wrong direction with respect to contemporary problems, so my poetry was quite superior. To prove it, he added: "Because, evidently, Bulocchi somehow pisses on academic traditions."

Everyone laughed at the word *pisses*. I did, too, despite the fact that it's not true; I always use the bathroom except, of course, in case of an emergency—from which no one is exempt.

"Where did you get this fairy?" I asked my father in a very low voice.

"Shhhh!" he exclaimed fearfully. "He might hear you! He's a person with lots of connections; it's important for you to get friendly with him. But not too friendly, eh?"

"Come on, Pop, if there's one thing I've got an oversupply of, it's broads."

"To be an established author, it's essential to be able to count on the backing of the fag sector."

Gospel truth.

5

"Pop," I said to him after the debut, "it looks to me like we put our foot in it. That stuff about classifying me as a Marxist, isn't that going to hinder my circulation in the United States?"

"On the contrary," he declared sententiously. "Why the Americans are delighted when Latin Americans are Marxists; they're going to heap prizes and translations on you."

"Do you think so?"

"What do you think? Just look at Cortázar, García Márquez, and Vargas Llosa; they act like Marxists, and things go great for them in the United States. Later on you'd do well to take up residence in Western Europe."

"Are you serious?"

"You bet your life on it."

Gospel truth.

6

My father worked diligently. I've always admired his foresighted, organizational spirit. One afternoon I found him making up little packages with copies of my book; among the pages of each volume he placed a check.

"There's nothing as poignant," he said, "as finding a flower among the pages of a book. Here, take these packages around to the editorial rooms of the newspapers and magazines."

In a few weeks, glowing reviews of my book began to appear. When they saw the undeniable signature of Pigafetti validating my creation and the forceful signature of my father validating their check, the most severe, demanding critics declared me a sublime poet. Of all those reviews, I recall with particular fondness the first one, which appeared in the *Voice of the Swine-Breeder* in the tiny town of Guaminí. It began with these words:

Miguel Bulocchi, a young poet from the little provincial town of Carapachay, has just brought out the second edition (after the explosive success which swept the first edition from the bookstores of the whole country) of his book of poems, *With Cavities in My Teeth* which (allow us the jest, the joke, the facetiousness, the *castigat ridendo mores*, the Aristophanic, Molièrean, Goldonian, Gudiñokiefferesque[12] touch) bites hard (despite its sickly, pessimistic title—a sign of the times—, lacking in calcium, to have recourse to a therapeutic metaphor which the great Argentine poet Esteban Echeverría, would not have disdained) into the dozing, hypocritical conscience of the bourgeois pig. To the extent that no more and no less than a critic of the stature, the height, the substance, the stuff, the magnitude of Mirindo Pigafetti (a philologist—if ever there was one—little given to lavishness in praise and dithyrambs) endorses the poems in his terse, analytic prologue with these measured words: "A ferocious tide of antiprotocolic life experiences . . ."

From this point to the end, the review reproduced verbatim Pigafetti's whole prologue and it occupied practically the entire newspaper, so that the subscribers to Guaminí's the *Voice of the Swine-Breeder* were deprived, in honor of Polyhymnia,[13] of their routine farming news about corn, bran, phosphoric mineral supplements, and the swine plague.

One bitter note. In a typically McCarthyistic action, the editor of the *Voice of the Swine-Breeder*, Dr. Cochon,[14] decreed the dismissal of the review's author because he found the association established between the words *pig* and *bourgeois* "improper, arbitrary, and capricious."

In the face of this injustice, the influential sectors of Guaminí mobilized in heated protest. There were demonstrations in front of the newspaper building, paid published statements appeared, insulting anonymous letters were sent, and a feeling of uneasiness took root in the bosom of the army, the navy, and the air force. First the province of Buenos Aires and then the entire nation stirred indignantly to the pulsebeat of a crisis that shook national institutions to their very foundations. Finally, Dr. Cochon, the mayor of Guaminí, and the governor of the province of Buenos Aires all resigned from their respective offices.

But it was all *Much Ado about Nothing*, and *It's an ill wind that blows no good:* my book sold more than ever, my name was on everybody's lips, and no one failed to point out that the pen had shown itself to be a weapon as mighty as the sword for overthrowing tyrants and keeping watch over human rights when they are being trampled upon.

7

After this triumph, I was now resting on my laurels, but my father was untiring. "I'm going to see if I can line up a good interview for you," he said, taking out his checkbook.

He got one immediately. One day there showed up at our house a tall, skinny, ugly, bespectacled woman with a short, fat photographer and a tape recorder. I had unwisely left my cigarettes within their reach and every few minutes they'd filch one on me.

The reporter asked me: "What are you doing now?"

"I'm working on a novel, a book of short stories, a Greek tragedy, a musical comedy and a volume of *conceited* essays."

"What's each one about?"

"The novel deals with the student movement of the Ona Indians;[15] the short stories with the frequent incest among public administration employees, a sociologically verified fact; the Greek tragedy, I don't know yet; the musical comedy is about the *Lumpenproletariat* within the context of the Vieytes insane asylum."[16]

The photographer was climbing around on the furniture like a little monkey, taking picture after picture of me from every angle and profile.

"And the essays?" the bespectacled woman exhaled absent-mindedly as she filed her fingernails.

"Well . . . Here I play around a bit with concepts, or *conceits*, as they were called in the XVIIth century, in the style of an English writer named John Donne, who died recently. As I was saying, I play around with conceits, y' know—expression-wise that is—with the word *syntax*, for example, playing on *sin*, as in the Ten Command-ments, and *syn*, which in Greek means *with* or *together*, and *táxis*, which is Greek for *order* or *arrangement*, so that *syntax* means ar-ranging things together, as in the word order of a sentence. But *syntax* also sounds like *sin tax*, that is, a charge placed on various things by the government. In this case, it would be a tax on sin, y' know? So in these *conceited* essays I'm attempting to communicate the notion, or *conceit*, that . . ."

"Isn't that entomology stuff a bit passé?" objected the bespectacled woman.

"Well . . . , that depends . . . I think that . . ."

"Do you believe in marriage?"

I paused slightly to think: "Basically, I believe in the mate."

"Bye-bye," she said, but not without first snitching one last ciga-rette from me.

"Is that it?"

"Yep."

Two weeks later I held in my hands the issue of *Anthropoids* maga-zine containing the interview they had done with me. The caption of the article read: *Good-looking. Young. Modern. An Up-to-date Guy. Happy and Personable. In Love with Life. Come On, Get to Know Him.* Anthropoids *Really Got Close to Him and Asked Him Questions about Absolutely Everything. His Name Is Miguel Bulocchi and He's a Poet.*

I read the text and found myself passing opinions with remarkable versatility on Zen Buddhism, Franz Kafka, the macrobiotic diet, the ocean, the myth of Carlos Gardel, the national soccer team, the Beatles, the incorrigible Brazilian lack of culture, the existence of God, voyages to the moon, premarital sexual relations, abortion, di-vorce, Schopenhauer, love, death and the Argentine woman. Con-cerning the latter, it turns out that I had said:

"She's the most elegant, the most beautiful, the best dressed woman in the world, but . . ."

I see Miguel is hesitating slightly at this juncture. But I'm a gal who's a reporter; I know my job, and my responsibility is to get at the truth:

"But what?" I ask him.

I put my finger on a sore spot here. Bulocchi gets nervous, and it's obvious he'd rather not answer. He still has time to pilfer one of my cigarettes and light it. Finally, there's a flash of light in his beautiful, Japanese cherry–colored eyes, if the cherry trees of Japan were gray.

"But," he finally decides, "the Argentine woman still hasn't managed to fulfill herself—sexual freedom-wise, that is—or in the areas of social and occupational equality."

But I'm a woman, too, and I'm Argentine. I'm myself, after all, and I can't put up with this kind of stuff. For a moment I set aside my journalistic objectivity and reply: "And have women perhaps attained their total liberation anywhere in the world?"

Bulocchi looks embarrassed; he wishes he had bitten his tongue, but it's too late to back out now. "Yes," he finally answers while swiping another of my cigarettes, "without looking any further, British and Swedish women have achieved their total liberation."

Why the hell do I get myself into things that are none of my business? In the next issue of *Anthropoids* three letters by as many women readers were published. They were laconically titled: "Argentine Woman (I)," "Argentine Woman (II)," and "Argentine Woman (III)." Give or take a word or two, the three erudite women said the same thing: they attacked me ferociously. Nevertheless, the second one stood out for her display of a style that I judged eloquently original and expressive. She said:

Anthropoids, you really bug me. You cheated me, what more can I say? I thought you were an up-to-date magazine, a sensational magazine, a cool magazine. Cool from the year one. Every Thursday I plunked down my $4.30 for a heap of beautiful things you always presented me with. Because in your pages I found the real, true country. But now, no way, I'm mad and I'm laying it right on you. And I'm laying it on you because now it turns out that you do an interview with a "poet" (yes, I'm writing it that way, in quotes, because there's really only one authentic, vital, lucid Poet, Poet with a capital letter: his name is John Lennon). You do an interview with a Mr. Bulocchi (Where did he get that last name? From the island of Sicily?), a man who brags about being a misogynist and a foreignizer, and who attacks the Argentine woman. Doesn't that guy have a mother? Was he born from a head of cabbage, like the ostriches? Gimme a break, *Anthropoids*, get off my back. Tell that guy I'm an Argentine woman—and proud of it. 27 years old. A woman who lives, works, studies, loves, struggles, dreams, and suffers right alongside men. A woman with guts, who's not trying to bug out of anything. A swinging gal, not a bummer. I'm in, not out. I'm turned on, not off. I'm a woman who doesn't try to shy away from her commitment to Life (like that, with a capital letter). A Woman (also with a capital letter) who doesn't need to be compared to British or Swedish women or anybody. Together with my mate, who lives, works, studies, loves, struggles, dreams, and suffers right alongside me, we've wholeheartedly assumed our role as young people. As people who . . .

"Pop," I consulted him, showing him that cruel denunciation, "what am I gonna do with this nutty dame who's laying all this stuff on me? Shall I maintain a dignified silence in the face of my unjustly offended righteousness?"

"Don't even think of it. Give her any answer you want, but be sure to put in something about the consumer society. You'll see how many more get into it. Readers love to debate in magazines over stupid things. They're happy because that way they think they're exercising their right of opinion, and they're giving you free publicity."

Gospel truth.

I grabbed my typewriter. My fingers ran over the keys almost at random; I wrote the first drivel that popped into my head. But toward the end there was a virulent paragraph seasoned with some of Pigafetti's unintelligible phrasing that was sure to have an effect.

. . . and inform that Miss or Mrs. Asciugalascimmia (I assume her last name didn't originate in Kent county),[17] who says she has assumed her role mate-wise, inform her, I repeat, that the here and the now, the *hic et nunc* of this coruscating twentieth century demands not only that the pubescent or impuberate, the virginal or deflowered, Miss or Mrs. Asciugalascimmia should have resolved her sexual problems outside the framework of the prudish, straight-laced priggishness of the petite bourgeoisie. It's necessary to take on something more than a mate; I, as an intellectual of today, tell her it's essential to accept the social challenge that the daily struggle in this consumer society imposes upon us and to occupy—to win for herself and hold it—the first line of trenches . . .

My father was reading over my shoulder: "That's it," he said. "Now you'll see what happens; there's not a nitwit alive who, faced with the term *consumer society*, won't consider himself a revolutionary of the pages of a current events magazine illustrated with lots of advertising."

Sure enough, an avalanche of letters plummeted down upon *Anthropoids*. Some readers defended me as if I were a physical and mental cripple; others were ready to tear me apart and throw my remains to the dogs; finally, others understood nothing about anything and shifted the debate toward remote areas lacking the slightest relationship with the original topic. They finally ended up fighting among themselves.

"Let them kill each other," said my father, quite satisfied. "You've already gone beyond that stage. Anyway, poetry isn't a very profitable genre. What you need now is to win first prize in the novel contest being organized by the Macaco Publishing Company."

Gospel truth.

8

"Take advantage of today and tomorrow to go to the movies if you want," my father said to me that Saturday. "Are you still going around with Benjamina Buffattelli?"

"She's better than nothing," I replied. "Besides, she's a girl who moves in literary circles."

"She doesn't have much of an audience. Get rid of her. What'll do you some good now is to take up with some young modern music starlet. The kind that dance while they're howling out onomatopoeic songs. Shooby-dooby-doo . . . Boop-bop-a-dop! Shooby-dooby-doo . . . Boop-bop-a-dop! See what I mean?"

"Yeah, but . . . what about my prestige in the world of letters and the arts?"

"Just imagine," my father went on, without hearing me, "every time *Radioland* or *Antenna* magazine does an interview with your future fiancée with her tits hanging out, they're going to mention you."

"Hey, right!" I caught on. "And I may even get my picture taken with her and everything. She'll appear in it with a worried face, because starlets are always confronting serious problems. I can just see the headlines now: *Vanity Narcissa and Miguel Bulocchi at a Crossroad*; or maybe *Shadow Hangs over Romance between Vanity and Miguel*; or *Stork Soon to Visit Vanity—Miguel on Cloud Nine*; or even *"They'll never succeed in separating us!" Vanity Narcissa tells us. "Miguel is the man of my life!"*

"But there's plenty of time for that," affirmed my ever practical and realistic father. "Go to the movies with anybody you want today and tomorrow. On Monday you have to begin your novel. And, remember, the contest deadline is almost upon us."

Artistic creation is a high priesthood. At ten o'clock Monday morning I plugged in my recorder and began to write my novel about the Ona Indians; in the face of so much literature on foreign and historical subjects, an up-to-date native theme was in order. For three straight hours I talked into the microphone until I filled the tape. And this productive work pace was kept up like that for fifteen days. In the afternoons a third-year high school girl contracted by my father typed up what was on the tape recording, put in punctuation, and endowed it with reasonably correct spelling. The novel was finished on the sixteenth day. My father hefted it with both hands.

"That's good. Over eight hundred pages. Your success is assured: everybody'll buy it, but nobody will dare read it." It was obvious the old man was happy: "Here," he handed me 1,000 pesos. "Go take Benjamina out for ice cream, because I have something urgent to do."

As if already sensing my future success, Benjamina was kind of physically demonstrative that afternoon; she had no way of knowing my heart already belonged to Vanity Narcissa. But that's life.

I returned in the early evening, still licking the chocolate, caramel, and pistachio from my lips. Toying with his checkbook, my father told me: "I already know who the members of the judges' panel are. They're coming to dinner tomorrow."

They came. They ate, they drank, they smoked, and they talked about themselves.

"Mikey admires you gentlemen very much," said my father. "He's basically a poet, but he's crazy about your novels."

The three of them got all puffed up and glowed with self-satisfaction.

I, of course, had not read their novels, because I don't like to read, but on the other hand I did remember the titles. I mentioned them quickly; they savored them as if they were candy.

"I just recently finished a novel," I added, "in which your influences are obvious. But . . ."

"But what?" one of them urged me on, in the hope I'd go on talking about their works.

"I don't know if I'll be able to find a publisher. My novel contains a lot of denunciation of the system. I sweep away everything that's familiar. You know . . . People don't like to commit themselves."

"The trouble is, in this country," said another one, chewing voraciously, "the only religion is a full belly."

"That's right," added the third, "when the old-fashioned ideals . . ."

"Would you gentlemen like some whiskey?" asked my father.

They would. After five or six drinks, one of them said: "Why don't you participate in the Macaco Publishing Company's novel contest?"

"Oh no, I couldn't," I said sadly. "Judges' panels are usually so arbitrary."

"Not always," they replied. "To be precise, we three make up the panel this year."

"No!! Really?! And do you think there might be a chance?"

There was. That same weekend they came to our country place at Tortuguitas.[18] They splashed around in the swimming pool, sunbathed, ate pounds and pounds of barbecue, closeted themselves in the study for ten minutes with my father, and agreed to come back soon.

9

Before we sent the final version of my novel to the publisher, my father gave it a cursory reading.

"This paragraph," he pointed out:

The clock sifted the minutes slowly, every sixty seconds. He remained still for a few moments until his eyes became accustomed to the darkness. His breathing gradually became more regular, and he finally fell fast asleep. Wearing that concentrated, typically Buenos Aires expression of tenderness, she nervously puffed on her cigarette as she always did when she was nervous. She thought: "And what about Marcela? Could she have been swallowed up by the earth or . . . ?" Meanwhile, the old woman's gnarled hands kneaded the fearful specter of Communism. She thought about Nicola, her husband. He had died years before in Italy. The doge, Marino Faliero, had ordered him poisoned. But his men, merely a handful of men, had managed to cross the desolate, stony, sinister plains of Hungary, striving to save the heroic Nicola's foot, even if nothing else. And now, so many years later, Giuseppina still kept her husband's right foot in an old shoe box in the attic of the big, inextricable, dark, macabre, gloomy, lugubrious, old mansion in the Nueva Pompeya quarter of the city. It was a foot. Only a foot. With five toes. But how much that foot had meant to the old lady! When they were young newlyweds, Nicola used to tickle her navel with its big toe. When she remembered that, the old lady shivered with retroactive voluptuousness. That foot was a compendium of the Italian soul, which was filled with poetry; that right foot, faithfully accompanied by the left, had traversed the entire Italian peninsula. The old woman took a bath. She was very dirty, with an interior, metaphysical filth. That bath was the symbol of a Better World. The water was the Ultimate Truth. The soap, Access to the Impenetrable Secret. But then his sensual lips kissed Suzette's white neck, her supple shoulders, her round turgid breasts, which seemed to give off a luminous, malignant vapor. In that position, with her vacant stare, she looked like an El Greco figure . . .

My father stopped.

"Something wrong?" I asked fearfully.

"No. In principle I like it, because you can't understand anything; that's going to give you the reputation of being profound. The figures of speech are very original. How did you think of that part about the clock sifting the minutes? And that stuff about sensual lips and supple shoulders?"

I smiled, flattered.

"I wonder why it is," my father added, "there are more El Greco figures in novels than there are in El Greco's paintings?"

"God only knows."

"Nevertheless, you're lacking something essential: experimentation. You've got to innovate, my boy! For example, why don't you write this same paragraph with the words written backward? Like this: *Eht kcolc detfis eht setunim ylwols, yreve ytxis sdnoces* . . . , etc. Isn't that beautiful?" my father looked excited. "Creativeness and renewal! New expressive forms! Revolution in Art! The search for a new aesthetics! A plunge into the infinite possibilities of the language! A hot, vibrant language! See what I mean?"

I saw. Following this advice, I wrote chapters with inverted syllables, chapters that read from right to left, vertical chapters like neon signs that read from top to bottom, chapters that were continued fifty pages farther on and then went back forty pages, chapters without punctuation, chapters with punctuation but without words, chapters in three columns, chapters with all capital letters, chapters with numbers instead of letters, chapters with blank pages, chapters with some words transliterated into the Cyrillic alphabet and others into the Greek alphabet. In short, I wrote all kinds of chapters.

"Great!" my father encouraged me. "You're going to drive the type-setters crazy!"

Following my own initiative, I finally turned to the infinite expressive resources offered me by the keyboard of my Olivetti and I came up with this discovery:

After scratching her right armpit with an artist's brush made of capybara-hair, Suzette said: "&1/2$ . . . , or, on the other hand, £%m/nN . . . ê3? You swine, you're not the father of my child!"

Drying the anguished sweat beading on his forehead, Jean-Paul replied: "I would never have assumed that (°è$&&&& . . . At any rate, there are worse things . . ."

Proudly, I thought: "It would never have occurred to Cervantes, Dickens, Dostoyevsky, James, or Kafka to do such things. And yet, they're famous!" However, I was not embittered by this injustice.

My father was delighted, but: "That's fine. There's enough pornography, dirty words, demagoguery, and typographical doodads. However, you're still lacking something important; you have to put in some racial persecution."

"How'll I do that?" I asked, half-annoyed and half-confused. "It has nothing to do with the Ona Indians."

"I don't know. You work it out. You're the writer. In a proper novel some racial persecution is indispensable. The best-selling novelists never leave it out."

"Well, what shall I include?"

"I don't know. Let's see. There's the map of Europe. I've got it! Stick in a British student, for example. A British student who comes from ancient Europe to this promised land," my father half-closed his eyes dreamily, "with just his suitcase full of hopes, and because he's an Anglo-Saxon, the Ona Indians discriminate against him by not allowing him to study nuclear physics at the University of Ushuaia."[19]

"Wouldn't it be better to make him a black from the Congo?"

"No, you numbskull! What power, money, influence, or means of communication do the blacks of the Congo have? What generosity can you expect from them? The trick is to present the victimizer as the victim, and vice versa. And in finding a powerful victimizer so he can yield you some revenue. Do you get it, nincompoop?"

I got it: "And shall I say that the Englishman had a shy, humble, melancholy character and that his sad meek eyes reflected the ancestral burden of an age-old pain?"

"Of course. And if you get lucky, you might even nail down for yourself a free trip to Great Britain to give some lectures at Oxford."

"Lectures? On what?"

"You ask more dumb questions! There's plenty to talk about. You can talk about the pillaging carried out by Mahatma Gandhi and his minions against the humble English peasants. Or you can tell about how the Zulus got rich transporting British slaves to the Antilles. There are lots of things to say."

Gospel truth.

I submitted my manuscript to the Macaco Publishing Company's novel contest, and *Humanization of the Penguins* won the unanimous vote of the judges' panel. Later on, at a simple but emotional public ceremony, I was awarded the prize, abundantly photographed, and interviewed at great length. At last I was able to fulfill the dream I had cherished for so long: to meet the three members of the judges' panel who had thus honored a novice writer overflowing with youthful ideals.

10

"Things are moving along rather nicely," said my father when we got home. "But I haven't seen you on T.V. for quite some time. I'm going to ask Agrippina da Pistoia to invite you to one of her famous Television Luncheons."

At that time this talk show was seen by a lot of people. Its hostess, the above-mentioned Agrippina da Pistoia, would bring together around a congenial table provided with interesting hors d'oeuvres and tasty food five personalities whose only thing in common was that they were the object of more or less widespread public attention owing to the most diverse reasons.

The afternoon I was invited, I shared the table with the powerful boxer Brutus Fourpaws, the well-known choreographer and male ballet dancer Fairyfoot de l'Antoinette, and a community business leader, Gino Sarducci, owner of, among other similar establishments, the sophisticated nightclub The Wild Gaucho. In addition to the four of us, who in greater or lesser measure belonged to the sportsworld-artistic-intellectual set, there was a strange character, a sort of fish out of water. He was Mr. Huakaspa Opa, a newcomer to the city, who had just won a billion pesos in the sports-predicting contest (the acronym of which is SPOPRE). Due to this unforeseen turn of the wheel of fortune, Mr. Opa had even had the distinguished honor of being received in private audience by the minister of social welfare himself, Mr. Perique.[20]

All well and good. There we were, the five guests and our hostess.

Agrippina da Pistoia said: "Let's see, Brutus, shall we start with you? Tell us something about your last fight at Madison Square Garden."

The boxer stood up and began to flaunt feints and jabs: "Da fight was easy!" he explained. "Da black guy comes at me 'n' tries to gimme tree jabs, like dis: bim, bam, boom! I close my arms 'n' fend off his tree blows. Den I take a step back 'n' I let 'im have it wit tree punches o' my own: bim, bam, boom! He went down like a sack o' potatoes!"

"*Knockout?*" inquired Agrippina, and the English *t* danced on her teeth for a moment.

"Dey carried 'im out on a stretcher," confirmed Brutus.

"Sensational! Fascinating!" exaggerated Agrippina. "A *knockout* right in Madison Square Garden, the great stadium in New York, the densely populated city of the United States of America!" her voice was that of an American actress parodying another American actress. "I suppose most of the people in the crowd were United States citizens."

"No," corrected Brutus, "dere was a lot o' Americans dere too. Dey froze when dey seen my punches, dey did! Bim, bam, boom!"

"Ha-ha-ha!" tinkled Agrippina's clear laughter. "Oh, this Brutus, always so genteel, pleasant, and witty. And now, tell me, Mr. Opa," she added, while the boxer went on talking to himself, feinting, jabbing, and making threatening gestures with his gigantic fists, "what did you think, Mr. Opa, when you suddenly found yourself . . . , that is . . . , owner of what . . . , well, in short, and in round numbers, suddenly amounted to the tidy sum of what . . . , well . . . , in the final instance and in short, was nothing more and nothing less than a billion pesos?"

"Huh?" asked Mr. Opa, dizzied by this flood of words and choking on a coca leaf pasty.[21]

"I mean," smiled Agrippina da Pistoia, simplifying her text, "what did you think when you won the SPOPRE?"

"Well . . . uh . . . , I said to myself . . . uh . . . Huakaspa . . ."

"Louder, please!" Agrippina exhorted him.

"Huh?"

"Louder, we can't hear anything you're saying, Mr. Opa! And our viewing audience out there, who follow us so faithfully day by day, is anxious to hear you!"

"Huh?"

"Louder!!" and now off-mike and under her breath the sweet Agrippina muttered, "Damn you, you deaf shit!"

"Oh, yeah. Well uh . . . , I'd . . . uh . . . only made one bet. I thought to myself: 'The Río de la Plata soccer team always loses.' I'd bet on 'em to . . . uh . . . win . . . Then I bet on 'em to uh . . . lose, 'n' uh . . . , I won."

"Oh, how interesting! What marvelous intuition!"

"Huh?"

"And what are you going to do with all that money?"

"Well I've uh . . . I've uh . . . stuck it in the bank. Later on I'm uh . . . gonna buy me a Chevy."

"Please, no advertising, Mr. Opa!"

"Huh?"

"And haven't you also thought about buying yourself a pretty little house?"

"Uh . . . yeah, that too. If the . . . uh . . . money goes far enough . . . uh . . . , I'll . . . uh. . . buy me a house, too."

"How marvelous and how talented! How fascinating and how amusing you are, Mr. Opa, with that witty charm and highland plains expressiveness of yours! And now, a commercial break for these timely messages, which will come in handy for all of us. And we'll be right back."

"Huh?"

After the break, which she used to retouch her make-up, Agrippina turned to Sarducci: "We know you've just returned from Europe. Where were you?"

"Well, we did Spain, Italy, France, England, London, Germany."

"And what pretty things did you bring back from the Old World, from that fabulous, marvelous, eternal continent?"

"I didn't bring back too much," said Sarducci in a disillusioned tone of voice. "The truth is that in night life, in the matter, that is, of the night, of where the action and carousing is, we have nothing to envy the Europeans for. From what I saw, I think shallow people here unfortunately don't know how to appreciate the great strides in progress we Argentines have made, night life—wise, that is. We've got to give some serious thought to this," he added with heartrending sadness: "Argentines aren't very patriotic. They think the country ends at General Paz Avenue; they're unfamiliar with Ramos Mejía or Olivos."

I loved that novel metaphor about General Paz Avenue.[22]

"But didn't you bring back something fashionable in the way of interior decor?"

"Yes," replied Sarducci with an air of mystery, "but that's a secret. You'll all see it as soon as I unveil my branch of The Wild Gaucho in Ramos Mejía."

"Oh, what an adorable man this fellow is! And will you invite me to come and see that marvelous place?"

"Sure! You and all these pleasant folks who are with us at this pleasant, congenial table which you so pleasantly host with so much . . . , uh . . . , so much pleasantness."

"Huh?"

"And you, Fairyfoot?" Agrippina proceeded quickly on, paying no attention to Mr. Opa. "What are you putting together for the upcoming season?"

"*Ooooh*, Agrippina, you *are* the indiscreet one!" exclaimed the choreographer, with an incredibly effeminate voice and gestures. "How do you know I've got something hidden in my garter belt?"

"When it comes to you, one always expects the *dernier cri de la . . . de la . . . de la choréographie. Non è vero?*"

"How simply awesome you are, Agrippina, you know so many languages! The only one you need to learn now is Quechua so you can discuss the secrets of *haute couture* with Mr. Opa."

"Huh?"

"But we're here to learn about your work, Fairyfoot," Agrippina said modestly. "Tell us about your dreams, your projects, your illusions, your . . . uh . . . , about your plans."

"Oh, but *dahling*, you're so hip to everything! How up-to-date you are! It's just as I always say. When Agrippina leaves Buenos Aires, Buenos Aires is no longer Buenos Aires, Buenos Aires doesn't exist, because Buenos Aires *is* Agrippina! Yes it is! Buenos Aires *is* Agrippina! And let there be no arguments about it! Oh, dear me, oh, me, oh, my!" Fairyfoot was getting excited.

"All right, you little rascal," Agrippina cut him off. "But don't get off the subject on me. What secrets are you cooking up for the season, *pour la saison*, to be clearer."

"Will you forgive me, Agrippina *dahling*? Tell me right now that you forgive me or I'm going home this very instant, take ten pills for my nerves, and I just won't be seeing your adorable little Scandinavian doll face anymore."

"I forgive you, Fairyfoot," Agrippina acquiesced, smiling pleasantly.

"Then I'll tell you with complete frankness, with my britches down, as they say. It's a secret! A great big secret!! You'll find out when we debut."

"My, my, today certainly is the day for mysteries! What *will* our beloved viewing audience, who follow us so faithfully day by day, think about all this?"

"So it would seem!" replied Fairyfoot. "Te-hee-hee, te-hee-hee!! But wouldn't you rather question this young man, who's *sooo* good looking and *sooo* nice? Surely he has something wildly interesting and *faaabulously* brilliant to tell us."

"Of course," said Agrippina. "But first we'll pause again briefly for these helpful messages, and we'll be right back."

I took advantage of the break to drink a demitasse of coffee and thereby evade the drooping eyelids with which Fairyfoot was attempting to seduce me.

"This young man who's so good looking and so nice, as our beloved Fairyfoot accurately defined, described, and designated him, is Miguel Bulocchi, recent winner of the Macaco Publishing Company's prize in the novel. He is in some manner a writer, in a certain way an intellectual, in some form a poet, in a certain measure an artist. A promising young talent of our short story production, our poetic lyricism, our essayistic thought, our novelistic art, and our . . . ."

"Thank you, Agrippina, but it's not all that much," I interrupted her for fear she might say something like *theatristic*.

"Tell me, Mr. Bulocchi . . . What did you feel when . . . ? Will you let me call you Miguel? You know, that way there's established an . . . , uh . . . , a current of affection, cordiality, perhaps . . . , which uh . . . , in the final instance . . . ."

"Of course, why not? Call me Mike."

"Well, Mike, what did you feel when you won the prize? Were you very excited? Or did you expect them to give you the prize?"

"Well, in the areas in which one achieves success, as you have, one always has expectations. You must have had them too. That optimism which uh . . . in some way, makes . . . uh . . . ," I was having trouble putting my thoughts together smoothly.

"That's true!" Agrippina acknowledged. "One doesn't get anywhere without optimism, without confidence, without faith in the future."

"Right. As I was saying, one always entertains expectations."

"Some entertain them and others cherish them," Sarducci pointed out.

"Sure . . . , but you know . . . , that is to say . . . , judges' panels are usually so demanding."

"Exactly," replied Agrippina. "The point is that contemporary novelistic art demands more and more every day . . . , uh. . . , in a word . . . , uh . . ."

"It demands more," I suggested.

"That's it, it demands more. And who were the members of the judges' panel?"

"I think they were . . . ," I tried to recall, ". . . Pablo Segovia, Ginesillo de Parapilla, and Lázaro Monipodio."[23]

"Oh, my God, I know all three of them!!" shrieked Fairyfoot, startling me. "But among their intimate friends they have such nicknames that I'm splitting with laughter just to think of them!"

"Come on, Fairyfoot, tell us what they're called," the ever-smiling Agrippina exhorted him.

"Oh, dear me, what *will* those boys *say* if I reveal their secret! They'll get naughty and uppity, that's what they'll do! No, no, no, a thousand times no!!" Fairyfoot exclaimed, underscoring each negative with a little stomp on the floor.

"Come on, Fairyfoot, tell us, *please*. Don't leave us in suspense."

"Oh, well, all right!" said Fairyfoot, making up his mind. "Oh, my God! Well, here goes. They're called Poochy, Coochy, and Smoochy! Te-hee-hee! Hee-hee-ha-ha-ha! Har-de-har-har!! Don't murder me, boys," he added, looking straight into the camera, "'cause I'm an unwed mother!"

"Oh, this Fairyfoot is just too much!" commented Agrippina. "Always so charming, talented, clever, fascinating, and amusing!"

"I didn't know anything about their nicknames," I said. "The truth is I didn't even know those gentlemen at all."

"What's the thematic thread of your novel?" asked Agrippina. "Tell us . . . rather, tell our friendly viewing audience who follow us so faithfully day by day, because I, of course, *naturellement*, have already read it."

"Well, the scene is . . ."

"What's the title of the novel?"

"*Humanization of the Penguins*. The scene is Tierra del Fuego. The main characters, two Ona Indians. He, a man; she, a woman. Basically, it deals with the problem of uprooted youth, a generation gap. Jean-Paul and Suzette are in love. On the surface, it's just an ordinary love affair, without ups and downs, with negligible action in which the messages are connoted through complex situations underpinned by a precise ideological alignment. But it also has a sociological backdrop; that's why they each evolve within diametrically opposed roles. She, a Dadaist painter, is the daughter of Chief Chamizo. By contrast, Jean-Paul is a traveling salesman of latex condoms. They live together . . ."

"And despite their sociocultural phase displacement," Agrippina butted in just for the pleasure of hearing herself talk, "there's real love between them . . . , and the symbolism is really . . . , uh . . . , it's in some way uh . . . , well, it's brutal, primitive, bestial, wouldn't you say?"

"Yes," I wanted to make this delicate point perfectly clear. "That love is real, within what is, what can be, what can become, or what may have been able to become, a love encompassed within the emerging petit bourgeois guidelines for the living together—cement jungle intercorrelation . . ."

They were signaling us from behind the cameras to hurry up.

"Time is a tyrant in television," said Agrippina, varying her approach. "So, to finish up, Mike . . . Well, at any rate we're going to bring you back again some day soon so you can talk, in some way, more at length about your novel."

"With pleasure, Agrippina. I'm at your disposal."

"To conclude, do you believe in marriage?"

I paused slightly to reflect: "Fundamentally, I believe in the mate."

"And you, Gino?"

"If I didn't believe in marriage, I wouldn't have married again for the fourth time in three years."

"And you, Fairyfoot?"

"Oh, please, don't give me any headaches, Agrippina *dahling!*"

"And you, Brutus?"

"Yeah, sure, I believe in marriage as long 's da wife is nice 'n' understandin', and she's up to my level o' intelligence. If my wife wasn't like dat, I'd grab 'er 'n' punch 'er out. Bim, bam, boom!"

"And you, Mr. Opa, do you believe in marriage?

"Huh?"

"And so, that's it for today, dear viewing audience out there, you who follow us so faithfully day by day. I'll be waiting for all of you tomorrow at this same time and over this same channel for another Television Luncheon and a chat with some extraordinary guests who, like those of today and those of every day, will be simply . . . sen-sa-tion-al! Until tomorrow, friends!"

11

When I got home, my father said to me: "I watched the program. You were fine, but you didn't talk much. Why did you let yourself be interrupted by that Marie Antoinette?"

I shrugged my shoulders: "How do I know? I have no experience at that sort of thing."

"Well, all right. But the time has come for me to start getting back the money I've invested in your literary career. Luckily I've already managed to have your novel turned into a best seller."

"What?" I was astonished. "But just yesterday it was in the process of being bound."

"Look," he showed me a page in the newspaper.

Sure enough, my *Humanization of the Penguins* headed the list of best-selling works.

"I haven't been idle," my father explained, wielding his checkbook. "I've been taking certain cultural measures. I've talked to critics and journalists. Your book will appear for two whole months on the best-seller list; that'll be enough to turn it into a real best seller right away. I tried to rent the space for half a year, but they told me at the newspapers that, since they already have the whole year sold out, they would agree to assign only two months to each book. Those are very reliable people, people who keep their word. In short, Miguel, the world is yours! There'll be multiple editions, you'll be translated into every language, young American university students will graduate in Spanish-American literature with theses on your life and works. You'll make a lot of money. Naturally, you'll have to reimburse me for all the dough I've invested in this business."

"Of course, and some profit too."

"That isn't necessary. What greater satisfaction for a father than to have a talented, enterprising son?"

I was touched: "Pop, your words give me the encouragement I need to go on dedicating myself body and soul to the muses. To overcome tenaciously, as I have until now, the lack of understanding and the materialistic obstacles thwarting the poet who lugs his artistic fantasies onward and upward. This is a passion, a calling that one carries in the marrow of his bones, that seethes in one's blood . . ."

"Yeah, yeah," he interrupted me. "But it won't be necessary for you to write anything anymore. I've now contracted four young men with their own writing business and good typing skills. One writes novels and short stories; another, essays; another, theater; and the fourth, poetry. Then you just sign."

I stood there, bewildered: "And, in the meantime, what'll I do?"

My father looked at me disapprovingly: "What do you mean 'what'll I do'? The hardest part's been left for you. You'll have to spend all day on television, on the radio, and in newspaper offices. You have to get yourself seen at art exhibitions, at all the private viewings, go around kissing everyone, males and females alike, show up at all the theatrical and film premieres, be a judge for idiotic television contests, get involved with all the right people who form part of the 'in' group, become friendly with the doctors who are now holding their office hours over the television channels. In short, there are so many things to do, you won't have time enough to work them all in; literature demands great sacrifices. By the way, did you get yourself a young singer as a girlfriend yet?"

"Not yet," I said, a bit ashamed at my indolence.

"Don't worry about it. I'll get one for you. In addition, you'll have to be signing paid published statements, articles supporting or protesting unknown causes, but always coming out, of course, on the side of the strongest party. You'll also have to visit jails, hospitals, and insane asylums, issue statements on the political situation in countries whose location you don't even know, become the champion and symbol of Latin American youth who are so deserving of everything . . ."

"That's all fine," I observed. "But who'll guarantee me our ghost writers can write well?"

"Don't make problems for yourself. Anyone can write better than you."

"Maybe," I said, somewhat resentful. "But what about the mixture of styles?"

My father let out an uproarious burst of laughter: "Who's going to notice?"

Gospel truth.

I had just turned twenty-one. The rest of it (my successes, my triumphs, my apotheosis) is a well-known story. But at that moment I was looking ahead toward the bright future. The world of art was magnanimously opening its broad portals to me. And I, proud and erect, was about to pass through them,

crowned with ivy and eternal laurel.[24]

El mejor de los mundos posibles, pp. 173–206
Buenos Aires: Editorial Plus Ultra, 1976

NOTES

SANITARY CENTENNIAL

1. Argentine general (1876–1943) and president of Argentina (1932–1938). This president's correct name is Agustín P. Justo. Pronounced rapidly in Spanish, the complete name sounds something like *Ah-goos-teen-Pay-Hoosto*. In his inimitable style, Luke Spettanza has written it as if the middle initial, *P* (pronounced *Pay* in Spanish), formed part of the last name, Justo (pronounced *Hoosto*).

2. The Spanish includes a playful ambiguity, since the word *grifo* means both "faucet" and "griffin."

3. Charles Édouard Jeanneret Le Corbusier was a well-known Swiss architect who lived in France.

4. The Spanish, *el varón domado*, is also the title of a book by Ester Villar.

5. Baltasar Gracián (1601–1658): Spanish Jesuit; philosopher and writer of the Baroque period; author of *El Criticón*, a criticism of the science and civilization of Gracián's time. The saying alluded to is *"Lo bueno, si breve, dos veces bueno"* [What's good, if brief, is doubly good].

6. José Ingenieros (1877–1925): Argentine thinker, professor, critic, and writer; author of *La simulación en la lucha por la vida* [Pretense in the struggle for life] and *El hombre mediocre* [The mediocre man]. Sorrentino drew my attention to Ingenieros' "affected style" at the beginning of *El hombre mediocre* and indicated that he was parodying such affected style in Luke Spettanza's repeated pedantic use of the phrase "inasmuch as" (*por cuanto* in Spanish).

7. Jorge Luis Borges, Manuel Mujica Láinez, and Marco Denevi are, of course, three of the most eminent Argentine writers of the contemporary era.

8. Alfredo Palacios (1879–1965): Argentine politician distinguished as the first socialist representative elected to the national parliament; later, ambassador to Uruguay (1955–1957).

9. The Atlanta Athletic Club is one of many such organizations in and around Buenos Aires and other major cities throughout Argentina. These clubs, in addition to sponsoring professional soccer teams, also provide sporting and social activities for the membership.

10. Another of the many *barrios*, or quarters, of Buenos Aires.

11. Juan B. Justo (1865–1928) was the founder of the Argentine Socialist Party, the members of which originally advocated a somewhat ascetic existence, including such things as abstinence from tobacco, alcohol, and so on.

12. *Maté* is a tealike, South American beverage, drunk hot, which is very popular in the River Plate region. Made from the leaves of a species of holly (*Ilex paraguariensis*), it is often drunk out of a gourd, also called a *maté* in Spanish.

13. "Elective affinities," a term taken from eighteenth-century chemistry, refers to the sometimes strange attraction of apparent opposites. Goethe used the German term as the title of his novel *Die Wahlverwandtschaften* (1809).

14. In Hispanic countries, and in most European countries in general, the number seven (7) is usually written with a kind of cross bar (7̄) and would, hence, resemble a capital *F* when inverted.

15. The Green Directory is a special Buenos Aires telephone directory that lists the name and address corresponding to a given telephone number. In a separate listing are given the name and telephone number corresponding to a given address.

16. With the phrase "all oblivion was always novelty," Sorrentino playfully inverts Francis Bacon's quotation of Salomon's statement, "all novelty is but oblivion" (Francis Bacon, *Essays*, LVIII). The full quotation from Bacon appears as the epigraph to Jorge Luis Borges' short story "El inmortal" [The immortal], Sorrentino's source for the phrase.

17. The Spanish of "so as to make . . . routine" is "*por no hacer mudanza en su costumbre.*" The phrase, an eleven-syllable verse, is a direct quotation of the last line of a famous sonnet, "En tanto que de rosa y de azucena . . . ," by the sixteenth-century Spanish poet Garcilaso de la Vega. The sense of the line is that time changes everything except its own unchangeable custom of changing everything. As is evident, Sorrentino is fond of working quotations from many sources into his writings, often with satiric or parodic effect.

18. According to Sorrentino, a parody of the language of Structuralism.

19. A place where civil marriages are performed; a city hall or some similar place.

20. Los Troncos is a very exclusive section of Mar del Plata, a popular summer resort city on the Atlantic coast of Argentina, approximately 250 miles south of Buenos Aires.

21. The phrase "the arduous students of Pythagoras" ("*los arduos alumnos de Pitágoras*") quotes part of the first and last lines of Jorge Luis Borges' well-known poem "La noche cíclica" [The cyclical night]. The phrase involves a figure of speech called hypallage, in which there occurs a reversal in the expected syntactic relation between two words, as in "her beauty's face" for "her face's beauty." Borges frequently attributes an adjective to a different noun than the one expected, as in this particular use of hypallage. In this instance, the students' work or their study is "arduous," not the students themselves, but Borges attributes "arduous" to the latter. Sorrentino also uses hypallage occasionally in his descriptive passages, often with startling stylistic effects.

22. Sorrentino's Spanish ("*cambiar los mojones por ganar heredat*") is a direct quotation of a verse from Miracle XI, "El labrador avaro" [The miserly farmer] of the *Milagros de Nuestra Señora* [Miracles of Our Lady] by the thirteenth-century Spanish poet Gonzalo de Berceo.

23. An old quarter of Buenos Aires, located near the waterfront and dock area.

24. Italian: *Signor podestà* means something like "lord potentate" or "lord of the manor." *Palazzo*, of course, means "palace." *Ah, quanto bella era Enza Quasimoda!*: "Oh, how beautiful Enza Quasimoda was!"

25. Another well-known *barrio*, or quarter, of Buenos Aires in which the Cementerio del Oeste [western cemetery], or simply "Chacarita," is located. In the streets surrounding the graveyard, there are many stores selling crosses, monuments, tombstones, and so on. This explains why Don Carmelo was able to buy marble at cost from the gravestone dealer nextdoor, to be used in the manufacture of the Spettanza line of Royal washtubs.

26. José de Espronceda (1808–1842): famous lyrical poet of the period of Romanticism in Spain.

27. Sorrentino borrowed the adjective "turbaned" (*turbantado* in

Spanish) from Jorge Luis Borges' "Pierre Menard, autor del Quijote" ["Pierre Menard, Author of the Quixote"]. Borges, in turn, took it from Shakespeare's line "Where a malignant and turbaned Turk . . ." In "Pierre Menard," after commenting on Cervantes' (or Pierre Menard's) "effective combination of two adjectives, one moral and the other physical," Borges is reminded of the same stylistic device in the above-mentioned Shakespearean line. Interestingly, Sorrentino uses the same adjectival combination here ("turbaned" combined with "inscrutable" and "exotic") as well as in other descriptive passages.

28. *Inodoro* is the Spanish word for "toilet," but the term "inodoro" also means "odorless," as the pedantic academician points out. The humor here is patently untranslatable.

29. Avenue of the Liberator: a wide, main avenue in Buenos Aires, named for the liberator Gen. José de San Martín (1778–1850), Argentine hero of the Wars for Independence fought against Spain (1810–1824).

30. Jacques Bénigne Bossuet (1627–1704): French bishop, writer, and famous sacred orator. His *Funeral Orations* appeared in 1689.

IN SELF-DEFENSE

1. A monument in downtown Buenos Aires, dedicated to the founding of the city.

THE LIFE OF THE PARTY

1. In del Campo's famous Argentine gaucho poem (*Fausto*, 1866), a gaucho (Anastasio el Pollo) describes to his crony, Laguna, a performance of Gounod's opera *Faust*, which he had witnessed by chance when he wandered into the old Colón Theatre during a visit to Buenos Aires. Part of the poem's artistry and humor resides in the gaucho's interpreting the opera's incidents as real and in the recounting of them in the rustic, picturesque (but stylized) gaucho dialect of the pampas. (My translation of verses from *Fausto*.)

2. With ironic humor, Sorrentino unmasks Vitaver's ignorance by having him recall here an almost unforgettable character who appears, however, not in *Fausto* but in *Martín Fierro* (1872; 1879) by José Hernández. The latter work is undoubtedly the most famous and finest gaucho poem and is read by most Argentine schoolchildren. Had Vitaver read the poems, he could not possibly make such a blunder.

3. Arthur now quotes from what may well be the most famous poem in the Spanish language, Jorge Manrique's *Coplas a la muerte del Maestro don Rodrigo, su padre* [Verses on the death of Commander Rodrigo, his father]. Rodrigo Manrique was an eminent, fifteenth-century Spanish nobleman and knight-commander (*Maestro*) of the military chivalric Order of Santiago [St. James]. When Rodrigo Manrique died, his son, Jorge, was so deeply grieved that he composed this immortal elegy in his father's memory. Among other medieval themes included in the poem are a solemn meditation on the transitory nature of wealth and other worldly, material things and a consideration of the brevity of power, beauty, nobility, and human life. (My translation of verses.) In mythology, Fortune is often depicted as a goddess with a wheel; her constant turning of this "wheel of fortune" raises the unfortunate to lofty heights of wealth and power, only to cast them down again, and vice versa. Arthur's subsequent recitation of "five or six stanzas" more of Manrique's poem then prompts him to expand on the medieval work's meaning for the crass, phony Vitaver. The explanation reaches a humorous crescendo with Arthur's reference to Adidine's possible future infidelity to her husband.

4. Latin: "Where are they? Where are they? etc. Where are the table and six chairs?" The words *ubi sunt* ("Where are . . . ?"), in Latin and other European languages, were frequent opening lines as well as the principal motif and theme of many European medieval poems emphasizing the transitory nature of all things. Perhaps the best-known example is François Villon's ballade with its famous line *"Mais ou sont les neiges d'antan?"* [But where are the snows of yesteryear?]. *Ubi sunt* is now a term used to identify the theme of such works, which have continued to be written on down to modern and contemporary times. Arthur's insistent repetition of the phrase is particularly appropriate in light of his previous quotation from Jorge Manrique's *Coplas a la muerte del . . . su padre*, the principal theme of which is, of course, *ubi sunt*.

5. A Buenos Aires suburb.

THE FETID TALE OF ANTULÍN

1. Avellaneda is a main industrial suburb of Buenos Aires. Despite its name, the Rácing Club is a soccer team whose great traditional rival in that same area is the Club Independiente. Their rivalry is in-

tensified by the fact that the respective stadiums of the two teams are in very close proximity to one another.

2. The original title of this chapter, "*El sueño, autor de representaciones*," is a line from a sonnet by the Spanish Baroque poet Luis de Góngora y Argote (1561–1627).

3. A popular summer resort city on the Atlantic coast of Argentina, approximately 250 miles south of Buenos Aires.

4. The Spanish title of this chapter is based upon that of a French detective novel by Gaston Leroux (1868–1927), *L'homme qui revient de loin*.

5. The original title (*"Descripción de una lucha"*) is the Spanish translation of a story by Franz Kafka, *"Beschreibung eines Kampfes."*

6. The Spanish landlady is from Galicia, a bilingual region of northwestern Spain that borders Portugal on the north. Since many of the less-educated inhabitants of the area speak primarily the Galician-Portuguese dialect, their command of Castilian Spanish is occasionally somewhat substandard. An effort has been made to convey in the translation something of the peculiar, humorous effects of Doña Encarnación's speech.

7. See note 13 above, under Sanitary Centennial.

8. From the Japanese word *ikebana*, "the art of arranging flowers." Sorrentino satirizes here the "florid" or "flowery" style of oratory used by certain political-revolutionary types. The entire passage that follows is characterized in the Spanish by a humorous, ironic style and tone seen, for example, in the ridiculous name of the numbers man's political party. Here the author plays with the name of the revolutionary movement that overthrew Perón in 1955 and later became known as the Asociación de Afirmación de la Revolución Libertadora [Association for Affirmation of the Liberating Revolution]. In the historic Recoleta graveyard, the oldest, most traditional, and most elegant cemetery of Buenos Aires, are buried the great, the famous, the wealthy, and many of the politically conservative of Argentina. In the Spanish, "the productive economic sectors of the cemetery" reads *"las fuerzas vivas del cementerio."* The literal meaning of this phrase is "the living powers of the cemetery," humorous enough in itself; however, Sorrentino achieves a further ironic touch with this term borrowed from economics by alluding satirically to those who control most of the wealth of the Argentine nation, that is, the rich politicians, cattlemen, industrialists, and businessmen.

9. The author here plays upon one of the well-known philosophical concepts of José Ortega y Gasset (1883–1955).

10. This title is a parody of that of a well-known sonnet by the Spanish Baroque writer Francisco de Quevedo (1580–1645). The poem is titled "*Amor* constante más allá de la muerte" [*Love*, constant beyond death]. (Italics mine.)

11. In some Spanish-speaking countries, including Argentina, there are sometimes two marriage ceremonies, religious and civil. The religious marriage is usually optional.

ARS POETICA

1. The epigraph ("*Un padre que da consejos . . .* ," in the original) is taken from José Hernández's famous gaucho poem *Martín Fierro*, Part II, "*La vuelta*" (1879), Canto XXXII, line 4595.

2. The narrator's ridiculous pedantry and ignorance are humorously satirized in this phrase, which, in the original medieval Spanish, not "Latin," is "*Lo que Natura non da, Salamanca non presta*" (literally, "What Nature does not give, Salamanca does not lend"). Since the city of Salamanca is the site of one of the oldest universities in Spain, this venerable Spanish proverbial quotation asserts that formal education and college degrees cannot make up for a lack of natural intelligence and talent. Bulocchi states it, of course, not in the "language of Homer" (i.e., ancient Greek), but simply in old Spanish, which he further mistakenly believes is Latin. I have sought to maintain a modicum of the original's humor by rendering the idea in Latin ("What Nature doesn't bestow, education can't provide").

3. The suburb of West Lanús (Lanús Oeste) is a small independent municipality located about twelve miles south of Buenos Aires.

4. In Argentina, a public auctioneer enjoys a kind of semiofficial status and must, therefore, pass examinations to be granted the title. He has, for example, the power to impound an automobile if the owner fails to make payments. The fact that the father is "nearly" a public auctioneer subtly implies that he hasn't passed the examinations.

5. San Isidro County, located about twenty miles north of Buenos Aires, is a fashionable area inhabited, generally, by well-to-do Argentines who commute by train to the city.

6. The fictitious newspaper name is, in reality, a line from the patriotic *Himno a Sarmiento* [Hymn to Sarmiento], thus suggesting a certain liberal bent in the father's politics. Although only a tiny town

in San Isidro County (see previous note), Carapachay does boast a train station on the commuter line.

7. Another example of the narrator's silly pedantry. The French phrase most certainly does not mean what Miguel Bulocchi has it say in his original (but nonsensical) Spanish translation, which reads "*yo me asemejo a tus ventas*" (literally, "I resemble your sales"). The French words, written *je sème à tout vent*, form part of the logo of the Librairie Larousse, publisher of the famous *Petit Larousse* dictionaries. The aim of Pierre Larousse and Augustin Boyer, founders of the Librairie Larousse, was "to teach everything to everybody"; hence, the logo's phrase, meaning something like "I sow [knowledge] to the four winds." The logo depicts a woman blowing the seeds off a flower, hence disseminating them in all directions.

8. A large important quarter of Buenos Aires, which usually fields a good soccer team.

9. One of the major Buenos Aires newspapers.

10. José de Espronceda (1808–1842): well-known Spanish romantic poet, but considered mediocre by some critics. Joaquín V. González (1863–1923): Argentine politician, historian, educator, and prolific writer; also generally considered to be a poet of very minor importance in Argentine literary history. Sorrentino's juxtaposition here of two major European poets and a pair of rather secondary Hispanic poets results in a humorous reductio ad absurdum.

11. The Galería del Este (Eastern Arcade) is a fashionable covered shopping mall or arcade in the last block of the Calle Florida (Florida Street) in downtown Buenos Aires. To be found there are typical tourist attractions, such as antique shops, high-fashion clothing stores, and expensive gift shops. Since the arcade also contains bookstores, it is perhaps appropriate that Miguel's literary debut should be held there. The Galería del Este became a frequent haunt of young, long-haired, marihuana-smoking, usually wealthy intellectual types. This incongruous juxtaposition of a commercial place of business and artistic intellectual pursuits points straight at Sorrentino's theme, the debasement of art in a materialistic contemporary society.

12. Eduardo Gudiño Kieffer (1935–): Argentine short story writer and novelist. While again juxtaposing the names of world-famous writers with that of a Latin American author who is comparatively unknown outside his native land, Sorrentino also pokes fun here at the

tendency of Hispanic critics to create adjectives out of practically any author's last name, which may sometimes take on rather humorous forms, as seen in this instance.

13. The Greek muse of music and dance and, hence, poetry.

14. The word *cochon* means "pig" in French.

15. An Indian tribe of Tierra del Fuego in extreme southern Argentina.

16. A very old public mental hospital located on Vieytes Street in the Barracas quarter of Buenos Aires.

17. The words *asciuga la scimmia* mean "dry the monkey" in Italian.

18. Tortuguitas is a town about twenty miles northwest of Buenos Aires. Many wealthy city people own elegant *quintas*, or country houses, there where they frequently spend weekends.

19. Ushuaia is the capital of the remote Tierra del Fuego at the extreme southern tip of Argentina. "The University of Ushuaia" would be tantamount to saying in English "the University of Timbuktu."

20. The Spanish, ". . . el propio ministro de Torrefacción Glacial," is untranslatable. Francisco Manrique, an Argentine minister of social welfare in the 1970s, created the Pronósticos Deportivos (Sports Predictions) or PRODE (its popular acronym) as a federal national lottery. It is based on the results of soccer games, which participants must predict successfully to win, and the proceeds go to various welfare, health, and educational programs. In Spanish, the phonetic similarities between "ministro de Bienestar Social, señor Manrique" and "ministro de Torrefacción Glacial, señor Perique" highlight Sorrentino's humorous word play.

21. Huakaspa Opa is obviously an Indian from Argentina's northwestern region near the Andes Mountains, who is quite out of place in a modern Buenos Aires television studio. (Agrippina subsequently refers ironically to his "expressiveness of the [Andean] highland plains," or *altiplano*.) His last name, Opa, means "idiot" in Quechua, the main native language spoken in the Andes, and the word *opa* has entered popular Argentine Spanish as synonymous with *tarado* (dumb or mentally retarded). Because of the sparse oxygen content in the air of that mountainous area, which is high above sea level, many Indians and others customarily chew the leaves of the coca plant (also used in the making of cocaine) for their stimulant properties to give them-

selves energy and strength. Sorrentino is, of course, exaggerating in good humor by having Mr. Opa eating (and choking on) a coca leaf *empanada*, or pasty.

22. The Avenida General Paz is a kind of outer drive or belt encircling the city of Buenos Aires, which marks the municipal limits. The narrator's use of the word "novel" (*inédita*) is ironic because statements like "the country ends at General Paz Avenue" are quite commonly made by many people in Buenos Aires, often with social or political connotations. The notion is analogous to the state of mind frequently attributed to New Yorkers and expressed in the idea that "there's nothing beyond the Hudson River but wilderness." Ramos Mejía and Olivos are both nearby suburban municipalities; there are some nightclubs in the former and many in the latter. As seen a bit further on, Sarducci is clearly getting in some free advertising for his new night club soon to be opened in Ramos Mejía.

23. All three recall names of characters in famous Spanish picaresque novels. The first and third judges' names evoke those of Don Pablos, the hero of Quevedo's *El buscón*, and Lázaro, the protagonist of the first picaresque novel, *Lazarillo de Tormes*. Monipodio, moreover, is the name of the leader of the thieves in Cervantes' picaresque novelette *Rinconete y Cortadillo*. Ginesillo de Parapilla is quite similar to the derogatory name given another Cervantine rogue, Ginés de Pasamonte, when he angers the guard keeping watch over him and the other criminals condemned as galley slaves in Chapter XXII of *Don Quixote*. Sorrentino thus humorously brands the members of the judges' panel as a triumvirate of corrupt rascals.

24. The Spanish, "*de hiedra y lauro eterno coronado*," is a line of poetry. Penned by the Spanish mystic poet Fray Luis de León (1537–1591), this verse forms the second line of the last stanza of his famous ode to "La vida retirada" [The retired life], sometimes titled "La vida del campo" [Country life]. The poem, a "lira," is a reinterpretation of Horace's "Beatus ille" ode.